The
Book
Of Isabel

ANTHONY OTERO

ISBN:0990515907
ISBN-13:9780990515906

DEDICATION

For all the people in my life who have been affected by cancer. To Titi Clara, may you rest in peace. To Titi Terri, you are stronger than you think. To my father, my cousin Karen, and my friend, Monique – you have shown me never to take life for granted.

Memorial Sloan Kettering
December 19, 2015
7:26 a.m. ET

I'm not a fan of hospitals. I always feel like something fucked up is bound to happen. I have to admit, I'm nervous. I haven't seen Naomi in a few weeks. She's been like the long lost sister that I never had. We've been friends for many years, but we lost touch after I moved to Syracuse more than a decade ago. Nayo, what we call her, is one of the people I made sure I regained contact with when I moved back to New York City last year.

We met during the Summer Institute Program back in 1994 at Syracuse University. I could immediately tell that this black girl from Brooklyn didn't want to be there any more than I did. If I recall correctly, they placed her in the wrong math class and she wasn't happy about it in the least. We were standing on a significantly long line in the Hall of Languages Room 500 waiting to "register" for our classes. Nayo was the last person in line and I was right in front of her. Her face said it all and even though I had a hard time speaking to women in general, she made me feel comfortable when I cracked a joke about being there.

I remember looking behind me and saying, "If it takes this long to register for a summer program then I can't even imagine what it's like during the school year."

Then she responded, "Or maybe this is how they corral all the black kids and fool us into thinking we might actually belong here."

I turned around fully and introduced myself, "Hi, I'm Louis." From that point on, we bonded over our mutual disdain over spending our last summer of freedom in Syracuse taking classes instead of going to Coney Island or Jones Beach. Once we thoroughly shared our mutual love for New York City and our general mistrust of everyone else, we became fast friends.

In college, we saw many things and survived many people. She was there for me during my worst breakup and I was there for her when she needed a shoulder to cry on. In fact, we shared several key emotional outbursts together. We both cried several times when Biggie and Tupac died, we got angry when the Knicks lost in the NBA Finals, we cheered when O.J. "allegedly" got away with double-murder, and lamented Syracuse's loss during The Final Four. After college we tried to maintain our friendship. Before I moved, we would hang out at Battery Park often eating lunch during my brief stint at the Borough of Manhattan Community College. I thought I lost her once, but she managed to get out of the World Trade Center before it collapsed.

It has been 21 years since we met and I find myself having a desire to make every moment with my friend count. Only God knows how much time she may have left. I walk into the elevator at Memorial Sloan Kettering and press the button for her floor. I put the headphones back into my ears because it would've been rude to talk to the lady at the front desk while listening to music. The doors close and I turn my music back on. I really try to be in better spirits these days, but I feel like I'm always either sad or angry. I look at the newspaper I bought this morning and the headlines are always the same, *Police Kill Another Person of Color.* I fold the paper and put it into my bag. Perhaps listening to "Be Free" by J. Cole wasn't a good idea after all.

I'm frustrated with my life for so many reasons, but I need to keep a straight face for Naomi. There's no problem that I can possibly have that can measure up to what she's going through. She was diagnosed with pancreatic cancer last year and I feel terrible for not being the friend I should've been. I was too busy dealing with the problems that revolved around my divorce. After my car accident, she was one of the first people to call me when I got out of the hospital. When I moved back to New York I made it a point to mend all broken fences in my life and Naomi was on top of that list. I've learned that true friendship can survive distance and minimal communication.

I chose to visit on a Saturday morning because I plan on being here for a while. We've talked on the phone many times since she's been diagnosed, but as much as I've tried to see her before she was admitted, it never worked out. Today, I want to spend as much time as I can with her. It's the least I can do to preserve our friendship.

She was admitted because of the massive amounts of pain that had been shooting through her body. We all fear that the chemo is no longer working. She told me a few months ago via text that she has a tumor somewhere near her pancreas that might be metastasizing. Because of her age, the doctors have been aggressively treating it with chemo in hopes they can shrink the tumor and then remove it. The process has been extremely painful for her. She's lost much of her hair and her appetite in the process, but on Monday she goes in for a surgery that may determine her future. The doctors have told her that despite all her pain, the tumor is indeed small enough to remove. Of course, there are always risks with surgery of this nature.

I walk out of the elevator and look around for the signs directing me to her room number. The smell of the sterilized air is palpable. I walk down the hallway, make a few turns and I finally arrive at her room. I look at my watch and it's still pretty early. I can tell by the silence on the floor I'm one of the few people who are taking advantage of the early hours. Visiting hours start at 6 a.m. and I really tried to get up earlier but this unusually warm December air, combined with the warm body of my girlfriend, and the snooze button delayed me a bit. But, it's about 7:30 a.m., so it isn't too bad considering I don't get up this early to go to work.

I show my visitor's pass to the nurse at the desk then turn off the music in my headphones before I walk into Nayo's room. It's a nice-sized space with light green painted walls. Her bed is against the far wall on the right and the overhead fluorescent light is on. There are several chairs around the room. Naomi considered herself lucky that she got the side of the building with the window facing York Ave. Even though she's connected to all these machines, I can tell from here that she's lost a lot of weight. It looks like she's still sleeping.

I walk into the room slowly and quietly so that I don't disturb her. However, I feel like my boots are going to betray me. It's wet outside because of all the rain we've had over the last few hours. I put my laptop bag down on the chair underneath the flat screen television mounted to the wall. I turn my back to her so I can take off my jacket and place it behind the chair. I leave my long gray scarf and my Mets cap on because I'm still cold. Despite the warm weather as of late, temperatures this weekend have dropped below 50 degrees due to the rain. The last thing I want to do is get sick.

"You're late," she says weakly.

4

Her voice startled me. "Oh, you're awake. I didn't want to wake you up any earlier than needed."

"I don't really sleep much these days." She squints a little to avoid the light coming from the ceiling.

"You want me to shut off the lights?" I point to the light switch behind me.

"No. It's fine. I just need some water." I rush over to the bed and hand her the small plastic cup of water that was sitting on her tray. I watch her drink it. From this close I can see her pale brown skin. She's lost so much color. Her thinning hair is pulled back and I can see a few white strands. We're the same age and yet she looks 10 years older. They say black don't crack, but this is an extreme situation. All I want to say out loud is Fuck Cancer!!!

"Was that water sitting there all night?" I ask.

Naomi shakes her head then replies after a few more gulps. "The nurse came in to check on me about an hour ago. I asked her to leave some water out for me."

I'm not used to seeing her like this. I remember the days when we would laugh at people and each other. We spent so much time together doing homework and enjoying funny stories. There are no smiles right now. I grab one of the chairs and sit down right next to her bed and grab her hand. "How are you really doing? You have me very worried here."

She turns her head towards me and smiles, "I will be ok."

I can tell she is lying but her smile provides some comfort. My eyes start to water a bit. "You sure?" I ask.

"Don't do this Louis. Not now. I'm not dead yet," she says

softly and she pats my hand.

"I know," I wipe my eyes.

"Besides, there's another reason why you're here and I've been waiting this long, so let's see it."

"Now?" I ask as I pull back not expecting to get into this so soon.

"Yes, now. Is there somewhere else you have to be?" She chuckles.

She has a point. I did come here to see her but I also came to show her something that I've been working on. I get up and walk over to my bag and I pull out a book wrapped in a brown plastic bag and I bring it over to her.

"You wrapped it in a bag?"

"Well, you know the comic collector in me. I have to protect the cover."

She looks at me with confusion and shakes her head. "But this is just a proof. I don't understand why you would protect the..." I pull the soft book out of the bag to reveal the cover. It is an elegant marble colored cover with strands and traces of blue and red. The words in the center of the book read, *The Book of Isabel.*

Naomi just looks at it. She grabs the book and touches the cover with her right hand. Her fingers trace the words of the title. There's only silence. I can only imagine what's going on in her head. She seems a bit speechless. "Do you like the cover?" I ask.

She nods her head with tears in her eyes. "I love the cover. I'm so happy for you." She gives me a hug. I know where the tears are coming from. Back in undergrad we took English courses together. We dreamed of days when we would write novels and go to each other's snobby book readings. Those days are long gone and I know deep in her heart she regrets not following that dream.

I sit back down as she continues to admire the book that took me a little less than a year to write. She wanted to read it right away and we both knew that this might be her only chance to do so. Once I had a working draft that I felt was decent enough for her to read, I arranged for a proof to be mailed to me. I gave her the impression that it was just some tired old manuscript I had been working on. Nayo had no idea, until now, how far along I really was in this process.

"Who did the cover?"

"Honestly I took a picture of a marble table and Zenia did the rest on Photoshop. Something about gradients. She's a bit more advanced than me." I chuckle.

"How's she doing?" She asks softly.

"She's doing well, making much more money than I am and I love it! But, as I told you on the phone yesterday, I can't imagine my life without her."

"Does that mean you're going to marry her any time soon?"

I smile. This is a question that I've thought deeply about. A part of me feels that it's silly to admit this because of everything I've gone through with the ex-wife. Another part of me has already been bookmarking websites because if and when the time comes, I need to make sure that I know the difference between a princess cut and an emerald cut diamond. "I think it might happen soon enough. I'm just hoping that all my friends can attend."

Naomi tries to hide her tragic smile as she continues to stare at the book. She turns it over to look at the brief bio, as well as my headshot. I feel the need to break the silence after my last comment.

"The back cover isn't exactly where I want it to be yet. I already spotted a few typos that I need to fix. Don't get me started on the picture." The typos annoyed me because it was Zenia who pointed them out to me last night. Before I could get too angry, she calmed me down by reminding me that is just a proof. I'm equally unhappy with the picture. The endeavor of self-publishing has been expensive and sacrifices had to be made. The headshot was indeed a selfie that I pulled from my Instagram account. If I write another book, I will need to invest in a decent photographer.

Nayo remained silent.

"You ok?" I ask.

"Yeah, I'll be fine. It's interesting that after all this time you can write a book like this. I've known you for like 20 years and it's so good to see you finally getting your work out there." Her voice cracked a little.

Nope. I'm not gonna to do it. I told myself before I left the apartment that I was going to be strong. I wasn't going to cry. "Look! I'm not here to cry!" I say laughing as I fight back tears, "Are you ready to read this book or not? I brought it here for you." I throw my arms up to exaggerate my point.

Naomi laughs. Thank God! I just needed to lighten up the mood. "Yeah, I think I'm ready."

She opens the book and begins to read.

THAT NIGHT

I waited for her. The airport was empty and the fluorescent lighting gave off an aura of pale emptiness. At least I wasn't alone. My roommate's new girlfriend, Madison, drove me to the airport. It was the least she could do since she seems to be living rent-free in our apartment these days. Besides, I don't have a driver's license yet. I'm one of those New Yorkers who keeps their learner's permit for years in hopes of actually getting a license one day. Even still, I feel a little uncomfortable with my present company since I'm waiting for my girlfriend to come back from her trip to Colombia.

Isabel's plane is scheduled to arrive in about 10 minutes despite the fact that it's snowing like crazy outside. This is a typical cold ass Syracuse day. It must be about -5 degrees outside and I won't even think about the wind chill factor. The weatherman is always quick to tell us what it feels like outside when it really doesn't matter after the temperature goes below freezing. I just consider this ball-freezing weather. When I walk outside I can actually feel my nuts crawl back up into my body. On days like this is when I begin to question my commitment to pursuing my master's degree.

I'm about to start my second semester in the Higher

Education program and I would be lying if I said that the first semester didn't kick my ass. Somehow I was able to maintain a 3.1 grade point average. While that's decent for an undergrad, it's totally unacceptable for a graduate student. I decided to stay up here after I graduated primarily to be in the same city as Isabel. She's currently in the last semester of her senior year as an undergraduate.

We have this whole thing planned out. I will stay up here for grad school, which would allow us to be together. Isabel would then apply to the Maxwell School to get her master's degree in International Relations, which is a one-year full time program. Since my program lasts two years, we would get our degrees together. I often think about how dope it would be to graduate together and proverbially ride off into the sunset with diplomas in hand. I really think she's the one. This plan is foolproof.

At least, I would like to think that it's foolproof. These last few months have been filled with worry. I've been getting this uneasy feeling of something being off, but I don't know where it's coming from. It almost feels like I've been on a runaway train with no control over where it's going. As much as I hated the idea of Isabel going to Colombia to visit relatives over the holiday break, there was a part of me that felt it was necessary for us to spend time away from each other. I think back to the letters that we used to write to each other when we first started dating. It's easy to tell that we had a thing for each other. I just hope that this time apart was good for us. I mean, I really miss her and cannot wait until she walks through those doors.

Amazingly her flight is not delayed and her plane lands safely. I try not to be too anxious but I can feel my stomach turning in knots. Why am I so nervous? Is it because I know that I've not been the best boyfriend? We've been dating for over two years and it's been absolutely great for me. Sure we've had our fights, but I'm not sure that I could love any woman more than I love her. However, my conscience is jabbing at me. Should I come clean and tell her what I did? Something like this is usually grounds for an automatic breakup. That's why guys will way say if you ever get caught out there: Deny! Deny! Deny!

The terminal doors finally open and out come the passengers. I wait patiently as face after unrecognizable face walks past me. She must've boarded this plane because she called from her mom's place before her dad drove her to LaGuardia Airport. I turned my head for a second to look at the board that displays the flights and when I turn back, I see Isabel walk in through the tunnel. She looks exhausted, yet radiant.

A big smile flashes across my face. She looks at me as she tries to manage a smile of her own. Maybe she's too tired to be as excited as I am to see her. She looks beautiful with her South American tan and dark brown shoulder-length hair. If I didn't know any better I would say that she lost some weight because her bulky winter coat engulfs her. Clearly, she enjoyed the weather down there. I approach her with full intentions of giving her the biggest hug. We embrace. "It's so good to see you. I've missed you so much," I say.

"I missed you, too," she replies quietly. I can sense something's wrong. I take her carry-on bag and introduce her to Madison. I almost forget that Madison wasn't in the picture when Isabel left. She has no idea what has happened in the three weeks she's been gone. Madison is very bubbly and says hello enthusiastically but Isabel is being her usual introverted self and only manages a small smile. I can already tell this is going to be a long ride back to campus.

We head over to baggage claim, which is at the bottom of

the escalator. I ask Isabel if she's ok, but she insists that she's tired from all the traveling. She just got back from Colombia a few days ago with her family. She stayed in Queens briefly and then flew up to Syracuse before classes start on Monday. Maybe she really is tired and I'm overthinking this whole thing.

Once we're at baggage claim all I can do is talk. I tell her all about my winter break and how I actually saw my mother during Christmas, which is a very big deal considering our relationship is strained. There's no response from her and I can tell she's trying her best to be polite by nodding her head with a seemingly condescending smile. It's a look that I dread because it usually means we're going to have an argument when we get to her place.

Perhaps Madison being here has thrown her off guard, but I did tell her that Madison volunteered to pick her up from the airport. I automatically start thinking that perhaps I did something wrong. Was she expecting flowers? Did I say something over the phone a few hours ago that bothered her? Perhaps it's that woman's intuition, I call it a "spidey sense", that is going off in her head since I'm feeling quite guilty about what happened a few weeks ago. Whatever it is, I hope I find out sooner rather than later.

The baggage claim wait isn't long. Hancock Airport is almost eerily empty at this time of night. The only people that are around are those from the same flight she was on. I don't have a watch but it can't be much past 10 p.m. At this point I just want to get her home and figure out what's going on. Even Madison is getting the hint that perhaps something's a little off about our interactions. I will try not to be too presumptuous. I really thought that this break we had from each other would be worth it. There's no secret about the fact that we had been arguing a lot before she took this trip. It was always over little shit. But slowly I kept feeling that I was losing whatever control I had over the situation.

I had a dream the other day that we were on a train going to God knows where and Isabel was the conductor. I needed to find a comfortable seat and she offered to assist me. We moved from car to car until we reached the last car of the train. When I entered it, I turned around to see her still standing in the other car showing me the pin in her hand that connected the two cars together. She was looking at me, as she twirled the pin around her finger, in her conductor's outfit. She even had the hat too.

I froze in horror as I realized she disconnected me from the rest of the train! Isabel wore that same condescending smile as my car violently derailed. I even think she waved too. I tried to grab on to anything I could find to stabilize myself and then I felt the fall. I woke up in a cold sweat knowing that the car fell off that bridge we were crossing into a mountainous ravine like you would see in the movies. With my luck, it wouldn't have been a quick death via fiery explosion, but instead I would land in a lake where alligators were waiting to devour what was left of me.

I have issues.

Somehow the small talk lasts us from baggage claim to the car. Isabel does manage a few replies when I asked, "How's your mom?"

"She's good." She replies.

"...and you brother?"

"He's good too."

As we get into the car I ask her, "How about your dad?"

I'm really reaching with asking about her dad. He never seemed to have many words for me. I often got the impression that he didn't care that his daughter was dating a dark-skinned Puerto Rican from the Bronx. I never once saw anyone as dark as me at any of her family gatherings or in photos. I'm not saying I was looking for Edgar Rentería, but still, someone has to be dark in this family.

"Same," she replies.

This is going to be a very long trip back to campus.

Thank God I'm riding shotgun because she cannot see me rolling my eyes. I turn the radio on to Z89, the campus radio station, just to not feel so awkward. *All My Life* by K-Ci & JoJo fills the air and I fight back a sarcastic smile. This song came out last year and won all these awards and yet, I still feel they play it too much. Madison looks over to me. I think she noticed my silent scoff at this song. She looks back at the road and tries to fight back a little laughter.

I fold my arms and leave the radio on that station. I look out the window and it's nasty out. The one thing that I can say about the city of Syracuse is that they really know how to clean up their snow. The roads on Route 81 aren't too bad at all, but I still have no idea how Madison can drive through this. The flakes seem like the size of quarters as they hit the windshield, but she keeps going as the defroster and wiper combination on her 1990 Ford Taurus Sedan work perfectly. I'm not sure I could drive in this weather.

It takes us about 25 minutes to get to the South Campus section of the University. Most of this trip was spent in silence while we listened to the radio. The conditions take a turn for the worse as we pulled into Isabel's campus apartment on Farm Acre Road. I jump out quickly and thank Madison for her services. I pull out Isabel's large suitcase from the trunk after I help her out of the car. She walks up to the door with keys in hand. I hope she said thank you to Madison. It would be rude if she didn't. I close the trunk and wave her off. She pulls away and I lug the suitcase into Isabel's apartment.

These South Campus apartments are bigger than they look. These units are segments of housing that have several connected apartments in each complex. From what I've heard they used to be old military housing. From the outside, it looks like each unit is small until you walk inside and see how spacious it really is. She lives in a two-bedroom apartment, which has a small kitchen overlooking a decent sized living room area. There is a sliding glass door toward the back in case you want to frolic in the snow. The best part about this place is that the bedrooms are located upstairs. There are other apartments on South Campus that have three bedrooms, but they only have one floor.

I can hear Isabel talking to her roommate as I carry her suitcase up the stairs and into her bedroom. Her roommate, Sasha, is also a senior but major's in Television, Radio, & Film Production at the Newhouse School. I place the bag in her room and I see Isabel walking out of Sasha's room smiling. Well, at least someone can get her to smile because I know I wasn't doing it.

Sasha and I wave to each other before she closes her door. She's always been the type to go to bed early and wake up at dawn for a jog around campus before her classes and on weekends. She's probably waiting for her boyfriend, my good buddy Jason, who is still at work at this hour. He's another friend of mine who decided to stay here for the love of his woman. Isabel walks past me and takes off her coat. She places it on her bed and turns around to look at me. She folds her arms very uncomfortably and then she looks down.

"What is it? I feel like there's something wrong," I say, as I close the door behind me.

There's an unsettling silence in the room. She turns around and looks out the window. It's practically whiteout conditions outside. The only color that can be seen is that ominous orange glow from the street lamps.

Isabel remains silent. I hate when I ask her a question and she takes forever to answer. It forces me to just stand here like an idiot looking at everything else. Although, I must point out that her room is immaculate. You can tell that no one has been in this room since winter break started. The bed is made up neatly. The top of the dresser with the small color TV is bare. The desk she's standing in front of only has her purse on it.

"I can't do this anymore," she says.

"Excuse me? What do you mean, you can't do this anymore?" I have no idea what's happening right now. Did I do something wrong? It can't be that, I haven't seen her in about a month.

She turns around and looks at me. Her energy has changed. Not just from the first words that she spoke, but her body language is a mixture of coldness and sorrow. Isabel's arms remained folded and her stance screams confrontation. However, her eyes betray her. I can see pain in them. "I don't want a boyfriend anymore."

Bang.

I feel like I've been shot in the face. Why is this happening? We were good just a few weeks ago, weren't we? "I... I don't understand. You were gone for like three weeks. How's this even possible? What happened?" I can hear myself coming up with more questions the more I thought about it.

Very calmly she responds, "I've done a lot of thinking during my time away from you and I decided that I just don't want to be in a relationship anymore."

"Just like that," I respond.

"Yes, just like that," Isabel's quick and direct response almost throws me for a loop. I feel my neck snap back as I look at her with disbelief.

I don't know what to say. I feel a wave of pain filling my chest cavity. Do I even try to argue this point? I can't force her to be with me. What does it look like to beg for someone to stay with you when they've already made the decision? "Can you at least give me a reason? Did something happen in Colombia? Did you meet someone?" I already hear my flurry of questions becoming pathetic pleas.

"No. I told you, I've thought about this. I just want to be alone," she says firmly and with a tone of ultimate finality.

"Really? So all of a sudden you just want to be alone? So, after two years you're just done?"

"Yes."

"Wait, so what about our plans? What about the graduate school at Maxwell? We had all of this figured out. We had discussions about a possible future together."

"There is no more plan and there are other schools. I've already begun to apply to some other programs. I just won't continue up here," she replies very dryly. Now I can feel my anger. This is complete bullshit. I don't even get a say in this because SHE doesn't want be in a relationship anymore? I want to put my fist through a wall, but I hold myself back.

This time I'm the one who replies with a firm tone, "Fine. I guess we're done then."

I wildly open up the door and storm out of the room. The door makes a loud bang and I'm about to head downstairs, but then I turn back and yell, "I just want you to know that this is complete bullshit that you cannot give me a reason why you don't want to be with me anymore. I tried my best to be a great boyfriend. I love you, doesn't that even matter to you?"

"Louis, don't make this any harder than it already is," Isabel replies as I hear Sasha open up her door. I guess I'm being too loud.

"Answer the question, does it even matter?" I yell.

Isabel looks at me for a moment. "No. It doesn't."

A LONG WALK

January is one of the worst winter months in Syracuse. The days are grey and the nights can be so dark that it makes you wonder if the sun is ever going to shine again. When it snows like this, there is no one on the roads. All you see are snowed over footprints of some poor bastard that braved the night walking to wherever they needed to go.

Right now, I'm that poor bastard.

After Isabel told me nothing I felt remotely matters anymore, I just left. I took two steps and I immediately regretted not calling Frank or Madison to come get me. I just didn't want to stay another second in that house with her. Imagine me stomping down her stairs while Sasha tries to figure out what's going on and I stop to grab their phone to make a call? Nope. I needed to get out of there.

I didn't want to stay and argue. The pain in my heart is just too great. She and I have had many arguments over the past two years but nothing felt as final as this. This was an absolute ending to what we were. Even though I know she cried when I stormed off, I knew it was over and now I'm trudging through this snow talking to myself.

I've made this walk several times over the last few months, just not in these conditions. Frank and I moved into an apartment complex at the end of the summer called Clarendon Heights. It's a nice little area filled with mostly graduate students. While I decided to go for my master's degree, Frank decided that he wanted to just find work here since he didn't want to move back to Buffalo with his parents. We originally planned on living with five other guys whom we hung out with during our undergrad years, but one summer in a house with them was enough for the both of us to seek housing elsewhere.

Fuck! It's so cold out here. If I had to guess, my apartment is about a mile from South Campus. There is no direct route either. It almost like a U-shaped route because I have to walk around this wooded area on East Colvin and Comstock. Of course there is no real sidewalk here either so every step is just snow and slush. This is why my Timberlands get so fucked up in Syracuse. With all the wetness and rock salt, I may have to buy another pair before February.

I'm having a hard time trying to wrap my thoughts around this. She doesn't want a boyfriend anymore? She couldn't have just come up with this decision lightly, could she? This was not part of the plan that we had set for ourselves and yet she already applied to other schools. We were supposed to be on this journey together. Now, I have no idea what I'm gonna do.

When I told people that I was planning on staying in Syracuse to do the grad school thing, they were happy. But then my dad starting putting this together and figured out that the real reason why I'm up here is because I wanted to be with her. Of course, it turns out that all my friends thought the same thing and now look where I am. I can't even say that I know what a breakup is supposed to be like. Isabel was my first real girlfriend and my true love. I know the thought of us ending up together and possibly getting married sounded a bit much for recent college grads, but we talked about it several times. Now those plans mean nothing.

I remember when I gathered up enough courage to actually ask her out. I was so sure that she was going to say no. We were in Maxwell Auditorium and the student government meeting we attended had just ended. She was sitting on one side of the room and I was on the other. Up to this point we only knew each other in passing via mutual friends and the student committees we sat on. I was way too shy to start a real conversation with her. After taking a few deep breaths, I walked over to her before she could leave and I asked the only question I could squeak out: "Would you like to go to the movies with me?"

Thank God she said yes. I had told myself that I would stop the self-pity because I wasn't getting laid as much as my other friends. So after a very bad experience with this girl, Brenda, I made a list (in my head, of course) of all the girls that I should ask out on a date. I could only come up with three names and Isabel was on the top of that list. I was almost sure she was going to say no.

The next couple years I learned so much about women and myself. I gained confidence in myself in ways I never had before. I figured out how to talk to women and express my emotions. This *was* my first real relationship. I mean, I did have a girlfriend before her but I'm not too sure she counts.

I now wonder if this is how Ingrid felt when I broke with her right before I graduated high school. I knew then that I was going to leave The Bronx to come up here to Syracuse for my undergrad degree. We had only been dating for a few months, but with her still being a junior in high school and me starting college, I didn't want to deal with the hassle of a long distance relationship. I felt it would ultimately be unfair to her if I got to campus and then cheated on her. I didn't want to be that type of guy. Ultimately I was happy with my decision. Yet, Ingrid wasn't happy about it. What I saw as a simple decision she saw as a complete disregard for what we were. Is this how karma works?

I could only assume that this is how it works because when I went home this past December, I found out that Ingrid is now dating my cousin Ruben. While this is something that shouldn't really bother me, I find myself so annoyed by this. Not that I should care whom she dates, but Ruben is family. It has been years since I have been intimate with her, but why now? Ruben should know better but I never got a chance to really tell him how I feel about this. Not that any of this matters right now.

I can feel my ears getting numb. I just made the right turn on to Thurber Ave. I hate walking down this street after dark due to the unnecessary amounts of small graveyards on this block. It almost doesn't fit the look of the rest of the street. I begin walking as fast as I can against the wind and the blowing snow. If I ever write a book about this place I cannot forget about how creepy these graveyards are. It's like something out of a George Romero movie.

I now regret leaving my CD Walkman in my apartment. At least I would've been able to distract myself with a little Wu-Tang Clan. I pull my skullcap down a little further past my ears. It helps, but not much. The snow is sticking to my coat and my jeans. These jeans are damn near soaked through, so I feel the stinging of the cold in my legs. My gloves are of little use at this point. Between the wind and the wet snow, these gloves are just a glorified covering. I try to keep my gloved hands in my coat pockets as much as I can, but it's hard to keep my balance on these snowy streets. The last thing I want to do is fall on my face. The best thing I can do is use my arms for balance and try to think of the hot shower I'm gonna take when I get home.

I shake my head. Home is where Frank and Madison are. For as long as I have known Frank he has never had a woman—not for lack of opportunity. The guys made several jokes in the past about all the ass he passed on during his days on the football team as a walk-on. Even our crazy friend, Ellis, used to say all the time that if Frank had dated a few white chicks, like the rest of the team, he might have seen more playing time. There was also an inside joke between the two of us about how him and I never seem to have a woman at the same time. We even chuckled a few days ago about how times have changed now that Madison's in the picture.

Yeah, times have changed indeed. I finally get to the entrance of Clarendon Heights. From here it's just a short walk uphill and I can finally rest. This has been the hardest walk of my life. The cold has been almost unbearable and somehow it all seems like a hazy, waking nightmare. I've been trying to fill my mind with thoughts that are not Isabel and it isn't working. I suppose I should feel fortunate enough not to be crying on this journey. The tears would probably freeze on my face and then I would get frostbite.

Did I mention I have issues?

Isabel filled a void that no woman has ever filled. I never thought that I could find someone that made me feel the way she did—both good and bad. I've learned so much from her on how to act proper in public while igniting a passion in private. I remember the first time I saw her naked. It must have been after date three or four. We spent all night out and I was just dead tired. It wasn't the first time she stayed at my South Campus apartment, but she never was in any real state of undress. I respected her and her wishes and to be honest, because I knew how conservative she was going into this whole thing, the pressure was off. I didn't need to act like "a man" who was going to knock the boots.

However, on that particular night when I tried to get some last minute reading done before I drifted off to sleep, Isabel decided to take a shower. When she was done, she walked in with nothing but a towel on. She had this look on her face of inspired embarrassment. I dropped my book as I looked at her and then, in kind, she dropped her towel. Her's is a beautiful petite body that was an almost perfect hourglass shape. From all our other encounters, I knew she was thin but what I didn't know was that she was still very curvy. My eyes soaked in everything I saw from her brown nipples, to her neatly kept pubic hair, and her perfectly manicured toenails. She promptly jumped into bed with me and we rolled around with wild abandon.

We didn't have sex that night. In fact, we never did. One of the things that she confessed to be during our first date was that her family was very Catholic. She wanted to do everything she could to make sure she remained a virgin and that meant waiting for the right man. I respected that because I went to Catholic school for 12 years. I know the bible pretty well and if that's what she believes in then who am I to tell her otherwise? Did I really not want to be in a relationship with her because sex was off the table?

Besides, there were other things that we did. We enjoyed the pleasures of oral sex and dry humping. She became bothered by the fact that I had a small collection of porn tapes of women that do "unspeakable acts" (her words). Maybe I shouldn't have laughed it off because Isabel was no saint in my humble opinion. Mine was not the first dick to be in her mouth (her words). So yeah, we never had intercourse but that was never an issue for me. Well, it wasn't an issue until about two weeks ago when temptation got the best of me and I let Madison give me a hand job.

I know! I beat myself up about this all the time. Maybe I do deserve all this. But she wasn't with Frank at the time. She hadn't even met him yet. This was just an incident that I wanted to sweep under the rug and not tell Isabel about. One incident shouldn't destroy a relationship, right? God forgives and so could she, right? I want to believe this. I don't want to think about how maybe it was never meant to be between us. Maybe I can change her mind tomorrow.

I fumble for my keys and then I finally open the door. The smell of marijuana hits me so hard that I almost choke. I walk in and on the couch is Frank and Madison looking completely baked sitting in front of a bong on the coffee table. Madison is underneath a red knitted blanket with the appearance of being topless and her hair is all messy. Frank is sitting right next her with no shirt and his orange Syracuse University basketball shorts. Clearly, I've disturbed more than just a weed session.

"Dude, I didn't expect you here tonight, is everything ok?" Frank asks with his red glassy eyes looking at me.

I close the door and lock it. I kick snow off my boots and shake off the rest of the snow from my body. I slowly take off my coat and place it on the coat hook by the door. I know the silence is a bit awkward but I cannot seem to get the words out at the moment. I untie my boots quickly and place them by the door. I step in snow on the carpet with my damp socks. This irks me. Finally I reply, "We broke up."

Frank looks at Madison, then at me and says "What? Are you serious?" If it wasn't for the fact that I'm so upset right now, his reaction would actually be hilarious. This man is so blunted right now that his surprised reaction is stunningly slow.

It's mind boggling to realize that he was never a pothead until about a week ago.

"Wait? Did you just walk here from her place?" Madison asks. She's the veteran weed smoker and the person who got Frank to love this habit. She can be completely baked and not show it as much. A functional weed head for sure.

"Yeah. I just walked. I couldn't be there anymore."

"I knew there was something up with her! She was acting all funny. What happened?"

I hold up my arms and let them drop to my sides, "I don't know. She just told me that she doesn't want to be in a relationship anymore."

"That is fucked up." Frank replies.

"I don't get it. Did she say why?" Madison asks.

"No. She just said that she's been thinking about this for weeks," I say as I put my head down. This is going to be the question of the year. From this point on, when anyone asks why we broke up, the conversation will be just like the one I'm having right now, except without the weed. This will be an endless nightmare that I'm going to hate to relive over and over again.

"I'm sorry. You should have called, I would've come back to get you," Madison replies.

I want to shake my head and say, *and disturb the naked weed session you got going on? Hell no.* I don't have room for witty remarks. I already feel too tired for this conversation. "I didn't think to call. I just ran out of there."

"Damn man. You gonna be alright?" Frank asks.

"Nah, I'm fine. I'm gonna be in my room."

I walk into the small hallway and make a right into my room. I close the door and I lean my back against it. I take my wet pants off and throw them across the room. I slowly bend my knees and sit on the floor. I take off my socks and ball them up. I throw them too out of frustration. The sock ball harmlessly hits the wall and lands on my bed. I begin to rub my cold legs as I look around the space I call a room, a wide room with a walk in closet that leads to the shared bathroom. I picked this room because I thought Isabel would be over here a lot. I didn't want to disturb Frank with our all night sessions of non-sex. In any case, it would give her freedom to use the shower and not worry about crossing the main room of the apartment.

That was me thinking about her needs while trying to figure out my own living situation. The rest of this room is pretty empty except for the full-size bed and 20-inch television on the floor. At least the floor is carpeted.

I just sit here. Rubbing my cold legs. Thinking about what the hell I'm going to do now.

Memorial Sloan Kettering
December 19, 2015
8:13 a.m. ET

"Are you sure you want to do this?" Naomi asks. She puts down the book on her lap and looks at me. I'm almost surprised that she read through the first two chapters so quickly. I did take comfort in the fact that she laughed at a few parts however.

I'm still sitting on the chair I pulled up next to her. While she was reading the book, I was going through some emails on my phone. I have a terrible habit of not sorting my email and I end up paying for it when I'm trying to search for something I need. I put down my phone and reply, "Do what? Write a book?"

"No, write about this. I remember all of this and this was a tough time for you. Are you sure you want to go there?"

She has a point. I've been asking myself a similar question ever since I totaled my car last year, *why the hell am I writing a book?* "I consider this to be part of a cathartic process that I need go through. When I look back at my life in college and all the things that happened, I used to ask myself, why's this happening to me? Then as I got older, I begin to realize that was the wrong way to look at it. These things didn't happen to me, I allowed them to happen based on choices and non-choices. Yes, it was a hard time for me, but I'm willing to put it all out there. Besides, what better way to create a debut novel than to base it on your own life?"

"I guess you're right. I just never had the courage to do something like this myself and now look at me. I'm stuck in this hospital until God knows when."

I'm reminded of the constant battle that she's in. The pain and agony of knowing her body refuses to cooperate. I avoid the entire thought process that revolves around the idea that I could lose such a good friend so close to my age. I've had discussions with my dad about how he's losing so many of his friends the older he gets, but he is like 72. I'm almost forty and I refuse to think this can happen to me at such a young age. "You know, it's never too late. I'm sure you can write that great novel that I know you have inside of you."

She regarded me and smiled. It's a look that I know so well. It's a smile that conceals the pain within. "I really do love the fact that you are so optimistic of my chances to survive this. You're one of the few good friends that actually texts and visits me. People can act so brand new when they find out you have cancer. They never know what to say. Some just tell me to feel better as if all I have is a simple cold. Others look at me like I have a death sentence. I can sense the pity coming from them. But you've always been so optimistic about me walking out of here."

"I have to be. You're too young to be lying up in this hospital. I know in my heart you can beat this. After Monday, you will be on the long road to recovery. I know it, I can feel it right in here," I pound my heart.

29

Naomi looks down. "Maybe. God willing." There's an awkward silence. What do you say to friend who might be dying? Before I can say anything she continues, "I hope you plan on changing the names in this book."

I chuckle, "Uh, yeah, I probably should. I had planned on changing the names before I publish it."

"But, you're still keeping the title the same?"

"I think I will. I just love the sound of it." I put my hand in the air like I'm sliding a bracket in place and say, "The Book of Isabel. It's kinda simplistic, yet biblical."

"Biblical?" Is that what you're going for? Why not just title it 'The Gospel According to Louis'". She chuckles.

"Hey! Don't laugh! I thought about that but I thought that would be too self-serving. Besides, I would then have these right-wing conservatives buying the book in hopes of finding a Latino gospel and thus the key to our vote," I say mockingly.

"Well I think they lost that vote the moment Donald Trump started talking about Mexicans being rapists."

"That's true. Him and his 'no more PC' rhetoric is great for all those gun-toting, islamophobic rednecks but it's getting old really fast for the rest of the country. He must've felt illegal immigration was strictly a Mexican issue when he first said it, but I'm sure it never occurred to him that Latinos have long memories and when you mess with one of us then you mess with all of us."

"Does that include the Dominican Republic?" Now she's pulling my cape. This was such a hot topic earlier in the year. With everything else going on, I almost forgot about the issue with Haitian citizenship in the Dominican Republic. I love Dominicans and their passion for life. I've met so many of them in my time at Syracuse and when I came back to New York, I moved to Washington Heights. Yet, the issue of the treatment of Haitians had everyone I know up in arms. What's considered to be an immigration issue for the people on the island, turned into a race issue for the people in America.

"Hey now. I never said that." I chuckle. "I still have love for Dominicans, I just hate the policies of their government. Not that I should talk, Puerto Rico can't seem to get their shit together either. Pretty soon it will only be tourists that live there." I've tried my best to not talk too much about Puerto Rico or the Dominican Republic since I don't live in either place. The bad thing about being second generation is that I know I don't have as strong of a connection to Puerto Rico as I should.

"Very true, it's not like those GOP Hispanics care very much about that." She scoffs.

"Of course they don't, they have no ties there. Cruz and Rubio are children of immigrants that don't care about other immigrants. They'll have this faux outrage about this wall that Trump wants to erect, but then talk about the need to reject Syrian refugees as if we don't see how dangerous their rhetoric is."

"Well, I hate the politics of our own government. How many theaters and churches are going to get shot up before people start waking up? How many videos of black people getting killed or beaten do we have to see before people wake up? Black Twitter can't be the only people in this country that sees all this bullshit happening." Nayo roared back.

"We live in a country that has a intricate love affair with

guns. As long as there is a perceived threat from terrorists (and I mean the Muslim kind and not the white-hooded kind), we will have people crying about gun rights. There will also never be a real discussion about the "mental health" of a police officer that can unload his clip into a guy walking across the street. The blue wall of silence is strong in every city," I reply, thinking about the newspaper headline from this morning.

"But the minute we decide to apply for a gun license, the NRA will have a fit."

"Exactly."

This is what we do, discuss politics and social justice. This is something we always seem to get around to. Our days of protesting tuition hikes and racist cartoons in the student newspaper in college have given us the unique ability to question everything and everyone. This year made it easy for us to question everything because it was a banner year for racists. There were plenty of church burnings, police brutality, racist presidential candidates, shootings conveniently branded as isolated acts of the "mentally ill", cops killing black men, black women "committing suicide" while in police custody, and this new trend of transracial identifiers. It's 2015 and the KKK is still rallying. We found time to smile when the Confederate Flag in South Carolina came down, a serial rapist cop got convicted of raping 13 African-American women, and when the Supreme Court ruled in favor of marriage equality. It all seems like too much, especially when calculating all the mass shootings from San Bernardino to Paris. I'm just glad that I was able to finish this book while all of these historical events were going on.

After a few minutes of laughing about the fact that this year has been President Obama's "blackest" year yet, she changes the subject with a more serious tone. "Did you really have to put HIM in the story?"

"You must be talking about Ellis," I almost cringe when I say his name. Its one thing to write about him as a character but saying his name almost feels like I'm summoning Gozer the Gozerian. There's a lot of history there and I knew that when I was writing this book, but sometimes the best way to exorcise a demon is to call it out and confront it.

"God, yes I am. Do you even have to say his name?" Nayo asks this like she's almost wincing in pain.

When I started writing this book I didn't want to get bogged down with made up names. It becomes a chore thinking about a good name, then looking them up to see what they mean. I needed to go with what felt right, so for now I used the real names. Later, when I'm in the final stages of editing, when the book is to my satisfaction, I will change all the names except for Isabel. She is my personal demon that I need to call out.

"Oops, my bad. I will make sure not to mention him verbally again. But, yeah, regardless of our feelings for 'he who shall not be named', he's a part of everything that happened in college. Just remember that when all is said and done his name will be changed."

"I understand that. I just get a visceral feeling when I see his name in print. I think back to all the things he's done. Not only to me but also to you. I'm sure you know that I would just rather not hear his name ever again."

THE THING ABOUT MADISON

How do I describe this pain? It's this numbing, dull sensation at the center of my being. It feels like a chest wound, but when I put my hand over my heart there's no physical pain. I know this wound is completely emotional and psychological in nature, but the ache is palpable.

I haven't told many people about what happened. I don't even know what to say. I mean, I told Frank and his girlfriend. I had to tell Nayo because I tell her everything. But how am I going to tell my dad? He barely likes her as it is. Isabel was nothing but a brat in his eyes and I know he thinks I've enabled her to be that way. I can't have him hear me like this. I have to be a man about this and deal with it.

Men don't cry.

I have to put this all out of my mind. Saturday night was horrible. The breakup, the freezing walk, and all the outpouring of emotion while I laid alone in my bed. I certainly didn't cry but I got very little sleep. Yesterday was a whole lot of me moping around and trying to figure out where I go from here. Yeah, I called her a few times. I needed some answers and when she hung up the first three times you would think the fourth time would hurt less.

I had to get this all out of my system so I can be prepared for the start of classes today. I didn't want to show anyone that anything was wrong. It was so hard to sit in my first class of the semester and concentrate on theories of Higher Education. That numb feeling would take over every so often, especially when I start looking at things that would randomly remind me of her. After awhile it wasn't just random things, but it became anyone who remotely looked like her. By the time class ended, everything reminded me of her. This is horrible.

Men don't cry

I already feel like I'm barely getting through this program and now I have to check out from my emotions for as long as I can. Some of my classmates have come to know me as the person who asks a lot of questions because I like to be engaged. But not today, I just sat quietly. I felt listless moving from class to class this morning. As I now head to the Student Union, a sense of dread wells up in the pit of my stomach. *Isabel works at the information desk.* I'm not even sure if her shift is today but I have no choice but to pass by there. I was originally going to meet up with Nayo at the cafeteria, but I became extremely paranoid about the possibility of bumping into Isabel. So I called Nayo last night and told her to meet me in the auditorium.

I was one of those unlucky people that didn't get an assistantship when I was accepted into the program. This is my own damn fault because I applied too late, but I was lucky enough to still have a job as a temp technician for Event Productions on campus. This is the department that provides all the A/V and technical needs for all the events on campus. Frank should be in the auditorium testing the new soundboard that we got over the winter break.

I walk into the main entrance of the Student Union at a quick pace. I can tell from here that the person at the desk is not Isabel so I can now breathe a little easier. I will have to make a mental note that she doesn't work at the information desk on Monday afternoons.

The Student Union is an oddly-shaped building with glass door entrances on every side. At the center of the atrium is a circular set of stairs that leads to the floor below. The information desk is closer to the southern entrance where I just came in.

Today is also the first day of class for the undergrads as well, which is why the atrium is extremely busy at the moment. There are students everywhere mingling and walking through the main floor. The sound of music gets louder the further I walk in as people flow in and out of the cafeteria on the west side of the building. This place is a hub for Black and Latino students. This union is the only place where we can gather and hang out, particularly the Black Greek organizations. Unlike their IFC and PanHellenic counterparts, who have houses to reside and party in, NPHC makes good use of the Student Union as a base for recruitment and operations.

There are a series of wooden tables around the parameter of the atrium where students sit and promote their organizations. The buzz is unique and lively.as several groups have their CDs blaring. I immediately notice the Latino Students Association table by the north entrance. My heart jumps because I see Isabel's best friend, Lucy. Next to her is an empty seat, which could easily be meant for Isabel.

From my vantage point it looks like Lucy is busy talking to some other students so I walk quickly past the tables and head for the entrance of the auditorium located on the east side of the building. I know the doors are locked so I enter through the elevator, which has double doors, and opens from both sides.

I walk through and I already see Naomi leaning on the wall. Her black hair is pulled back into a small bun. She still has her coat on and is listening to her Walkman. She glances at me as I walk towards her. Nayo picks up her book bag from the floor and flings it over her shoulder. A clear indication she's ready to go.

"Hey" I say.

"Hey there. Are you ok?" she asks. A worried look crosses her face. My morose demeanor must be obvious.

"You know I'm not." I try not to look at her directly. For some reason I don't want her to see the pain in my eyes.

"Did you see her out there?"

"No. Was she there when you came in?"

"No. But, I got here 10 minutes ago. I did see Lucy so I thought there was a chance that she would show up. Did you figure out where you wanted to eat?" Nayo's tone suggests that she's trying to be upbeat. This is how I must sound when I try to cheer her up.

"Just not here."

"We can go to Acropolis."

"That's fine. I just need to check in with Frank. Do you know if he's here?"

"He's in the sound booth."

"Let me just drop off my bag. You don't want to leave your bag here?"

"No, I plan on heading straight to Newhouse after we eat."

I walk into the sound booth and I see Frank rolling up some microphone cables. It seems like he's enjoying himself as he bobs his head in unison with *Hypnotize* by The Notorious B.I.G. As usual, he has on a Buffalo Bills shirt.

The booth looks pretty standard even with this huge new 32-channel soundboard overlooking the auditorium itself. The Goldstein Auditorium is a multi-purpose event space that seats about 1,000 on the floor and 500 in the balcony. At the moment, the floor is empty, except for the large motorized lighting truss in the center of the floor. Frank must have lowered it from the catwalk above anticipating my arrival. Directly behind Frank are the amplifiers and sound equipment. I never really bothered learning much about sound because I feel like I'm more of a lighting guy. I would rather deal with the overall look of a show instead of how it sounds.

"Hey man. I'm leaving my bag here so I can grab some food with Nayo. I should be back later to focus the lights on the truss."

"That's cool. Where you headed?"

"Marshall Street. Did you want to join us?"

"Nah. I'm good. Madison is gonna drop by with some food soon." Even though I asked him to join us, I'm glad he said no. I fully intend on telling Naomi the story of me and Madison and I don't need him as an audience. I've already told him this story and I'm sure the closer they get, the more he wants to forget that certain things that occurred between her and I.

"Okay man. I'll see you in about an hour or so," I say. Then I leave the booth.

Naomi follows me back out into the controlled chaos that is the atrium. We both figured that being in a crowded place is just as good as being alone, particularly when you're a graduate student. Sure there might be a few people from the class of '99 or '00 that may know us, but for the most part I see a lot of freshman and sophomores.

Before I walk out of the double glass doors next to us I hear someone calling my name, "Louis!" I turn around and it's Lucy calling me from the LSA table. I look at Naomi and I mouth, "Fuck!"

Naomi stands by the glass doors while I walk over to the table. "Hey Lucy, how are you?" I say this in the liveliest way possible, even though her best friend ripped my heart out.

She gets up from the table and we hug. Lucy is a short, fair-skinned, Puerto Rican and is the current president of the Latino Students Association. The club is her life and she does everything she can to promote it. Her snugly-fitted LSA shirt has a design with a fist encircled by flags that represent the countries of Latin America. Lucy has a fiery personality, but she's also one of the nicest people I know. We've interacted a lot during my days in Student Government, so in many ways we have a separate relationship that doesn't involve Isabel.

We do the small chat stuff and ask each about our vacations. The main reason she called me over was to promote an event they're doing during Black History Month about black Puerto Ricans.

"This looks really interesting. I will see if I can drop by," I say dryly as I look at the flyers she hands me.

"I hope so! I know how much you're interested in this," Lucy replies.

"Yeah," I say. There is a slight pause in the conversation as I view the flyer. She's right though as I'm very interested in this topic. There have been several meetings over the last few years where we've discussed prejudices within various aspects of Latino culture.

"Also, the LSA Banquet is April 10th at Drumlins," she points it out to me on one of the other save the date flyers she gave me.

"Wow, you already know the date?"

"Of course, we're always on point, especially since it's not on main campus. You know this takes a lot of planning. I hope you come to this too. It's our 10th anniversary."

"With any luck maybe I will work this event."

"That's right, Isabel told me that you work events for the school now." Lucy caught herself. I know that she was only trying to cheerful. "I'm so sorry Louis," she says as she grabs my arm.

I look at her. "It's okay."

"No, I wasn't thinking. I didn't mean to be insensitive. Isabel told me you two broke up and I'm sure you're having a hard time with it. I can see it in your eyes."

Nope. Don't do it. Don't cry. "I'll be fine. I mean, shit

happens right?" I smile.

She stays quiet for a few seconds, "You're a good guy. Just know we're still friends."

Men don't cry

"Thank you for that, Lucy."

"One more thing..." Lucy says as if she noticed that I might be feeling down. "The submission deadline for the LUCHA magazine is in March. I would love it if you could submit one of those poems you supposedly write." She says this with a smile.

I brighten up a little bit. "Now, that, I think I can do."

I walk back to Nayo and she asks if everything is okay. I nod and we leave the building. I remain silent as we walk to Marshall Street. Naomi fills the air with conversation about the latest gossip that she's heard. She's a great friend that has known me since we started the college experience. She knows me well enough to know that right now I would rather be silent because I need to keep my emotions in check. *Men don't cry*. During my phone call with her yesterday, I explained everything that happened and while I didn't have the emotional release I should've had, she knew how devastated I was by this whole thing. She knows I feel like this breakup has come from out of nowhere.

Even Nayo had a hard time trying to explain why this would happen. What possible reason could there be? Of course, if I ask my dad he would probably say, "She fucked another guy." That is not the response I want to hear and the reason why I will probably avoid that fun conversation for as long as I can. Truth be told, Nayo agreed with that possible reason when I told her what he might say.

Right now I refuse to believe it. I would like to believe that Isabel's not that type of person. She's told me personally that she would never be the type of person to sleep around which is why she wanted to wait to lose her virginity. I know that I placed her on a very high pedestal because she meant the world to me. Don't I deserve some sort of explanation? Probably not and that's something that I cannot get out of my head. Maybe I deserve all of this sadness and guilt.

The walk to Acropolis is no more than five minutes. It's a medium-sized pizzeria that can hold its fair share of costumers. The line to order food is not very long. We sit down in a booth after we order lunch from the counter. Naomi is talking about this undergrad that failed really badly at flirting with her.

"I don't understand, is it really that hard to come correct to a woman these days?" She asks before taking a sip of her Lemon Tea Snapple.

"Maybe he didn't want to beat around the bush."

"Okay, I get that. I like sex as much as the next woman, but that doesn't mean that guys should be crass about it."

"That's true, guys are dumb."

Nayo rolls her eyes, "That's your answer to everything isn't it?"

"Yup and when it stops being true I will let you know." These conversations used to be livelier. I know that I should be joking more or even do the occasional chuckle but I can't. I'm broken on the inside. About another five minutes go by before they call out our pizza orders. As we begin to eat, I finally speak my mind.

"I feel this is all my fault."

"That makes no sense. Why would you say that?" She replies.

"There's something I need to tell you about Madison."

"Madison? As in…Frank and Madison?"

"Yeah. This is all karma coming back to me because I cheated on Isabel."

The story goes like this:

I met Madison at my other part-time job where I'm a telemarketer for an exclusive buyers club called The Direct Club. We're the people that call you at around dinnertime to get you to come see us in East Syracuse. The one major benefit of this club is that members can browse the catalogs and purchase from any major manufacturer in the country. So if a member just bought a new house, they could furnish their new place with furniture directly from a company like Natuzzi at the wholesale price.

This club is truly incredible, but there's one problem. The price of membership is insanely high. For $2,000, members can have access to these catalogues, which to me was crazy, but there are people who actually join and use the club. It's my job to "cold call" people and try to convince them to accept our invitation to the club. I would give my affirmatives over to Madison, who would then follow-up about a week later to see if they got the invite. She would take on the sale from there.

This is her full-time job and she's quite good at it. It's decent money for me and I do this for about three nights per week.

A few weeks ago, before I went home to New York for Christmas, the club had a holiday party. I wasn't going to go at first because I really didn't have a way to get there. I normally took the Centro Bus and while it works for me during the day, the evenings are always a problem. However, Madison was more than happy to come get me and take me to the party.

The party itself was not that great. I thought it would be just an employee party but it turned out that they also involved members of the club as well. The real purpose was to nosh and mingle with all those who can actually afford this club. This was Madison's opportunity to really shine. She is indeed one of the best salespeople there. She has a wit and charm about her that can be very attractive. On this day, she wore a tight red turtleneck sweater with a pair of dark denim jeans and dark brown high heel boots. This is was the first time I had really seen her body. Madison is a few inches shorter than me and has an athletic build.

She definitely had me wide-eyed, but I just took the sight of her all in and tried to not think anything of it. I mean it has been more than two years since I've had sex and in spite of that fact, I still had a girlfriend whom I loved. My thoughts were just to keep that in mind until we started drinking. Let's be real, there are plenty of women out there that look hot and when all else fails, masturbation is typically the final answer.

The club's manager made sure that all the liquor was top shelf, so a lightweight like me was feeling it after a few *Cuba Libres*. Madison had a few glasses of red wine and that's when the flirting became noticeable between us. When the members left the music changed and all the employees were really starting to have a great time. We danced a little too much and a little too close. So close that we snuck away to the loading area where I found myself making out with her while both of my hands were under her sweater. I really felt bad about that later.

The car ride back home was interesting. I felt guilty the whole way despite my alcoholic buzz. This was the first time I'd ever cheated on any girlfriend I had. Of course, I've only had two, but still, I didn't want to be that guy. When she stopped the car to let me out, we talked. I had opened up to her in the past about my lack of sex and she told me right there in the car she would be willing to be my outlet with no strings attached. I didn't have to answer her then, she told me to think about it.

I came back early from visiting the family, just a few days after Christmas. I wanted to get a jump on reading for the semester and make some extra money at The Direct Club. Madison convinced the manager to give me a few extra hours during the holiday break since she seemed to get a lot of membership sales through my cold calls. I really needed the extra hours for books. I always seem to barely make rent at times, but with the extra paychecks I planned to get a head start on the necessities.

Of course, Madison and I would exchange glances. I figured this would happen, but after my conversation with Ruben about all this, I felt that my resolve had strengthened. He pointed out that despite my up and down feelings about my relationship, Isabel had never done me wrong. I needed to do everything I could to be a better boyfriend and that started with two things: Not telling her what happened and never doing it again. I convinced myself that it was my one and only moment of weakness.

That all seemed fine and good until the day before New Year's Eve. It was snowing pretty heavy that night and

Madison had asked if she could crash at my apartment for the night. This wouldn't be the first time she asked. Madison lived with her mom in Truxton, which was a place I had never heard of before until I met her. It's about a 40-minute drive south of Syracuse.

"It's not snowing that bad. I've see you drive home in worse conditions," I said.

"Yes, I know. But the truth is my mom has a new boyfriend and I don't get along with him. I know it's an inconvenience and I'm sorry. I will just stay at a hotel," she replied.

Clearly I couldn't let that happen because I began to feel bad. Despite our make out session, she was the reason why I was getting more hours at the club. I finally gave into her.

"I can't let you do that. You can stay on the sectional couch."

"Are you sure your roommate won't mind?"

"He's still in Buffalo visiting his parents."

We get to the apartment and I showed her around. She really liked the off-white sectional couch. "This is so nice! Did you order this from the club?" She asked.

"No, Frank and I were lucky enough to know someone who was moving and wanted to get rid of it."

The couch is not that new, but the former owner took great care of it. It forms an L shape around a glass coffee table that we got at a garage sale. I went to the linen closet and pulled out a blanket. "It can get cold in here so this should help you out," I said as I handed it to her.

She took it and placed it on the couch. "Thanks, I do tend to sleep naked so this well help," she said with a laugh.

I raised my eyebrows. "Okay then."

"I'm kidding."

I don't think she was. I still felt the sexual tension between us. I wish I could say I didn't like it, but that would be a lie.

"Well make yourself at home. The television is right here and it works. I have some beer in the fridge too."

"Okie dokie, what're you going to do?"

"I got some reading to do. Then I may fall out." What I didn't want to tell her was the truth. Yes, I planned on doing some reading because Lord knows I needed to, but I really just wanted to write Isabel a letter so I can distract myself from a possibly naked woman on my couch. Of course, if all else failed I was going to jerk off and not worry about anything.

The night was uneventful. I had my TV turned on to ESPN most of the night as I tried my best to get some reading done. With the NBA lockout and boring ass college football bowl season in full swing, I managed to get a lot of reading done. Every so often I would hear her rustling out in the living room as she's watched TV. I also wrote a draft letter to Isabel. I told her how I much I missed her and how I wish she wouldn't be gone so long. Two weeks with no contact is such a long time. It really made me wonder about our future. I mean who really knows what she's doing in Colombia. Is she really the last woman I will ever be with? I'm 22 talking about marriage, which is kinda scary when you think about it.

I sighed deeply. Clearly I needed to get back to reading. The overthinking was not doing me any good. Usually, I liked to settle down with some milk and cookies. It sounds a bit childish, but to be honest its one of the things that calms me down. It goes back to when I was a kid and my mother used to give me milk and cookies before bed. There must be a connection there.

I opened the door to my room and headed to the kitchen. I saw Madison lying on the couch looking at the news. The covers were wrapped around her body while she was on her back with her head turned toward the television. I didn't think it was that cold in the apartment but then again, I'm always hot.

Still awake huh?" I asked.

"Yeah, I can't sleep."

"Is the couch not comfortable?"

"No, it's comfortable. My body is not cooperating," Her eyes remained fixated on the news. The weatherman was going on about lake effect snow coming in from the north.

"Alright, well I'm going to get some milk and cookies, do you want anything?"

"Aw, milk and cookies. Isn't that so cute," she replied playfully as she finally turned her head in my direction.

"Oh hush," I said as I walked toward the small kitchen that over looks the living room.

"But, I'm alright. I already grabbed one of your beers."

"Really, which one?" I opened the fridge and grabbed some milk. There was barely any left for a full glass.

"The PBR."

"Pabst? Yeah, that's Frank's. I don't drink those." I grabbed a glass and pour what's left from the carton into it.

"What? Pabst is great!"

"Yeah I'm sure you think so." I grabbed the bag of Oreos from the cabinet and walked over to the part of the couch that wasn't taken over by her.

"What's that supposed to mean?" She smiled.

"It means that I'm sure you love a beer that does nothing for me. I'm sure they're other things we don't have in common." I put the glass and cookies down on the table.

"I see what this is." She sat up still wrapped in the blanket.

"Excuse me?" I asked as I started to eat.

"Maybe you're trying to come up with reasons to decline my offer by saying we have nothing in common. I mean, it's fine, because it's not like I asked you to be in a relationship."

"I never said all that."

"You really don't have to. Be honest, you never said no to my offer. Not when I made it and certainly not within the time that I've been here," Madison proudly stated.

She got me there. I have to admit that I'm just a little too curious about her. I'd been telling myself how Isabel is in another country and all I've been really doing is fighting the feeling that's coming from my pants.

"Look, maybe you're right. I guess I have been debating your offer and thinking about whether I really want to do this. I've always told myself that I would never be one of those guys that would cheat on a woman and I've already kissed you."

"Yup. Technically you've already cheated," she chuckled.

Shit. Dammit. I had been trying to give myself reasons not to do this. "Well, aren't you being the tempting one." I gulped down the last bit of milk and continued, "Was this your intention the whole time to come here and fool around?"

"Nope. I mean, I'm always down for a good time but I can't force you to do something you know you want to do. I didn't force you to kiss me at the warehouse. You were pretty excited all by yourself," she chuckled. That was also very true. It was my idea to sneak away because I really needed to feel up on her.

"Ok, fine. It's absolutely true that I keep thinking about that night and I want to do things to you that I haven't done in a long time. But you know I can't."

"You can't or you won't?" She asked firmly but not maliciously. I've only seen her like this before when she was closing a deal at the club.

"What's the difference?" I fired back.

"There are plenty of differences Louis, but hey, I get where you're coming from. I've been thinking about that night too. You took charge and knew what you wanted and I kinda liked it but no pressure from me. But if you change your mind…"

I looked away. I was stalling. I looked at the television. "What are we watching now?"

"Looks like some expose about a Y2K problem."

"A what?"

"I don't know how to explain it but what really matters is that there's nothing on TV," she answered as I got up to put the glass in the sink and then the cookies away. Then she asks, "Going to bed now?"

"Yeah, it's getting late. I need to get up early to go my other job. See you in the morning."

She said good night and I walked into my room thinking about how close that was. I was this close to going to the other side of that big ass couch to see if she was indeed naked. I'm glad I didn't and, at that moment, the most important thing was to take a shower. I'm so glad that I have my own door to the bathroom. I can walk in and out whenever it's unoccupied in my birthday suit.

Before I got undressed I walked into the bathroom and turned on the shower. I adjusted the water temperature. As usual the water was pretty cold so I let it run from a few minutes. I walked back into my room and started taking off my clothes. In fact, I locked the door to my room in the process. I didn't need any surprises when I came out of the shower. I really didn't want to make any assumptions, but she just seemed like the type of person that would do something unexpected.

I knew the following day was going to be a long one. I had

to go to main campus and sort some cables with Brian. Normally, I would've had some more help, but Frank wasn't coming back for another few days so that process was going to take some time. Sorting cables is not the easiest job in the world. Most of what we do with events in both sound and lighting is about cables. If they can go bad, then they need to be replaced. More importantly, they needed to be sorted so that they're easier to find when we need them for major events like the annual Greek Freak and Block Party concerts that happen every spring semester. Brian is one of the students that works for Event Productions, he just happens to live in Syracuse. Sam, our supervisor, asked him if he could put in a few hours that week to help out. Once I was done with that I'd to go to The Direct Club and get on the phone for a few hours. Of course, somewhere in between all that, I would eat and study, so I was planning for a long day indeed.

I stared at the television and wondered how many times I could watch Sportscenter in one night. It had been more than a few minutes so the water should've been good. I walked into the bathroom and opened the curtain. Madison was in the shower, hair wet and naked. I was in complete shock. She must've used the other door to get into the bathroom. I never thought to lock that one.

She looked at me as the water hit her back and said, "I hope you don't mind." Her freckly white breasts were perky and I was right about her athletic build. I was just as intimidated by her shape as I was aroused by it. I noticed the tattoo right above her navel as well as a thin strip of pubic hair. Madison was the whitest woman I'd ever seen naked.

She smiled and I realized that I was just as naked as she was. "So are we just going to stare at each other or are we going to share this very awesome shower?" She said.

I made a very quick decision and stepped into the shower. "I'm still not going to have sex with you."

"Well that's your choice." Madison handed me the bar of soap. "The least you can do is wash my back."

I took it and reached for my washcloth. "I thought you weren't going to force me to do anything I may not want to?"

"I'm still not forcing you, but that doesn't mean I can't have fun," she smiled. Madison turned around and that was when I saw the elaborate tattoos on her back. At first glance it looked like several tattoos but I got a closer look, it was one huge tattoo. It started at the center of her shoulder blades with a drawing of the planet Earth then coming from both her left and right sides stretching down both sides of back were twisting vines that reached above her ass and reconnected. Right above that was quote that read: *I can calculate the motion of heavenly bodies, but not the madness of people.*

"Nice Quote." I said as I tried to figure out what her body was telling me. It's such a thoughtful quote on an elegant body.

"You like that? Any guess who said it?" She asked as she brushed her ass up against the erection that I couldn't hide. I put my hands around her waist and looked up and down her back.

"I have no idea." I tried to think of ways I could get out of this but I had to admit that this was way more fun than I was used to having with Isabel. I also heard this voice in my head telling me that I should really stop fronting and just have sex with her all over this bathroom.

"The quote is by Sir Isaac Newton," She answered slowly with a half moan. Madison continued to gyrate slowly.

53

"I suppose you are the heavenly body," I replied softly.

"What do you think?"

I pulled away and I began to lather up. Noticing this, she turned around again and I answered, "I think that I'm the person who's gone mad."

"You know what I'm absolutely fascinated about? You are a man of your word." She put her arms on my shoulders and continued, "I would've figured by now you would have..."

I began to kiss her.

We passionately kissed for a few minutes as the water rained down on us. I felt her breasts as I kissed her neck. I heard a slight moan coming for her. She grabbed on to my erection and tugged it ever so slightly.

Between neck kisses I said, "We're still not having sex."

Madison whispered, "I know."

Naomi is wide-eyed, "I'm not sure what surprises me more. The fact that you did all this or the fact that you're telling me this now. Wow."

I'm just about done with my slices of pizza, which tend to be relatively small. I ordered another slice.. Right now this is the best I can do considering that my appetite isn't where it normally is. "I admit I'm a little ashamed to tell you. I felt like you would look at me differently. I told you guys are dumb."

"It's not about that. I mean this girl was giving you no ass so I guess it was only a matter of time before you would seek it out elsewhere. What confuses the fuck out of me is how is

Madison Frank's girlfriend?

I sigh and sit back on my booth seat, "A few days later she drove me home and she wanted to stay over again."

"You fucked her this time?"

"No! I had ended it but again she wanted to stay over on the couch and since Frank was over I figured we would just ignore her and play Mario Kart. But then, they started talking and apparently they hit it off. One thing led to another and they were doing it."

"That same night?" Nayo scoffed and sat back.

"Yup, that same night," I say as I finish up my last slice of pizza.

"That's crazy. When did you tell him about Madison?"

"I told him the day after it all happened, but I guess her eyes charmed him."

"Her eyes?" She asked sounding perplexed.

"She has really nice eyes." I chuckle.

The one thing that pushes Madison's charm over the edge are her eyes. A pair of blue eyes, with a spark behind them that gives her an almost irresistible aura. Sometimes you can see the light behind someone's eyes and it tells you everything you need to know about them. Personally, her eyes told me that she's a huge freak.

"I'm sure the back tattoo had something to do with it" Naomi says as she shakes her head. I already know what she wants to say. She wants to talk about how black men always seem to have a soft spot for white women. We've had this discussion numerous times before over the four years of our undergraduate lives. The things we've seen and heard about athletes and successful alumni are something I should consider writing books about in the future.

THE BALLOON POPS

I don't know how it all started. One minute I'm fine, just trying to get through the day and then the next, I'm crying like a baby. I managed to get through this first week ok, but my heart is still heavy and I haven't eaten much. Somehow I've found the will to get up every day to go to class and then both jobs.

Today, however, was different. The pressure of everything must've gotten to me. The not knowing the reason for this breakup and the realization that this relationship was no more than a simple joke has wrecked my mental being. It all started with a phone call this morning with my dad.

I knew that I had to call him. I knew that I needed to tell him everything that happened with Isabel, but up until that moment I couldn't bring myself to do it. My dad tolerated her with a certain disdain that only I saw in his expressions. He considered her to be a diva and not in the good way.

It reminds me of my awful graduation weekend, which was a time that was supposed to be joyous, but this celebratory event led to too much drama. This is the weekend when my family first saw Isabel for what she really was. First it was

Ruben that decided to take me out to Dreamgirls on Erie Blvd on Saturday night. I'm not sure what upset her more, the fact that my cousin took me to strip club or the fact that I had "Happy Graduation, Love Vivienne" written on my bare chest in red lipstick. Either way, it lead to an argument at 4 a.m. in her South Campus apartment.

Of course, commencement festivities began at 9am. I was so tired that it was difficult to run interference between those two. All she wanted to do was dropkick him and he was too busy pointing out she should take the stick out of her ass, unless she was into that sort of thing. It was this back and forth type of situation that annoyed the shit out of my dad and my stepmother.

I know my dad agreed with Ruben. I knew that he felt she had a stick up her ass too. Isabel's whole nose in the air demeanor was not appreciated and he saw it first hand on the drive back to New York City later that afternoon.

Ruben wasn't the only person in my family that upset her that day. His brother, Desiderio was also there with his wife Joanne. I hadn't seen the two of them since the day they got married a few years ago. Isabel didn't like Joanne. I'm not entirely certain why, but I did notice they were hardly ever in the same room together.

Ruben told me at the strip club that he thinks it's a woman thing and that I shouldn't even pay attention to it. In fact, he straight up said "Fuck Bitches, Get Money." He had just gotten out of a relationship so I took this with a grain of salt. I should have listened when he told me to stay away from Joanne just to be on the safe side. "Try not to be overly friendly." My only thought was, whatever. Joanne is practically my sister-in-law so why would I start treating her differently?

Well, when commencement ended I found my way back to the family through the crowds. It took me awhile with all the hugs, the pictures, and the general realization that I may never see some of these people ever again. The family was waiting in the large corridor on the field level of the Carrier Dome. I greet them all with a big smile and I hug every one starting with the person closest to me, Joanne. Turns out that was not such a good idea. In my defense, I figured hugging my girlfriend last was a good gesture on my part because I was saving my biggest hug for her. I knew something was wrong the minute I hugged her.

My dad was very insistent on getting back to The Bronx before 8pm. He had to be at the firehouse by 7am the next morning and that meant he wanted to get home, relax, and then go to bed. So, once I walked across the stage, I was on his time. When the hugs were done, it was time to go back to South Campus, get my shit and hit the road.

It was when we were packing the car that Isabel made it clear that she did not appreciate being the last one hugged. "How dare you hug Joanne first! There was no reason why that should've happened. I felt like a fool waiting for my turn," Isabel said barely whispering. She never liked having an audience when we argue but she was so upset the whispering barely contained her rage. I couldn't believe what I was hearing. Was there something going on that I wasn't aware of? Was there some beef of some kind?

With all the business and drama of just getting my shit in this minivan my dad borrowed, I told her off. I said, "This is what you're upset about right now? Get the fuck over it. You've been on my ass since last night. This bullshit that my family doesn't like you is all in your head." I barely contained a whisper as well. I wanted to yell but then that would've drawn attention.

Isabel glared at me as if I just said the wrong thing. This time she didn't whisper, "Fuck you. I knew I shouldn't have stayed up here for your graduation." From that point on she shut down and went into the minivan to sulk. I looked around to see if anyone has just witnessed this. My stepmother glared at me from the other side of the minivan.

Isabel sat there and started to cry. I had no idea what to do. My stepmother pulled me aside, "What the hell is going on with you two? What did you say to her?" Ana, is a short Ecuadorian woman that can be the sweetest person in the world until you piss her off.

I'm almost speechless at this point. What am I going to say, that Isabel cannot stand her daughter-in-law? No, I have to play this down a bit. "We're just having an argument that's all."

"So she's crying in the car for no reason?"

"It's not like that. We gotta go and she keeps on nagging me about something that's not important."

"Women don't nag for something unimportant. Get it together. It's a long ride and your father is already annoyed that we're running late," Ana scolded me and then walked away. She was right and I had to figure out a way to fix this.

A long ride indeed. We did manage to pack the car and be on the road before 1:30pm. I will admit that I had a lot of shit, but the good news is that most of it was ready to go when it came time to pack the van. Meanwhile, It felt like Isabel sulked for the entire five hours on the road, but the worst part was when we stopped to eat in Scranton. She wouldn't get out the car. As a show of solidarity I decided to stay with her. The look my father gave me told me a story longer than this one.

I tried to talk to her, but she shrugged me away. "Isabel, I don't understand why you're being this way."

"What's there to understand? I'm sure your family thinks I'm this crazy little stuck up bitch because I don't want to eat with them. But you know the truth as much as I do. They don't even like me. Just admit it!"

"That is not true. Why would you say that?" I lied. This is not the time to talk about families not liking each other. I certainly don't complain about her dad and his indignation towards me.

Isabel scoffs, "Your fucking rude ass cousin has the nerve to say that I have a stick up my ass! Oh yeah, that's coming from someone who likes me. I'm not even sure YOU like me." She begins to cry even more. Either I didn't want to admit it at the time or perhaps hindsight is 20/20 but I knew her assumptions about my family were true.

At this point I began to worry if she had any tears left. I reply, "Why would you even think that? I love you. What's going on with you? Help me understand."

She pauses then says, "You didn't even defend me to Ruben and then you hug Desi's wife before you even hug me. None of this makes me feel good at all."

"Is there something going on with you and Joanne?" I figured this would be a good time to ask because I'm very confused as to what's going with them.

"She's just a fucking bitch. I tried to be nice to her and she was rude. I just don't want to talk about it."

That was the extent of that conversation and for the next

several days I had to try to piece back together our relationship. We got to the Bronx on time to unload the minivan. My dad reluctantly drove her to Queens afterwards and was on his best behavior when he dropped her off in Kew Gardens. But that ride home to the Bronx was just as brutal having to explain all her bullshit without making her look worse. I guess I refused to believe there was something inside of her that thought we were not meant to be. That was the point I knew he would never really care for her.

So when I called him to tell him that we had broken up, I expected him to be upbeat with an "I told you so" tone in his voice. I dreaded dialing his number but I had to be a man about this.

"Hello," My dad always sounds like he's yelling into the phone.

"Hey papí," I say with as much happiness as I could muster up but I know I failed.

"What's wrong, son?" He asks this and I already feel the emotion coming through my eye sockets. Today is the day this man wants to be compassionate. I was hoping for a bad mood so that it would be easier for him to tell me to forget about her.

"How can you tell something is wrong?" I chuckle a little bit to hide whatever emotion is now bubbling to the surface.

"You're my son and I know you. I can hear it in your voice. ¿Qué pasó?"

There's a short pause. I swallow so that I can save face and not break down on the phone. "Isabel and I…we broke up." At this point I'm expecting a laugh, a joke perhaps, anything sarcastic but that's not what I got.

"Louis, I'm so sorry to hear that. I know how much you cared about her. What happened?"

I slowly tell him the story that began with waiting at the airport for Isabel. He listens patiently and doesn't say a word. I get through the story without choking up and when I'm done he begins asking questions.

"So, she never told you the reason for the breakup?"

"No. Like I said, she doesn't want to have a boyfriend anymore."

"And you believe her?"

"I honestly don't know. I guess so."

"Son, I'm going to say a few things you're not going to like but just understand that I would never steer you wrong. But first let me just say that I understand your pain. I've been there papa." I can already feel the tears coming out. There are times when I can remember when I was a child when he was affectionate enough to call me "papa." It's like saying, "my little man." It always seems to happen when I'm most vulnerable. He continues, "I've had my heart broken more times than I can count. I've been in love with women you wouldn't believe and this was before your mother. Just know that you're not alone. These things happen and they will get better."

"Thank you." I say softly. I thank God that he cannot see the tears running down my face. I breathe in slowly so he can't tell I'm crying. I don't even want him to hear me sniffle. I cover the mouth of the cordless phone with the palm of my hand when I'm not talking.

My father continues, "Now for the bad part, I think she's lying to you son. I think she's hiding something that she doesn't want to admit to."

"What do you mean?"

"Let's think about this. You once told me she was a virgin, right?"

"Yes."

"Has that changed? I mean, if you don't mind me asking but have you had sex with her. Actual sex. Not the little bullshit foreplay you kids these days try to pass off as sex. I mean penetration…"

"I get it dad! No. We've never had sex."

"Maybe she has." He says bluntly.

Bang.

I feel like I've been shot in the head again. There are no more tears now. I just feel heat coming from my face "What are you saying?"

My father sighs. "Son, I love you but sometimes you're a little too gullible. You have to look at the world for what it is. Why would any woman suddenly feel the need to not have a boyfriend anymore? Why would she say that to you?"

"I don't know!"

"Ok, I think you need to be prepared for the possibility that she may not be a virgin anymore. Maybe she went down to Colombia and had a few guys plug her."

I literally almost choke. "What??"

"I'm sorry, I know that was a bit harsh, but you need to understand that women love sex as much as we do. Maybe she found some asshole that she liked and he slipped her some..."

"Ok! Ok...but then why would she lie then? Why not just tell me the truth?

"To save face. Maybe she doesn't want to hurt you more than she already has. It could be that she's being real selfish and doesn't want you to know that she cheated on you. I know it's hard to accept but you did put her on this pedestal as if she could do no wrong. Isabel doesn't seem like the type to admit to something like this, so she will just come out and say she wants to be single, which by the way, is a red flag that proves my point."

I really didn't know what to think. My father has always been a straight shooter in these situations, but it really hurts me to think this might be even remotely true. What does that say about her? More importantly, what does that say about me? Here I'm thinking this entire time that I was this complete asshole for succumbing to temptation with Madison. Maybe I did put Isabel on a pedestal. Maybe I ignored warning signs that she was unhappy. I stay silent because I'm not sure what I should say.

"Are you ok?" He asks.

"Not really."

"I know you have a lot to think about but I want you to know that I was like you oh so many years ago. I was very much in love with my first wife, at least I thought so at the time. But, after I came back from a few months at sea with the

Navy, I found out she was cheating on me. It changed my life. I wasn't one of those guys who fucked whores when we went to different ports. I always stayed behind because I knew I was married. Then I come back and she's taking it in the ass from some guy down the block."

"What did you do?"

"What do you think? I kicked her out."

"But what did she say? What was her reasoning?"

"All she said was that she was lonely. Of course she apologized, but later on I realized that she wasn't ready to be married and neither was I."

"How old were you?"

"I was 19."

"Whoa," I say stunned. My dad has never told me this story before. I did know that he was married before my mother but her never went into it.

"Yeah, so you will be ok son. In time you will get over this as I did. There will be other women in your life and you will have more failures at relationships. This is the way life is. I was not a complete angel myself you know that. I had my series of women and affairs but none of that really matters once you find that woman who loves you as much as you love her. I would tell you to forget her but I know you can't. Just try to move on."

"Thank you dad. I have to go now."

"You sure you're gonna be OK?"

"Yeah, I will be fine. I'm getting another call. I will call you back soon," I lied. I need to get off this phone.

"Ok son. Take care of yourself. I love you."

"I love you."

I hung up and then cried harder than I had before.

MY SECRET LIFE

This is my secret life wrapped up in damp skin, cheap perfume, and fake breasts. I started feeling the effects of the 40 oz. I downed 10 minutes ago after I said "fuck it," I'm going to Adult World. I need to get away from my life. I needed to stop thinking about the pure shit that's my existence.

I focus my attention and energy on a very sexy black woman that wraps her body around a pole that's at the center of a broad stage. Her well-built naked body is the best thing that my eyes can absorb today. Her stage presence is everything I need right now. I came here to see her, to get lost in her movements, her body, and her magic.

I know the days that Vivienne performs at Adult World because there was a time when I came here quite often to bask in her seduction. It's been a couple of months and I miss it. Today, I needed to get away, just for a few hours, from this meager existence of crying over a woman I can no longer have. I would rather be caught up in a fantasy starring Vivienne. I would rather get lost in her eyes and her scent. I would rather get lost in her breasts and her G-string. I would rather get lost in her smile even if it means that I'm paying for it.

Her slow movements on the stage elicits an erotic dance that's in perfect unison with the music blasting from the speakers. Most strippers dance to fast-paced music, but not her. She was dancing to *Sour Times* by Portishead and it's as if she's reaching into my soul giving it head. Her nude body and all her movements are speaking a foreign language that only a few people understand and she knows it. The men in the audience probably don't even exist to her.

I don't exist. I'm happy not to exist because there's no betrayal in non-existence. There is no pain in the vacuum of non-existence and yet all of her rhythmic maneuvering drags me back from the ethereal to reality. Her ever-evolving choreography constantly reminds me that we are privileged to be in the same room with her. There is no pain here, only her.

I love this place because I'm a non-entity. I'm just another paying customer whose life choices have lead him here, to this place, with the hope of being teased. I can sit in the middle of this small venue and fade away watching nude women come and go off that stage. I can choose whom I want a lap dance from and I already know it's from Vivienne. She won't reject me because I'm just another paying customer and our relationship is that simple, pleasure and anonymity. I pay for her to give me the attention I only wish I could get for free.

The fixed seating gives off a theater-like quality that doesn't resonate in other clubs. I do my best not to look up at the stage lighting because that only reminds me of my reality outside of this place. So I keep my vision directly on stage because it makes me comfortable to sit in darkness while I watch the show. My emotional numbness and disconnection to existence makes me feel better. It means the pain is not real. But from here she can see me if I wanted her to, I just have to give her a reason. I play with the singles I have in my pocket with my fingertips in anticipation of her coming into the audience. I know this game. I've played it before with her.

I pull out a dollar and I begin to fold it in half lengthwise. I smile while looking at her, hoping to get her attention during her routine. Vivienne does a long swing on the pole and gently lands on the ground. She crawls to the front of the stage and remains on her knees. She grabs her big fake breasts and licks her nipples as she scans the room. She notices the dollar I'm slowing waving and the game begins.

She smiles at me. There is recognition there. Her favorite customer has returned. How long has it been again? Weeks? Months? My invisibility now fades as she climbs down the small stage and provocatively walks towards my seat. Her platform heels make her look overwhelmingly sexy. Vivienne sits on my lap and never breaks eye contact with me. She smiles and says softly, "Welcome back, Professor."

She grabs my head and pushes it between her breasts. Her skin is cool, but unbelievably comforting. She smells heavenly and for a brief second, this is everything I want. This is where I want to live. She shimmies her torso from side to side. Once she's done, I lean back and give her the dollar. Vivienne, with her hands on her breasts, moves towards the dollar and I place it in her cleavage. She squeezes her breasts together and takes the money then mouths "thank you" and winks. She then gets up and continues her show.

I'm completely turned on by everything about her as I watch her bare ass walk away. Her sex appeal is off the charts. Other guys begin to give her dollars as well and this doesn't bother me. This is the business of being a stripper. There is an unwritten contract that all patrons must abide by once they sit in these seats. It states that we cannot touch the women unless they allow us to. They're also not property. Even though we're giving money to them to stroke our egos and make our dicks as hard a possible, they are in control. We are not allowed to disrupt that fantasy with our desires.. The only thing we control is the amount of money in our wallets and right now I have enough money for her to dance for me.

Her dance routine ends after another song and she collects her cash and her clothes before heading backstage. Amber, a tattooed blonde white woman, comes out on stage and begins her routine. She's a little too skinny for my taste and my interest in her fades, so I wait. It normally takes three to four minutes for any woman who performs on stage to count her money and get redressed before returning to the seating area to continue the fantasy by offering lap dances. I know there's a chance that I may have to wait a little longer than I anticipated. There may be a few guys here that want a lap dance from her a much as I do, but considering that all the guys in here are white and are focusing on Amber, I think I won't have to wait long.

As expected, Vivienne walks out in a short one-piece strapless dress with the same platform shoes and she heads towards me. She sits on my lap and we begin to chat. "Hey there professor, it's been awhile. Can I interest you in a little private time?" she asks.

I nod my head and say, "yes" without being too eager. She grabs my hand and I get up and follow her to the "VIP" section, which is just a fancy way of saying this area is for lap dances. Vivienne calls me professor because she knows I'm going to graduate school. She was fascinated by the idea of my becoming a professor even after I told her what I was really going to school for. Of course, I would never correct her because I'm not going to ruin a potential lap dance.

The VIP rooms are a small set of rooms separated by a curtain. This incredibly huge black guy that she nods to guards this area. We enter to the second room on the left and I sit down on the bench. She closes the door and I look around the dimly lit room. This looks like it could have been a dressing room from the Gap. There are mirrors on the walls and ceiling in case anyone wants to see all angles of the ass.

She takes off her dress in one quick motion and turns around to face me. Once again, she's totally naked and I grin. Vivienne has always been the perfect stripper to me. There are no blemishes that can be seen in dim lighting. She has no tattoos so her clear brown skin looks flawless. This all comes together with her voluptuous curves and a thin pubic hairline. This is another reason why I love coming to this place. Adult World is the only adult club in Syracuse that is fully nude. The draw back is that due to New York State law, they cannot sell alcohol if the women are bottomless. Thankfully I'm still buzzed from that 40 oz. I drank outside.

She used to work at Dreamgirls, which is just a topless establishment. I went there to see her because a black woman stripping in this town was a rare sight. When Ruben told me was she working here, I knew I had to come visit her. It was almost a weekly visit during the summer before school started back up.

She sits on my lap again and begins to gyrate. This is where I can touch her a little bit more. My hands are on her back tracing her curves. Lucky for me the mood has been set by Amber's second song in her routine. *Closer* by Nine Inch Nails is blasting over the speakers, which is notoriously a stripper song.

This quickly becomes a chair dance that she controls and once she senses my arousal she takes her gyrations to another sensual level. She guides my hands on to her breasts allowing me to feel on them as she dry humps me hard. She moves her head closer to me and begins to put her lips on my neck as if she's about to kiss it. I can feel her hot breath and she releases a well-timed moan that makes every hair on my body stand up. Then she gently bites my ear. She places her hand on my head and she vigorously straddles me while rubbing herself on my erection. Vivienne knows she has me.

Then she stands up and begins to dance. She turns around and bends over and I stare at her ass. She orders me to slap it and I do. She sits back on my lap and I get a view of her back as she moves back and forth. I look to the mirror on my right and I see what this all looks like from the side. I reach over and grab her tits again and she leans back while we do our erotic chair dance. As she moves, I move along with her.

She gets up again and turns back around then places her right leg on my shoulder while doing pelvic thrusts in rhythm with the music. I get a view of her belly button ring and a very faint landing strip right above her clitoris. Then she bends her leg, which thrusts me, face forward stopping inches away from her vagina. Then she kicks her leg straight and I'm sitting upright again.

"You're such a bad boy. I can tell by looking at you that you wouldn't mind putting your face in between my legs," she says as she sits back down on my lap.

I nod my head in agreement and the song ends.

She smiles at me. "Would you like another one, my bad professor?"

I can't resist her. I should say no, but I know myself pretty well. I knew that I wasn't going to do just one song. I'm having fun and enjoying not thinking about anything else. "Yes, I would love another one."

"You sure you can handle it? You haven't been here in a while and it seems like someone's about to burst out of their pants."

I smile, "I think I can handle things on my end."

The next song comes on. Another rock song that I cannot place. She begins to gyrate slowly. "How's that stuffy girlfriend of yours?"

"We broke up."

"Oh no, well that's a shame." She says as she rubs herself on my erection again. I will not delude myself into believing that this isn't anything more than an act to get more money at the end of the night, but if I didn't know better I would almost think that she's actually taking pleasure from our interaction.

This time I grab her ass as we continue this chair dance together. She puts her tits on my face again. I grab them and she orders me to bite and lick her nipples. Vivienne let's out another slow moan and I start thinking about how long I can keep this up. I don't want to go home with a wet stain on my pants. If I'm not careful that could happen really soon.

I begin to breathe heavy to hide any moans and she looks at me as she goes faster. "You're not allowed to unload in your pants without my permission." She stops moving to look at me as if she's making sure her commands are being heard. Then in one swift move, she leans all the way back putting both of her legs on my shoulders with her feet resting on the wall behind me. Her hands are on the floor as she moves her vagina inches from my face. This beautiful sight dances in my face for only a minute, but it seems like forever.

I've always been amazed by her athletic build and her

ability to do something like this. I'm looking right at her pussy knowing that this is the one thing that I continue to get in trouble for, yearn for, and fall in love with. It's the most beautiful thing in the world. I would reach out and touch it if it didn't go against the unwritten contract that I signed the minute I walked through those doors. I'm renting this view. I'm paying to see what it is I'm missing from my life.

She pulls herself back up easily and I no longer wonder how she has such tight abs. Her legs are still wide open in front of me with her knees bent. She shakes her breasts. "Too bad about your ex-girlfriend. You should've brought her over. I could've given her a lap dance just like this," She says as she moved her left hand down her navel and on to her clitoris. She uses her two fingers to open her lips. There is no question that Vivienne is the sexiest stripper I've ever seen in my life. I keep coming back to her because my fantasy life is richer than my real life. This is better than any comic book or video game I can ever play.

I bite my lower lip.

"Maybe what she really needed was for me to sit on her face," she says as she rubs her fingers up and down her clitoris. She continues, "I could have wound her up so good she would be begging to come here every night with you." She puts her index finger inside then pulls it out and is about to place it on my lips then pulls it away.

She smiles and shakes her finger telling me no. Her pussy is not mine. I do not pass "Go" and collect money, but she will. I will shortly return to my nonexistence as a normal customer as she puts her finger in her mouth then spins off my lap onto the floor. Her moves are graceful. She crawls to me and places her hands on my lap, then starts stroking my legs and works her way back up to my erection. She buries her head in my lap and bites it gently. I almost scream in anticipated agony that quickly turns to pleasure.

The song ends. My mouth is still gaping.

She looks up and asks, "Would you like another one?"

Softly, I say no and I start going into my pocket for cash when she sits backs on my lap. "Don't let the pain of a broken heart define who you are. I'm only telling you this because you are one of my favorite costumers and I feel the pain coming from you. One day you will let it go and you will smile and say, 'Vivienne was right.'" She leans in and kisses me on the lips gently. I close my eyes for a moment and before she pulls away. She bites my bottom lip just hard enough to make it still feel good.

She smiles again. This dance has ended and the contract fulfilled. She gets up, her small dress slips on as easily as it came off.

I stand up and give her $50. "Thank you."

"You're welcome, professor. I will see you soon."

Yes. You will.

SERENE

I feel a little better. Over the past week, some people have suggested that I should see a therapist. I suppose that going to Adult World is my therapy. Somehow everything makes sense in the moment and Vivienne is certainly cheaper than any doctor I might see. I've also received other suggestions that I should start dating someone else. This is easier said than done. I do have someone that I've had my eye on so I just went with that idea.

Her name is Serene. When I asked her out I could hardly believe she said yes. But that's just typical of me to think that a woman would automatically tell me no. That's also the reason why I had to ask her out. I needed to change the way I viewed the women in my life. It was bad enough this breakup with Isabel still has me acting in ways I didn't like. I needed to change my perspective.

Serene is a beautiful name for a beautiful woman. She works at The Direct Club as a telemarketer. We normally split up the week since we're both part-timers, but there are a few days that we both work at the same time. Serene was hired a few weeks after I was and right away we began a little friendly competition for the amount of slips we could hand over to

Madison.

We were always friendly and never flirted even though I found her to be very cute. She has chocolate brown skin with a set of light brown eyes that will melt any man's heart if he's not careful. She never dressed inappropriately which made me use my imagination to figure out what she might be hiding underneath her jeans and sweatshirt. I could tell that she has a nice set of tits on her that were more than just a handful. She wore her hair naturally. Serene doesn't seem like that type to relax her hair, but I have to admit I don't know her all that well. I do know that her nails are always manicured and her eyebrows are always tight.

I must say that the day I asked her out I was feeling particularly horrible about myself. I saw Isabel on the Quad earlier that day. I was coming out of the computer cluster in the Physics Building heading toward the bus stop when I glimpsed her. I had the urge to say hi, but before I could I say anything this guy walked up and started talking to her. It was cold, as usual, so I wasn't going to stick around. I did notice it was Felipe she was talking to, again. I hate that guy. I won't even get into it right now.

For the entire bus ride all I can think about is this gap in my life. It has been three weeks since this breakup. Valentine's Day is around the corner and being alone is the last thing that I need. I'm not saying I need a girlfriend or even a date, but maybe a prospect, a possibility that perhaps I can get by all of this.

This made me wonder about Serene. Why shouldn't I ask her out? She's the kind of woman that normally intimidates me because of how attractive she is. She looks like a woman that you need your A game for and I'm not even sure I have my B-game on deck right now. Fuck it, I was going to ask her out anyway.

This was my last week at The Direct Club. I gave my notice last week because I can't work in this place anymore. My numbers were slipping and I'm barely keeping up with school. To be honest, I've lost all sorts of focus and if I'm going to get that back it should be while doing schoolwork. Besides, if I were going to quit one of my two jobs, it was always gonna be this one. My job as a lighting tech isn't nearly as stressful and I don't have to worry about satisfying a bottom line.

So, here I am in the break room when she walks in. Her hair is really curly today. When she walked in, Serene smiled at me as she went to the sink to rinse out her cup of whatever she was drinking.

"Hey Serene, how are those calls coming today?" I said. It sounded so fake and I hated myself for it.

"I'm doing OK. I think Chad purposely gives me numbers for Brewerton because he knows most of them will say no," she responded. Chad is the assistant manager who is in charge of the call center portion of the club. He makes the phone calls along with everyone else and he's extremely good at it. I have a theory that he gives her the harder areas because her voice is so damn sexy. Of course, I could be wrong about that, but I would find it hard to say no to her.

"So you're getting a lot of no's then?" I ask with a smile on my face. At least I can pull her leg by way of this friendly competition we have.

She shrugs, "Not really, they just need a little bit more coaxing to get that yes!" she smiles.

"Always be closing huh?" I finger quote that. This is

something Chad is always saying to the associates. Everything is about the final sale.

"That's right!" She laughs as she heads for the door.

"Um. Serene..." I needed to stop her because it's now or never. No one is in the break room, which is a miracle, and I will kick myself if I don't take this opportunity. For one moment I'm reminded of that day in Maxwell Auditorium when I asked Isabel out.

"Yes...Louis?"

Shit, I paused and now it's awkward. I can feel myself getting really nervous. I try not to shake. "I'm sorry. I'm just not good at this."

"Good at what?" She has a look of confusion on her face as if I told a joke without a punch line.

I laugh a little, a nervous laugh that probably broke the tension. "I just think you're a beautiful woman and I was wondering if could get your number." My face getting really hot and I'm already feeling the "no" coming. Serene's face changes from general bewilderment to surprise.

"Wow. That is so sweet. There's no reason to be nervous at all. I would love to give you my number. But, I thought you had a girlfriend?"

"We broke up a few weeks ago. I really didn't feel like telling anyone." I try my best not to be real excited right now. I'm so busy thinking that no woman would ever want me again that I almost missed out on this.

"I'm sorry about that. I'm in the same boat too. I've been

single for a little over a month now. Do you have a pen?"

Of course I don't. I would only carry a pen if I were used to asking women for their numbers. I do the "searching my body for a pen" routine with both hands patting various pockets. "Actually I don't," I say and I begin to smile.

Serene smiles back, "You are too cute. I have a pen at my cubical I will write it down or you." I wait for her to leave the break room before I pump my fist in the air like Allen Houston who just hit a three at the buzzer. It feels like my luck might be changing. I don't want rush back too quickly to my cubicle. I need to be cool and not seem like I'm a desperate fool. I take deep breath and leave the break room.

I walk back to the call center where people are busy in their cubicles on the phone giving their pitches and reading their scripts verbatim. On my desk, I see Serene's phone number on a yellow Post It note written perfectly with a smiley face under the numbers. Under the numbers was her AOL screen name, SxyEyes315.

I sit down and lean back thinking how awesome this will be. I look over my shoulder and Chad winks at me and mouths, "you're the man." He's a balding, slightly overweight man dressed in khakis and a light blue collard shirt. His cubical is neat with pictures of his wife and kids pinned up alongside all the scripts. The chord of his headset drapes down his shoulders and trails toward back of his chair where his sports coat is hanging from. His chair is spun toward me and he must be on the phone with a customer. I smile and then he points to the phone telling me to get back to work.

My last week working at The Direct Club was a breeze after that. I started feeling like I was on the right track. Frank noticed a change in my mood at work and at home. The days seemed just a little brighter. I started wearing my contacts again and I got my hair cut. I actually smiled in public while walking through the Student Union the other day.

Nayo commented that there might be hope for me yet. Just to think that last week I was this sniveling pile of a man crying about a woman who didn't love me. The best part of this week was that I really didn't have to call Serene yet, since I saw her a few times at work leading up to my last day. Also since I didn't have a computer at home, I made sure to visit the computer cluster a little more often. I was new to this whole online chat thing, but I remember making an AOL screen name a few months before I graduated. The internet just seems to get bigger and bigger every time I log in so I don't want to get left behind. I figured at some point I will get a PC at home if that's even possible. In the meantime, I could use the university's computer to do homework and chat with Serene.

She even drove me home on my final day. It made me give serious thought about getting a driver's license. Madison was happy for me too, but if I didn't know any better I swear I sensed a tiny bit of jealousy coming from her.

I want to take things slowly with Serene. I don't want to play any games with her. I just want to have a good time with no worries. It makes things easier because I feel like I could do this dating thing and while we really hadn't gone out on a first date as of yet, we did grab dinner together a few times after work. So our first kiss in her car seems very natural.

"I normally don't kiss a guy before he calls me," Serene smiles.

"Clearly, I'm a lucky man."

We kiss again before we say our goodbyes.

"So when are you actually going to take me out?" She smiles. We've had this discussion before in a playful manner but now that I don't have work breaks to navigate anymore. I need to step it up.

"Last time I checked you don't work Saturday."

"Ooh. You're swinging for the fences huh? I can do Saturday."

"Great, I will call you tomorrow then." We kiss one more time because...why not?

Thank God I'm not one of those dudes that had a lot of stuff in his cubical, just a few pictures and a digital clock radio that plays CDs. I pull my keys out and open the door to what I expect to be the usual sight of Frank and Madison blunted on the couch.

This time it is a much different feel. They're both on the couch looking rather sober and fully dressed. Madison is still in her work attire. Was I out that late? I leave my coat on because this is just weird. "What's going on?"

"Isabel was just here." Frank says very plainly as if he just wanted to get it out quickly before I lose my shit.

"What? She was here?" I ask in disbelief.

"Yes." Frank answers

"My ex-girlfriend?"

"Yes." They both say this in unison.

"She was here?"

"Yes," in unison again.

"Isabel?"

"Look, I don't know how to say this but yes she was here." Frank says. I would say it's refreshing to hear the sarcasm coming from him right now, but honestly, I'm not amused.

"What the fuck? Why was she here?" I ask with in complete exasperation. I'm both angry and disappointed. I wanted to be here when she showed up and I missed out on it.

"She came by to drop that off," Frank points to a box next to the door filled with fairly familiar things.

I kneel down to look through it. "I don't understand. This is all the stuff I gave her."

"Isabel said this was all your stuff that she's giving back to you."

I look though the box in disbelief. There are things in here that are definitely mine: the Big Punisher and Outkast CDs I've been looking for, a few ties, my extra toothbrush, a stick of deodorant, and my old pair of glasses. However, the rest of this stuff in here, I *gave* her! The Lauryn Hill album, *The Miseducation Of Lauryn Hill,* how can she give this back? She is also giving back *The Motorcycle Diaries* by Che Guevara. Are you kidding me? I don't even want to look through the rest of it. I stand up. "I can't believe this shit. When did she leave?"

"A few minutes ago." Madison says.

A part of me wants to run after her. It's not like she has a car. How else would she get here? Wait. "Was she alone? How did she get here?"

There's no way this woman walked that path and she doesn't know that many people with a car. If Jason drove her, Frank would have said it already.

"No. Felipe drove her," Frank says calmly.

THIS MOTHERFUCKER! I am seething. My night is now done. Actually, my entire week is just done all because Isabel picked this day of all days to return my stuff. I can tell from his face that Frank is waiting for me to lose it. I can't say I blame him. I'm the type of guy that will throw something against a wall because I lost a race in Mario Kart 64. I really want to kick this fucking box across the room but I promised myself no more emotional outbursts because of her. I'm just going to close my eyes and breathe. I need to remember the kiss from Serene. I need to remember that this weekend will be my first date in a very long time.

Frank breaks the silence, "Are you ok?"

I exhale. "I'm fine." I take off my jacket and place it on the hook. I bend down once again to pick up the box when I notice an envelope inside a book. I pull it out and it's addressed to me in her handwriting. I turn it over to see if there's anything written on the back. I open it and pull out a folded piece of loose-leaf paper and a credit card statement. The note reads:

Louis,

You still owe me $200 from the suit you charged on my Visa from graduation. You have 2 jobs so I expect to be paid back ASAP..

Isabel.

I am done.

Memorial Sloan Kettering
December 19, 2015
9:48 a.m. ET

Naomi closes the book and rubs her eyes. "I need to take a break. My eyes are heavy."

I've been sitting next to her with my laptop editing a copy of the novel. Even though she has a copy of the book in her hands, I still want to read it over and over again to check for typos and misspellings. This is my first novel so I'm relentlessly trying to remove all mistakes from this book. Naomi has already spotted a few things and points them out so I can make the edits in real time.

She looks up at the television. I turned it on earlier just to have some other noise around here. Of course it's still going to sound like a hospital, but at least the television drowns out some of the noise. I put on CNN and one of the news segments is recapping some of the events of 2015.

They're currently showing all the various Black Lives Matter protests that happened throughout the year. "I guess I should be happy that I didn't have kids," Naomi says just staring at the screen.

"Why would you say that?" I look at the screen as they first focus on the riots in Baltimore, then images turn into a montage of protests in Cleveland, Chicago, and the University of Missouri

"Besides the obvious? I mean look at this all this. It's not safe to have a black baby in this country. How would I ever explain to my son or daughter that the police can just take your life like that?" She snaps her fingers "You can't send them to the store, you can't let them go to a pool party, you can't let them play outside, and God forbid they get stopped by the police. This is 2015 and they got us rioting like it was the 60's. The Klu Klux Klan was marching out in broad daylight in favor of the Confederate flag. Nothing has changed since the time when our parents were kids."

Naomi is absolutely right. Police brutality is nothing new in this country. We've only seen it so much because camera phones are so widely used now. Just last week I was watching someone getting stopped by the police in Washington Heights and I pulled out my phone and started recording just in case something happened. It's almost like second nature these days. We have been seeing so many instances of unnecessary force used that it's almost maddening. Yet, both of my parents will be the first to say that they never trusted the police since the days of their youth.

One of the last things Naomi and I did together before she got really sick was attend the Millions March last year. There were quite a few of our friends who went with us, Ruben, his girlfriend, my girlfriend Zenia, and Naomi's brother Malcolm. We started out at Union Square and walked up to 34th Street and then marched back down to One Police Plaza. We marched, chanted, and made fun of all the oblivious white people who were either shopping or dressed up for Santa Con.

"I wish I had an answer for all this. I would love to have a kid you know that. I know that Zenia and I have talked about it few times but I can't force her to be a mother if she's not ready to be one." It's weird for me to talk about children these days. I spent so much time assuming that I would never have one particularly after my divorce. It's not like I didn't try to have a child with the ex-wife, it just never panned out.

"Being a mother is hard enough as it is. I've seen my mother go through so much of the bullshit with my brother. Yeah, Malcolm was a good kid and turned out to be good man but do you know how on edge my mother was every single time he came home late? The times she cried when he told her how the NYPD patted him down for little to no reason? It happened to him too many times while he was a student at NYU. That is why he was out there on those cold days protesting at Times Square and shutting down the West Side Highway. Mom hated that Malcolm was out there even if it was marching against injustice. I don't know if I could ever have the strength she had."

"I think you're stronger than you give yourself credit for. You're battling a disease that keeps knocking you down but somehow you keep coming back. That is a strength that few people have."

Naomi looks at me. "Yeah but for how long? I'm not sure I can keep doing this. This chemo saps every last bit of energy I have. This may be my last surgery for the good or bad. I pray for the strength my mother has."

"I bet that if she heard you say that, she would tell you that she wishes she had your strength."

"I guess. But being a black woman is so damn hard. I spent all this time being hard on myself because I didn't have a man. Brothers will try their hardest to get the ass but will put a ring on the finger of some light-skinned chick that never had to work hard for anything. You remember all the hoes back in school? They're all married now with children. Me? I'm in bed dying with no man, no kid, and a master's degree I can piss on."

We've had this discussion so many times over the years and each time we talk about it, I'm at a loss for words. I mean what should I do? Do I nod in agreement? No. Do I laugh because she is so damn blunt that it can be hysterical? No. I do what I always do. I just stay silent and listen.

Naomi drinks a cup of water. "I wish I traveled more. I always wanted to go to Morocco."

"Maybe you still can."

"Ever the optimist."

"I have to be. You're the negative Nancy."

"Well duh. You've been insufferable ever since the Mets made the playoffs. Not that I would know why. They lost in the World Series. I almost expected you to be in a perpetual bad mood." She smiles.

I laugh and say, "You know how hard it is in these streets to be a Mets fan? I live and die with that team. Just making it to the World Series is a miracle and since we always seem to be on the wrong side of history, I will take what I can get. Besides, I'm not the same negative person you used to know."

"At one time, I would've found that hard to believe, but when I read this, I remember just how negative you really were." She holds up the book.

"Clearly, I've changed."

"Oh yeah? What changed?" Nayo asked almost skeptically.

"I got older and more mature. I dunno, maybe it was working with all those kids in Syracuse or maybe it's working with theses kids at Columbia University now. I see the light in their eyes. They have more of an idea of what they want from life than we ever had. Shit, I didn't know what I wanted when I was 18 years old. In fact, I didn't really know what I wanted until about 3-4 years ago." I chuckle because at that moment I realize how fortunate I really am right now. "To be completely honest, the biggest thing that's changed in my life has been Zenia. She has really made me rethink everything in my life."

"Well you do look happier and that's good."

"She gives me hope that maybe life does indeed get better as we grow older. I mean, I wish I had more money now that I'm older."

Naomi puts her hand on her forehead and slow rubs her head from front to back as if she is trying not to stress out. "I hear you. If I really do survive all this, I'm not sure I can survive all the bills. It's bad enough Christmas is next week and I'm stuck in this hospital."

I try not to think about how horrible this would be if Nayo didn't make it. The holiday season may not be the same after that. I try to keep it light. "At least you don't have to go Christmas shopping. My broke ass barely has enough money after I buy gifts."

Naomi begins to chuckle and I turn my attention towards her. She replies, "But you have money to see Star Wars."

This is the Naomi I know. She is still the woman I remember with the quick quips and the snarky remarks. It doesn't really matter that she's right. I did see the midnight showing of the new Star Wars when it came out which was less than 36 hours ago. "I always have money for Star Wars," I responded with a smile.

"You're going to see it again though right?" She maintains her weak smile.

"I fail to see your point. I totally budgeted at least two more showings before the new year," I grinned evilly.

"Did the black guy die?" She asks. Her tone is a little bit more serious then she continues, "I know how Hollywood is. They will give us a black man or woman to cheer for and before you know it, they're dead by the end of the movie or worse."

"Or worse? What's worse than death in a movie?" I knew where this was leading. In fact, I knew the answer before I even asked it. I just wanted to keep the conversation going like the good old days.

"Don't play dumb. You know exactly what I'm talking about. There's always some stereotype that is played up or some trope that gets put on display for everyone to see." At this point she's not even looking at me anymore. Naomi eyes are focused on the television.

I turn around and look at the screen. We watch images of a black man getting shot in the back as he runs away from a police officer. The footage was taken from a camera phone. Then there's footage of another black man getting gunned down in the middle of a street by a police officer. "No. The black guy doesn't die."

I looked down letting the point of what I just said sink in for a few minutes. I think about all the discussions I've had about this. I feel so strongly about the need to be represented positively in the television, books, and film but the reality is we can't even be shown in a positive light in the media.

"I don't know how you can be optimistic about the future because sometimes I really do believe we are fucked," she says.

I grab the remote and shut the television off. "Maybe we should just focus on the book, eh?" I put the remote on her tray and sit back down.

"I'm just gonna shut my eyes for a little bit. I will begin again in a few moments." Naomi closes her eyes and before I know it, she's fast asleep. I smile because of how peaceful she looks. I revert my eyes back to my laptop and begin reading again.

WHAT ARE FRIENDS FOR?

I need to get a computer. I've been putting it off because I would like to think that it's more of a luxury than a necessity. I get the impression from some of my classmates that having a computer is no longer a fashion statement. I guess this makes sense because I'm getting pretty tired of the routine of staying late at the computer cluster, then running to make the 2:30 am South Campus/Vincent Apt Bus only to miss it and then make that 10 minute walk to my apartment. I can't even imagine what it would be like to write a paper at home.

I also need a distraction from my life. There's a lot of confusion and anger going on right now. Isabel and her impeccable timing have thrown me off balance. I can't believe that she felt the need to return my things on the very same day I kissed Serene. Of course there's no way she could've known that was going to happen because I really didn't know. It's like she has some type of "spidey sense" where she suspected I may be trying to get over her.

For these reasons I'm in Carousel Mall right now looking to get a desktop computer with money I shouldn't be spending. On the bus ride over here, I was going over the list of reasons why I need this computer. I only have three items listed: schoolwork, talking to Serene, and watching the *Star Wars: Phantom Menace* trailer over and over again. The trailer is two minutes of pure heaven and I really can't wait for this movie to come out.

I normally hate going to the mall but it's an early Tuesday afternoon and I won't have to endure the anxiety and stress of worrying I might randomly bump into my ex-girlfriend. This is why I picked today instead of the weekend. The possibility of Isabel being here is minimal, after all, she's in class and in the grand scheme of things, this mall is not all that big.

Right now, I'm focused on seeing how much a PC is going to run me. Best Buy is the only place I know of that sells computers. Every time I walk into this store, it always surprises me the amount of electronics this place has. It almost gives me chills because if I had money, I would be in this place all the time. It's bad enough that the only reason I would ever come here is for the video games.

I browse the personal computers and my heart just sinks looking at these prices. Most computers here are well over $1,000. The cheapest one is for $899 and I don't even have that. I have one credit card and that's been charged up for books. Minus that, the rest of my money goes to rent, the phone bill, and food. I won't even mention that I owe my ex-girlfriend money. As a matter of fact, I'm still not used to calling her my ex-girlfriend.

Well, I can't afford any of these machines, which makes this entire trip useless. I was hoping to chat with Serene online more but that will have to wait for another time. I'm not even sure I thought this whole thing through. Even if I were to get a home computer I would also have to invest in a dial-up connection and honestly, do I really want another bill? There's this new service called Net Zero that I've seen commercials for. Apparently, they guarantee free internet access, but I don't know how true that is. Nothing in this world is free. I will have to figure all this out later.

I get over my decision pretty quickly and I decide to do what's normal to me. I figure I'll check out the CDs and then make my way over to the video games. Perhaps I'll find something that will make this trip worth something. I walk to the hip-hop section in search for the DMX album I've neglected to get after all this time, *Flesh of My Flesh, Blood of My Blood.* I really do love DMX because he's so damn angry. I've been playing his first album almost nonstop since the breakup. I need more of this.

I pull out the CD and start to browse through other albums when I see him, the dude that I've been trying to avoid since last summer. Ellis just came from of the video game section. This is the kind of dude that when you see him walking on the same side of street, you want to cross over to the other side. However, it's too late for me, before I can move, Ellis sees me and heads my way. Shit, I really have nothing to say to him after what he did to Naomi. He's like a bad penny that always turns up.

We've known Ellis since freshman year and while he appeared to be a normal person with his Sega Genesis and his sense of humor, he had us all fooled with his bravado. He was a founding member of the *No Ass Crew.* This is what we called ourselves. There were seven of us in this group that included Frank, Jason, my college roommate, Dopeness and me. The only requirement for admission to this group was that girls seemed to ignore us.

At first glance it seemed like we were anti-everything. We were anti-Greek because these dudes would do all types of shit to cock block the rest of the Black and Latino males on campus. Those in fraternities were accustomed to having all the girls swoon over them the moment they put their letters on. To young men like us, we found it to be absurd. Of course, we all knew the benefits of being in a fraternity, we were just not willing to take those steps. I remember how we scoffed at a certain little fundraiser they had entitled "Let a Sigma Tuck You In" where the fellas would come over to your dorm room and tuck you in at night. Yup, Dopeness was quoted as saying, "That shit's ingenious!" But we all hated it. Clearly we were not the intended audience.

We were anti-athlete. Let's make this very clear, Donovan McNabb will always be the chillest football player we've ever known and the last major quarterback this school has ever had. Yet, all these other dudes seemed to think they owned the school. I would never tell them that they didn't because these guys were way too fucking big and the women loved them. There was always some fight between Greeks and the football team over some girl and in the end, it was the basketball team that managed to lay everyone and anyone they got their hands on.

Finally, we were anti-establishment. Once we took that AAS 112 (Intro to African American History) class, we hated every white person we saw for at least a year. There was not enough Public Enemy, Brand Nubian, Poor Righteous Teachers, or X Clan music in the world. Some of us joined the more socially progressive student organization to protest things like the constant tuition increases, Columbus Day, and the damn student newspaper with all their racist cartoons. The one thing that we did do together was attend the Million Man March.

Over the 4 years of school we stuck mostly together and while the name of our crew was funny it never really stuck because after a while some of us did break that motto. Yet,

Ellis seemed to go overboard with everything he said or did. If Jason had a girlfriend, Ellis made sure he had two. If Frank got a new pair of Syracuse basketball shorts, he would get the same shorts plus the jersey. If Dopeness landed an interview with Run DMC, then Ellis had to be the cameraman. If I got a new game for my Nintendo 64, he would try to get the same game for his Sega Genesis. It was always tit for tat but taken to another level.

I also learned from Ellis that guys love to gossip more than women do. If something went down on campus, he knew about it in some fashion. I could never tell if he was lying about a rumor he heard or if he was making it up. I personally believe that he's solely responsible for all the rumors tied to the "Great Herpes Outbreak" during the spring of 1995. It seemed like almost every other week there was a story about how some guy we knew gave it to a girl that we all liked. It was all surreal but there was absolutely no proof of any of it.

But, it got really bad when Ellis started doing drugs. I've never been one to believe that weed will get you all fucked up in life, but there's always been talk about marijuana being a gateway drug. Ellis may be the only case in which I've actually seen this come true. I'm not even sure what happened but all I know is that some time after junior year he went from smoking weed, to eating mushrooms then to taking LSD. It got so bad that he was arrested for indecent exposure in Thornden Park. Apparently he was walking around nude talking about he was the Son of God.

"What up, L," Ellis says. We do the customary hand grab that morphs into a bro hug. He's wearing a dark green bubble jacket, blue baggy jeans, and the standard issue Timberland boots. Basically he looks like he walked right out of an Onyx video.

"What's up? What are you doing around here?" I asked feigning interest. The truth of the matter is I don't really care what he's doing but rumor has it that he lives in Queens now, so for Naomi's sake, I need to know his whereabouts.

"Yeah, so I had to come back to SU to straighten out my situation." Ellis says this while looking around.

"Ok…what situation?" I already knew what he was talking about but I wanted to hear it from him.

"You don't know? These fucking bitches won't give me my diploma."

Yup, that sounds about right. "Why not?" Again, I feign a fake surprised interest.

"My record is showing that I'm one credit shy. You believe that shit? All those classes and now they want to circle jerk me over one credit?"

I totally believe it. "No way. That's rough, man. So, when are you going to talk to them?"

"I already did. That's what they told me. Of course, they were giving me some bullshit about how I need to take a one credit class and shit. I ain't trying to do that. Can't a nigga be finished in 4 years? It's probably because I'm black, you know Syracuse is a racist ass institution, right? That mothafuckin' Chancellor ain't tryin' to hear shit about niggas and their problems."

Here we go. I'm all for the movement. We went to the Million Man March together but I have never seen him at a Student African American Society tuition hike rally. I certainly never saw him at the anti-Columbus Day rallies. Ellis is the lightest brother you will ever see and can just about "pass" anywhere on this Earth and he knows it. Yet, he will only claim his blackness when it suits him. He quickly forgets that his drug abuse issues are the reason he's in this mess in the first place.

"Wait, but I thought you were in HEOP?" I ask.

"Yeah, so?" Ellis shrugs.

"Don't you have 5 years in which to graduate?"

"Man, don't get me started on this government shit. HEOP be buggin' out too. I should've gotten into the United Negro College fund because my mind is a terrible thing to waste."

I want to laugh, in fact, I almost did but then I realize he's not joking. What Ellis has failed to realize is that his arrest was the last straw for his counselor. From what I hear, HEOP may have pulled his funding. While I'm not entirely sure of that, I wouldn't be surprised.

"Ah, well that's rough," I say with the intention of trying to end this conversation. All I really want to do is buy this CD and go home. I start tapping the CD case with my fingers hoping he would get the hint.

"But, enough about me dog, what's up with you? What you got going on? Is that DMX? I have that album, that shit is dope." He's getting a bit loud now.

"Yeah, I was just looking at some things and I realized I didn't have this album..."

"Yo, how's Isabel?" He interrupts enthusiastically.

Damn it. Do I have to tell everyone about this now? I roll my eyes and say, "We're not together anymore."

"Whaaat?" That is crazy. When did this happen?"

"A couple of weeks ago."

"That's rough. She fucking another dude?"

"What?" I ask with a look of disdain that he ignores.

"I'm saying, it had to be her because you're just not that type. No offense, but you don't have it in you to cheat." Ellis begins to flip through CDs as if this conversation isn't that big of a deal.

I stand there watching him in disbelief having no idea what to say right now. I mean, I can totally cheat if I wanted to. In fact, I kinda did, right? "What are you trying to say to me, Ellis?"

He continues looking through hip-hop albums as if he's searching for nothing in particular. "Relax man. I'm just saying. She probably wasn't for you. I remember how much of a bitch she was, always being so bossy and telling you want to do. You were so pussy whipped," He says without looking at me.

"No, I wasn't," I snap back.

He finally stops and looks at me, "Yes, you were. You just couldn't see it because you were too busy with your nose in her ass. You ate her ass didn't you? I wouldn't be surprised."

"Stop. Just fucking stop." I say with my hand up. This is the Ellis that I know. The asshole that goes way too far. The guy that liked to say shit because he thinks he's being real and funny, when he's not. I walk away because I feel an anger boiling up inside of me. I'm not sure if it's because he's talking shit about her or perhaps he's right to say that I was whipped. Either way, I don't like it and I need to go.

"What? Aw, Come on. I was joking." He begins to follow me to the register.

"Don't follow me."

"I can't joke around? My bad man."

I turn around to him. "Everything is a joke to you and this is why most times I don't fuck with you." I turn back around and walk to the nearest line.

"Alright, alright. You right, I went too far."

"Why are you really here Ellis? If you got kicked out of HEOP and thus out of school, why are you still here? Don't you have some place in Queens to be?"

"Aight nigga look, I just needed to be out of the cold because I ain't got enough money to buy a ticket back home."

"I don't understand. You bought a one-way ticket? How the hell were you going to go home?"

Ellis shrugs like a little kid.

I roll my eyes. "Are you serious? So you're just wandering around the mall asking for money?" I ask. He doesn't say anything and within minutes the cashier is scanning my DMX CD. I quietly pay for it and after saying thank you to the cashier I walk out of Best Buy with Ellis trailing behind me. What am I supposed to do about this situation? "How much are you short by?" I ask.

He digs into his pocket and pulls out some money. "I need $30 for the bus," he responds. I give him a look because he knows how hard it is to be a student and still try to eat. "Come on, man. Aren't we boys anymore? You know I'm good for it."

See that's the point, we were boys but then he became less trustworthy as the years went by. Isabel slapped him once. She wouldn't tell me what he said or did but she slapped the shit out of him. He laughed it off but I always wondered what he said to her.

I also need to think about this. If this man stays up here then I have a feeling that Naomi will find out. If that happens then I'm not sure what she will do to him or to me if she finds out I didn't tell her. Sure, Ellis and I may be friends, but she's like my sister so I have to do what I feel is the right thing.

"Fine. I will lend you the $30."

"See? I knew you was my nigga." He comes in for a hug and I hold out arm to stop him.

"Yeah, whatever," I respond.

I reluctantly go the ATM to take out $40 because God forbid there's ever a machine that spits out anything other than $20 bills. Ellis is all too happy to take the cash with a promise that he's going to pay me back. I already know that's a lie so I consider this an investment toward my overall mental well-being. While I can stress out all day long about my ex-girlfriend, having him out of the way will make Naomi worry free.

It takes us about 15 minutes to walk from the Carousel

Mall to the newly built Regional Transportation Center. This place was all we could hear about last year as it was being built. It's supposed to bring new commerce and visitors to Central New York and the mall. I really don't care all that much for it, but this is a big time upgrade from the shit show that was the old bus station on Erie Blvd.

My plan was not to watch him get on the bus because I don't have time for that. I just wanted to make sure he bought the damn ticket. I didn't want to chance giving him this money and then seeing him back on campus with a bottle of St. Ides and some onion rings. Luckily for the both of us that the bus he bought the ticket for was boarding in 15 minutes. I suppose I could stay and chat with him since I'm paying for him to leave Syracuse.

"I really appreciate this. You know I was only playing with you back in the mall, right?"

"If you say so. You go too far all the time, which pretty much makes you an asshole." I say with my arms crossed.

"I'm an asshole for sure, but I will make it up to you." Ellis smiles.

"I doubt that."

"You really have a low opinion of me."

"You left me little reason to think any other way."

"Ok, that's fair. But in my defense I was high most of the time."

"I'm not sure that is a good defense, Ellis."

"Ok. So what exactly are you mad at? The thing with Isabel or the thing with Naomi?"

I drop my arms and turn to look at him. "Both, actually. Although neither you nor Isabel will tell me what happened."

Ellis has a smug look on his face when he says, "You're not gonna like it."

I fold my arms again. "I assumed that. What happened?"

"Aight, but don't say I didn't warn you."

"Just tell me."

"So last summer, if you remember, we were all in that house on Ackerman and I don't remember what I did the night before. I guess I must've passed out on the couch but I woke up to Isabel talking to someone in the kitchen. I honestly thought it was you because who else would she be talking to like that?"

"Wait, what do you mean like that?"

"Look, I know you think I'm crazy and dumb but let me tell you, Spanish or no Spanish, she was flirting with someone."

"I don't understand."

"Well let me finish then. So I sit up on the couch quietly thinking that maybe you and her are about to get it on and maybe I need to leave." That right there is a lie. I know Ellis better than that. If someone was going to have sex, he would find a way to watch. I say nothing but I will make a mental note of it. "So as I'm about to get up I hear her say something like, 'I can't wait to be alone with you when I get to Colombia.' So then I…"

"What?" I interrupt. My eyes open wide open.

Ellis pauses to see if I'm done, then continues, "So then I move toward the kitchen because I figured she had to be on the phone we had in there. Then she says some shit in Spanish. Not sure how you people do it, going from English to Spanish and all that shit. Anyway, so she hangs up and I walk in to the kitchen…"

"Who you on the phone with?" I asked.

She gives me a dirty look and says, "None of your business." Then she tries to keep walking by me and I stop her by grabbing her arm.

"Really? Because it sounds like you know this person very well and that person ain't Louis."

She pulled away from me and says, "How dare you? What are you trying to say?"

"How dare I? I mean I can just tell L that you were flirting with some nigga on the phone."

"I was NOT flirting on the phone with anyone. I was talking to my little brother."

"Word? That's the lie you gonna go with? So, you're not seeing your little brother when you go back to Kew Gardens in a few days? Or will you see him later on in Colombia?" I swear to you bro it was like I hit a nerve. She really thought I was bluffing. I think she was mad at herself for not being more careful.

"He will never believe you," she snapped back.

105

"What? Louis and I are boys. He's known me longer than he's been with you."

"Yeah, but I suck his dick and no matter how long he's been friends with a drug addict like you he will never believe you over me. You're not even trustworthy."

"Maybe I'm not trustworthy but I'm still gonna tell him, and he's gonna wonder why I know about this trip to Colombia."

"Fine Ellis, do whatever you want. But once he realizes that you're full of shit, you will never be friends anymore. I will make sure of that."

"You right. But let's be honest. Y'all think I'm stupid anyway as if I can't see the writing on the wall. You fight all the time over trivial shit. I hear it when he's on the phone or when he's complaining to Frank about you. Why do you still have him on the hook? Just be the free woman you want to be."

"You don't know what you're talking about."

"I don't? That's cool. But hey listen, if you want to play this charade go ahead. I won't tell him on one condition."

"Condition? You need weed money, let me tell you…"

"No, nothing like that. I won't tell him unless you deep throat me like you gonna do to that dude that in Colombia…"

Then she slapped me.

This motherfucker! I lunge at him. He flinches and blocks me. "waitwaitwaitwaitwait! WAIT!" He yells as he pushes me away.

I'm breathing heavy with anger and disgust. I can feel the

eyes of other people in the bush station looking at us. "What the FUCK is wrong with you?"

"I told you that you wouldn't like what I had to say!"

"You expect me to believe anything you say? You piece of shit, how dare you say that to her? Is that what you do now? You try get blowjobs from your friend's girl? I should beat the shit out of you right now!" I'm upset. People are staring at me and I am acting the fool in public. This is not what I wanted. This not why I walked him to the bus station. I was being nice and this is what it has cost me, my dignity.

"What does it matter? I'm doing you a favor by telling you how she really is! So, calm down dog, I ain't trying to fight you."

I just stare at him. I want to hit him with everything I have but what will that do? What will it cost me? I go over the scenario very quickly in my head, but what exactly will that look like. The truth is he is bigger than me and I may just lose the fight, but it just might be worth it just to let this anger out. "Why the hell didn't you tell me this before? This was like over six months ago!"

"Would you have believed me then?"

No. I wouldn't have. But I think I believe him now and that is what upsets me the most. I try everything in my power to calm down but I can't. I feel like I'm trembling.

"You ok, bro?"

I take a deep breath and then punch him right in his face. "Fuck you!!! I'm not ok."

I grab my hand. I never punched someone in the face before. Ellis is startled and grabs his upper jaw. I may have hit his ear. He looks at his hand to make sure he wasn't bleeding. "It's like that motherfucker?"

"It's like that." I'm scared but angry. People are starting to get nervous. They begin to back up. I can hear murmurs of people asking what's going.

I can tell that he's ready to fight, but then he relaxes and smiles. "You know what. I'm a give you that because that was a little bitch punch and you paid for my ticket. Next time, I will put you through a fucking window."

We stare at each other and then he walks toward his bus.

BACK TO SQUARE ONE

"I would have beat his ass," Frank says. I had just gotten home from the Regional Transportation Center. My hand is all sore and swollen. How do people fight like this? Besides, I just had to hit Ellis. I couldn't stand there and look at his face after that story he told me. I was so angry that I just had to take a swing, but the moment it happened I knew that I shouldn't have done it.

The first thing I did when I got home was wrap my right hand in an Ace bandage. Frank has a lot of them leftover from his football days. I put a filled Ziploc bag with ice on my hand so I can keep down the swelling. Of course, Frank was all concerned about what happened since he's the non-violent person in the group. That is, until I told him what happened.

"What would fighting have done? Get me thrown in jail or get me shot by some trigger happy SPD? Nah. I got my lucky punch in and now me and my dragon fists are retiring," I said as I was looking at my swollen hand. This is how the last few weeks have been. It doesn't matter how hard I'm trying to get over Isabel, something always brings me back to square one. The question that has been haunting and burning through me everyday has been...Why?

I thought I was fine. I felt like I was making progress in getting past this whole question of...why? I don't want to be one of those people that whine about their exes, but no matter how hard I try, I get back to this place. Now, I have to wonder if Ellis is telling the truth. Was she really excited to see someone in Colombia? This could all be some elaborate tale that he made up, but if that's true, what does he gain from it? Too many questions and not enough answers are going to not only drive me crazy, but it's going to cause me to fail my classes.

"I still would've beat his ass," Frank says. We're in the tiny kitchen in our apartment and he's cooking his meal while I standby the sink nursing my bandaged hand with a homemade icepack. Frank has one specialty dish, which is pasta with spaghetti sauce, which of course sounds pretty plain, but he does manage to make the sauce himself. Depending on the day and what we have in the kitchen, the sauce may contain many things from little pieces of frankfurters to leftover veggies. He throws everything in a big pot and after about 30 minutes it's completely edible. Just add whatever pasta we have like elbows, ziti, penne, and/or shells. Sometimes he just dumps the contents of the half empty pasta boxes into some boiling water and we are set.

"Maybe he was telling the truth," I say while I look at my hand.

"...and sometimes that truth requires a beat down," Frank replies. It's getting increasingly hard to take him seriously when he has on his South Park Chef apron on. The lettering across the chest reads, *O, suck on my chocolate salty balls. Stick 'em in your mouth, and suck 'em!*

"Look, you can talk about beating his ass all day because you're a big dude. Look at me, look at this hand. What am I supposed to do?" I take off the ice pack and show him my swollen knuckles.

"Well you can start by learning how to throw a punch, Daniel-san, but other than that are you really looking for me to tell you what to do?" Frank asks as he stirs the big pot of sauce with a wooden spoon.

"No, I just…"

"Because I already know how this is going to play out. I tell you what I think is the best answer and you do the opposite."

"What? I don't do that."

"Yes, you do."

"When?"

Frank puts down the wooden spoon he was using and turns over to open the fridge. He pulls out a Pabst Blue Ribbon can and opens it. "This conversation requires beer." He says before he takes a healthy swig. He comes up for air and burps then continues, "Remember the day after you two broke up and I told you not to call her? I told you not do anything but give her the space she needs. You remember that?"

"Yeah," I reply. Of course I remember that. I was a complete mess. I had this overwhelming feeling to talk to her.

"And what did you do?"

"I called her."

"Exactly. Not once, not twice, not even three times…"

"Yeah, I get your point! I called her four times."

"You sure it was four?"

"Yeah ok, it was five…"

"You see what I'm saying"

"But, in my defense, I needed to really talk to her. I needed to call her. Nothing she said made sense to me. I just needed some clarification."

"What you need? That's not a defense. That's an excuse. I mean, come on. There's nothing you could've possibility said to her then or now that she would listen to. She did all the talking. In fact, she's doing all the talking right now by not saying anything at all. I still think you should try your best to let this go. If you and her are meant to be, then it will be."

Words cannot express how much I hate that statement. Everyone is so quick to say the "meant to be" statement. I don't need to hear that shit right now. I get that fate is a thing that people want to believe in because they refuse to take their lives into their own hands. I want to have a say in what happens to me, I want to be in control of my destiny. Fate should not dictate what happens and neither should Isabel. However, I don't have a great response to Frank so I stick with my typical, "Whatever" reply.

Frank takes a few more swigs of his PBR before tossing the can into the sink. "Look, I get that you're upset but again, me giving you advice is like throwing sand toward oncoming wind or better yet, it's like you throwing a bad punch." He chuckles.

Here we go with his proverbs he read somewhere. I'm betting Buffalo doesn't even have sand, also his joke is not humorous. "It's funny, you talk about how I never follow your advice, but there are times you don't follow mine."

"Oh really? Please enlighten me," Frank folds his big arms in amusement.

"That night you convinced me to watch *Friends* a few weeks ago."

"What?" Frank says in disbelief and he begins to laugh before he starts again. "Really? Again with this?"

"Yup!" A few weeks ago, I wasn't in the best of moods. It was a Thursday night to be exact. Frank had suggested that we watch television. Maybe there was some show on that would take my mind off things. The Winter Olympics was the big thing on T.V. and that was something that I really didn't care about. We get more than enough snow here and I didn't need to be reminded of that.

Frank turned the channel to NBC 3 and on came an episode of Friends. I knew this would be a repeat because no station would really program against the Winter Olympics but I figured that maybe this would put me in a better mood, after all, this show is really funny. The best part was that this was an episode I'd never seen before. The worst part, this was the episode when Ross and Rachel broke up. I was not happy.

"How was I supposed to know they would play that episode? It's your fault for not checking the TV Guide." Frank continues to laugh.

"Maybe, but I did say that watching TV was not a good idea for me at that time."

113

"Ok man, whatever you say." Frank totally dismisses me.

"I get what you're saying but I really need to figure this out. What if Ellis is telling the truth? What if there really was another guy in Colombia? This may be the answer I've been looking for."

Frank checks the sauce again and stirs it. "First of all, that is a big if. Ellis has been known to stretch the truth on several occasions. He may be fucking with your head and clearly it worked."

"Yes, Ellis, is an asshole and a liar but there's always some truth in the things he says. I think I need to find out how true all this is."

"By doing what? Asking Isabel if she openly flirted with some dude and then was propositioned by Ellis? That's very thin, Louis. I don't think that is the best idea you've had."

"What else am I gonna do?"

"I know you're looking for answers but I don't think she's going to give them to you. The only thing you should do is study and try to get with Serene."

I know that Frank is right. I drop the subject and go back to talking about normal guy stuff like the NBA lockout. We both know that I'm going to end up confronting Isabel about this. There is something about all this that needs to be discussed. I just think that I should be afforded an explanation.

My plan is very simple. I need to head to campus anyway to do some work tonight. I'm supposed to meet up with Naomi at the computer cluster in the Student Union tonight because I need to talk to her about Ellis. Also, I can get some chatting time in with Serene when she gets out of work. Of course, during all this, I know that Isabel is working tonight in the Game Room. I can't help but know her schedule. Normally I would be working tonight too, but since I have work to catch up on, Brian decided to cover tonight's lecture in the auditorium.

As always, Frank's pasta dish is good. I eat fast and leave. The bus schedule is relatively accurate and if I miss it, I will have to walk to Manley Fieldhouse. Tonight, I barely make it. As I sit in the back of the bus, I do wonder what I'm going to say to her. Do I come off as aggressive? My problem during this whole time is that I feel like I've been on the defensive reacting to everything she's done, which has given her the upper hand in this situation. I'm tired of feeling that way. When I talk to her, my tail is in between my legs. Maybe there's a better way of dealing with this.

With the bus ride and the walk, I get to the Student Union in about 30 minutes. The computer cluster is located one level down from the main floor next to the copy center. I walk into this room that is long and narrow but filled with PC's on either side of the room. It is semi-filled with students and I can see Naomi at the far end of room. I walk towards her and I can see she put her bag in the seat next to hers.

"Hey what's up?" I say as I approach her.

"Hey man," She replies as she moves her bag from the seat. "You're lucky you're getting here now because this place is filling up quickly. Wasn't sure how long I could hold this seat for you."

I look around. "I see," I say as I put my book bag on the chair. I take off my hat and gloves and put them on the keyboard and then I take off my coat and put it behind the chair. "I will be right back."

Naomi looks up at me. "Where you going?"

"I need to take care of something."

"Uh huh," Naomi makes a face and looks back at the screen. She begins to type.

"What does that mean?" I smile.

"It means that I know you're up to something. I will be here typing away. Just don't be too long. I don't want to keep fighting off these nimrods about the empty computer." Then she looks down at my hand. "What happened to your hand?"

"I will tell you when I get back. I shouldn't be long." I was hoping that my Syracuse hoodie would have made my hand less obvious but clearly I was wrong. I will just have to keep my hand in the front pocket. I walk out and head toward the stairs on my left. The Student Union has four levels that consist of three floors and the basement level. Because of the weird configuration of the building and the fact it was basically built on a hill, the main level is actually the 2nd floor. The basement level is where the Game Room is located and I decide to take the stairs because it quicker than the elevator.

The other reason I love taking these stairs is because of the beautiful mural that is located in the alcove of the stairwell. To those who are not familiar with hip-hop or street art, this mural would look like random images of Black people highlighted by graffiti. However, when I look this mural I see the history of hip-hop. There are so many names highlighted on the wall like DJ Kool Herc and Afrika Bambaataa.

On a normal day I would marvel at these images of the

people spray painted on these walls in late 80's to early 90's Hip Hop attire mimicking dance moves but I'm in a bit of a rush. I know that Isabel's shift starts at 9pm and I'm about 10 minutes early. I don't want her to see me coming. I don't want her to be able to avoid me.

I walk in and I see a few people playing pool. The video games are in the back and the game room attendant is sitting at the desk reading. I walked up to him and ask for change for a $5 bill. I specifically ask for three singles and two dollars in quarters.

The game that I play is Tekken 2. This is a fighting game that I've been known to beat in a single turn, although I'm not sure how well I will do tonight with my hand like this. I frequented this game room as an undergrad. Since I loved playing Street Fighter 2, my goal was to always be the best. When I beat some of the Asian kids from Chinatown, I knew I gained a little bit of respect from the nerds on campus. This game is a little different, but I love it because the screen for this game is so much larger. It's twice the size of a normal coin-operated machine.

My goal is not to beat the game tonight. I just need to take out a little aggression on my computer-generated opponents while I wait for Isabel to clock in and take a seat behind the desk. There are other games that I'm sure I could play like Ms. Pac-Man or NBA Jams but that would put me within immediate eye-shot of her. By playing this game, I would have my back to her and she wouldn't really notice me.

I put in the 50¢ and begin to play. I pick the character Lei Wulong because he resembles Jackie Chan. I begin to play and I forget how easily this game comes to me. Despite the wrapped up hand, I do manage to beat character after character while occasionally looking behind me to see if Isabel has arrived. Two people actually decide to challenge me but I sit them down with relative ease. When I'm done with them, the game goes back to normal play mode. I look at my watch and I realize that Isabel is late.

The one thing that I know about her is that she's always been responsible. She never likes to be late to anything. But then, how well do I really know her now? Maybe Ellis is telling the truth. Perhaps she's become this untrustworthy person that I refused to see all these years. I lose focus and lose the first round of this fight. I should just concentrate on this game. If she's not here by the time I finish, I know that it wasn't meant for us to have this conversation.

I beat my next opponent and when I glance behind me, I see Isabel walk in. She has on her grey winter coat and a hat while carrying a bag from Burger King. She must have gone to the food court before she came here. I turn my head back to focus on the next character, Heihachi Mishima. This is the second to last boss. Good, I can just beat two more people and be done with it. I haven't practiced what I'm going to say to her so this is bound to be a shit show if I say the wrong things. I will give her some time to get settled. I've worked a few shifts in the game room before and I know that she will need to talk to the person she's replacing and count the money in the register.

I hear the door open and I look back, it's Felipe. He walks in with his a navy blue jacket with white arms and red fraternity letters. He's all smiles and gives her the drink in his hand. I really can't hear what he's saying. I turn back around to see my character getting his ass kicked. I almost salvaged the first round, but I lost. Damn it. My hand is now beginning to hurt. I may be holding the joystick a little too hard. I rub my palm before the second begins.

I turn my head around slightly and he's just standing there talking to her. Fuck! Not only did I not anticipate this, but also when I'm done with this game, I will have to pass her on the way out. The only other alternative is to just tell Felipe to get the fuck out while I try to have this conversation with her, but that's probably not going to work in my favor. Imagine me trying to have another fight after the day I've had? I need to calm down. I win the next two rounds and turn around to see if my options have changed.

She's now alone eating her food. He must've left when I wasn't looking because I don't see him anywhere in this room. Before I think about how good this is, I do have this nagging feeling that my window for this conversation is closing soon. Who knows if this dude is going to come back to keep her company. I hurriedly beat the game and I take a few deep breaths.

I turn around and she sees me right away. I can already see her tense up. Isabel continues to go about her business and continues reading whatever book is on her lap. This is how it's been when she sees me in public. She tenses up and pretends like I'm not alive. Sometimes I say hi and try to talk to her or sometimes I don't. In all cases, she's the one who dictates the situation. Not today.

I walk up to her, "Do you mind if we talk?"

Isabel doesn't move her eyes from her book. "I'm at work and studying so unless you need change or have the money you owe me, then no, we cannot talk."

I can feel the anger bubbling up. I swallow it. "Look, we need to talk. No more bullshit." I say this a little louder so that the patrons at the pool tables can hear me. I know that she doesn't like to be embarrassed.

119

Isabel puts down her book. "Alright. Fine. What do you want to talk about, Louis?"

Her abruptness throws me off. I really want to ask her why the fuck she's so angry with me all the time but I won't. I need to focus on what I need to know. "Fine, I will get right to the point. Ellis told me why you slapped him. I need to know if what he's saying is true."

Isabel scoffs in a type of way that shows this annoys her. "Really, is this what this is about? This is why you're here. Is your lunatic friend telling you stories?"

I don't bat an eye. I barely blink. "I just want the truth. Is what he told me true?"

She sighs, "You're going to have to enlighten me on the story that he's shared with you."

"He claims that you had a conversation over phone with some guy from Colombia. You were flirting with him and he confronted you on this."

"That is absurd, and let me guess, you believe him."

"I don't know what to be believe. That's why I'm asking you. I'm giving you the benefit of the doubt. I'm coming to the source so at the very least, that lunatic doesn't spread false rumors."

"You mean to tell me that you are that desperate to find answers on what happened between us that you would go to Ellis? Drug addicted Ellis. The guy who wanted me to go down on him, really Louis?"

She probably thinks that this is information Ellis may have

withheld from me. My hand aches thinking about that damn conversation. "Yes, he told me that, but yet you still have not answered the question."

"I think we are done here Louis. I don't owe you anything. You should know me better than that."

I think for a minute. "You're right about one thing. I should know you better. But, you know, I'm not really sure about that anymore. I'm not sure about anything when it comes to any of this."

She rolls her eyes, "I don't even know what you're talking about so I think it's time for you to go. If you haven't noticed I am at work."

"So that's it? You're not going to answer the question?"

"I did answer you and now you can go." She picks up her book as a sign that this conversation is over but I don't take the hint.

"Right, just like you answer all my questions, right? I never ever get a straight answer from you."

"What answer do you think you need? The fact that I simply don't want to be with you isn't a good enough answer? That you just have a desire to dig deeper? You're such a typical man to believe that a woman can't simply want to be alone. No, you would rather believe in some fairytale that involves me acting out in the way women do in those X-rated movies you love so much. Is that it? You think I'm riding two dicks at the same time?" Isabel puts down the book again and does a double-fisting motion towards her mouth.

"I never said that," I say softly. I begin to feel ashamed of myself. Maybe I'm totally wrong about this and I let my emotions, once again, get the better of me. Somewhere Frank is laughing while smoking a blunt.

"Of course, you never said that, you never need to say that. But here you are at my place of work being this stalker that can't simply do the one thing I asked which was to give me space. Do you remember me telling you this?"

I close my eyes. Yes, I remember this. The day after we broke up after I called her for the fifth time. She did answer and she told me to let it go and give her some space. I just never really knew what that meant. Was there a time period? What does it mean? "Yes, I remember. But that doesn't mean you have to treat me like I did something wrong to you."

"You should really stop playing the victim. It's not a good look for you."

I just stare at her with disdain. She returns my look. The tension is palpable. Before either one of us can say anything else the door opens. It's Felipe again.

"Oh look who it is, your shadow," I say.

"Really? Are you jealous?" She asks.

"Please," I answer as I roll my eyes in disgust.

Felipe walks up to me. "Is there a problem here?" I do not want to fight this guy. I barely escaped the last fight. This is not what I came here for but we stare at each other. I really start thinking about if this is what I've suddenly become, the college gangster that we used to make fun of all the time.

"Wait," Isabel gets in between us and looks at him.

"Felipe, he was just leaving." Then she looks at me and for a brief second I can see a flash of compassion in her eyes. "Right, Louis?"

I look back at Felipe. "Yeah. I was." I leave the game room and, once again, my tail is between my legs.

STALKER

I sit back on my chair in the computer cluster thinking about how far this whole thing has gone. Naomi can only sit there and listen as I tell her the whole story. I put myself in this situation and I know I acted against conventional wisdom.

The fact that I went down there, to her place of work, just to talk does seem very stalkerish. Is that what I'm slowly becoming? Am I that dude that cannot take no for an answer? The type of guy that turns up when you least expect it like... Ellis?

"There is no way you're like that asshole," Naomi says as she goes back to typing. It seems like she has been putting a lot into this paper she's writing. She has one ear bud of her headphones in while she listens to me with the free ear.

"I feel like I need to tell you that I saw him today. That's why my hand is like this," I say. I was thinking about waiting until another time to tell her this but since his name came up I might as well just get this discussion over with.

Naomi glances my way. "Saw who?" She asks defensively because she knows exactly whom I'm referring to. I suppose she just needs confirmation.

"Ellis. I saw him a Carousel Mall today"

"Are you serious? He was here?" She stops typing.

"He was. I bought his bus ticket back to Queens and then I punched him in his face."

"Wait. What?' She takes out her ear bud and spins her chair toward me. "You need to tell me everything."

I tell her the story of how I needed to go to Best Buy for a computer but left with a CD. Along the way I ran into Ellis and his broke ass and he tells me the real reason why Isabel slapped him. I tell her how angry I was and about what he did to provoke me to awkwardly deck him in his jaw. All of this leads me to confront Isabel in the Game Room in the most stalkerish way possible.

Nayo is animated during most of this story and for the most part she had to keep it down because, even though this is a computer cluster and it isn't a designated silent area, it might be considered a bit rude to be loud in here. Despite that, I cannot blame her for her anger towards him.

The issue stems from a complete violation of trust. Nayo was the only female member of our *No Ass Crew*. She was the type of person you never heard anything about. You never heard a rumor about her. Naomi kept her shit on the down low and because of that, both men and women thought that she had something to hide. She did have relations with a man here and there but no one would ever know that.

Her two roommates, on the other hand, were wild. Belinda dated a football player and Alice had a reputation for debauchery. I knew them through Naomi since we hung out a lot. Most of us would hang out in each other's South Campus apartments at one time or another, but most of the time we just chilled at her place. We would go over to borrow things because, to be honest, she had the nicest shit.

Nayo had her shit together. Run out of toilet paper? Go to Nayo's. Are you hungry and you have no money on your SUpercard? Nayo's cooking. Don't have cable and you need to watch Def Comedy Jam? Nayo's got HBO. That's how she rolled. Somehow she seemed to make her work-study wages last a lot longer than the rest of us.

Needless to say, we were all welcome at her apartment. What I didn't know, up until the point when she told me this story, was that Ellis seemed to frequent her place more than the rest of us. I always thought he had it bad for Alice but she would ignore him and his antics. He would always talk shit about Alice but we all knew he had a big time crush on her. Naomi had always felt that deep down Ellis was a needy person with mommy issues that needed to be taken care of, but she wasn't trying to be the one to lead that charge.

At one point during our senior year, before he declared himself Jesus, he came by her apartment late one night asking if he could take a bubble bath. Of course, Naomi found it strange, but it was late and snowy outside so she let him in. This wasn't the first time that he'd asked to use her shower and it certainly was not the first time he wanted to take a bubble bath. It could've been because him and his roommates never cleaned up their own bathroom but I know that once Jason started dating Sasha, there was one less person around using their facilities.

In any case, Naomi never felt like she was in danger or that anything out of the ordinary was going to happen. Out of courtesy, she pointed out where all the things he can use to make the bubble bath were in case he forgot. She also told him that when he's done in the bathroom he was welcomed to stay on the couch or he can simply let himself out. The door to the apartment locked from the inside so theoretically Ellis could leave and she wouldn't have to worry about the door being unlocked.

Naomi falls asleep. She has always been a light sleeper so when she heard Alice come into the apartment, she was not concerned. Since she did not hear Ellis leave, she figured that he was asleep on the couch, as he has done so in the past. Something told her to open her eyes. She's not sure what it was, perhaps it was one of those instinctual feelings that occurs when we feel we've overslept or someone is watching us.

Naomi opens her eyes. She's facing the window so she can see the light blue tint of morning. She can tell from this vantage point that it's still snowing outside. Naomi turns her head slightly and she sees Ellis with his pants down and his dick in one hand stroking himself and her panties in the other. All in one motion she gasps and screams while instinctually pulling up her comforter. "What the fuck are you doing??" She asks even though it was very obvious.

"I just had to… uhhh," Ellis manages to say a few words before releasing onto her panties.

Naomi is now enraged. "I cannot believe you just did that! Get the fuck out of my room!" Ellis begins to plead with her saying that he's sorry and that he was compelled to do it. All words that Naomi doesn't want to hear. He pulls up his pants and drops her panties and all the while she's screaming, "You nasty motherfucker!"

Just as he zips up his pants, Alice barrels through the door

127

with an aluminum bat. "What's going on?" Alice sees the sight of Naomi covering herself with the comforter and looks back at Ellis. "Did you just fucking rape her you asshole?"

Before Ellis can try to explain, Alice starts swinging for the fences. Naomi is in shock watching this unfold. Alice misses him and he manages to duck and roll past her and out the door. Alice asks Naomi if she is ok before going after him. By the time she's done asking the question they hear the front door open and close.

"I'm telling you there is no way you are like Ellis. He violated my trust and my friendship. I should've pressed charges when I had the chance." Naomi says as she turns her chair back to her computer.

"I still don't understand why you didn't," I say. I always felt that her reasoning was a bit fuzzy. I always figured in cases like these a woman should just report these things to Public Safety.

She rolls her eyes. "I've explained this to you. It becomes his word against mine and, as a black woman, they were going to make it seem like I used my powers to entrap this negro in my smutty clutches. Then before you know it, I'm the evil horny woman and he's the poor male victim that was lured by my Venus flytrap. Fuck him and fuck patriarchy. I'm glad you punched him in the face."

I know that Naomi is right. I have no idea what it's like to be a black woman, but I'm pretty sure that her assessment is accurate. I guess she's also right about me not being like Ellis, although I still do feel like a stalker. I've just been obsessed with wanting to know the answer. Maybe I just got my answer. Is it possible that everyone has been wrong about her? Maybe she just simply wanted to be alone. That should be an answer all by itself. Maybe there is some thing deeply ingrained in me to believe that there needs to be a deeper more sinister answer than that. Perhaps I've blinded myself with my own insecurities and lustful actions that I've not seen the real truth behind this which is she hasn't changed at all. Maybe it's me that has changed. I mean look at me and the way I'm behaving. I don't do this, in fact, I never do this. Fighting over a woman? Really?

I finally boot up the PC after what must have been about 10 minutes of me sitting here thinking about my life. I can pout all I want but that isn't going to make the work get done any sooner. I think it would make me feel better if I could talk to Serene. I pull out my books and my floppy disk as Windows '98 finally finishes loading. All the desktop items looks pretty much the same no matter which campus computer you use. A picture of the campus in the background and the standard Icons: My Computer, My documents, Recycle Bin, & Internet Explorer. Sometimes you get lucky and see the AOL Instant Messenger (AIM) Icon on the desktop other wise you would have to use the Start Menu to find it, which is what I had to do.

I find it in the menu and click it so it can start. I then put my floppy disc in the hard drive. The small AIM window comes up prompting me to enter my screen name: El_Jander1. I enter my password and my friends list comes up. It's a pathetic list, actually, that consists of a few people. Most of which are my classmates from the Higher Education program that I've had to do group projects with. The other three are Ruben, Naomi and Serene.

When people see my screen name they always ask me where I got it from since it is so unusual. Believe it or not, it took me quite a long time to think about this name. The first part is real easy, "El" stands for the first letter of my name. Those who call me a friend will shorten my name to just one letter so it made sense to just put that but change to make the whole name itself seem Spanish. "Jander" comes from one of my favorite books that I read in high school called *Vampire of the Mists* by Christie Golden. This was during my Dungeons & Dragons phase where all I did was role-play, play video games, and read fantasy/horror books.

Vampire of the Mists was book about a gold elf named Jander Sunstar who is, of course, a vampire that sets on a dark path of revenge where he meets an even darker vampire, Count Strahd Von Zarovich. The book is a lot of fun and I must have read it at least 10 times. What sticks out to me so much is how even the purist can succumb to the blinding effects of deep-rooted emotions. I always wonder what it would be like to be a vampire, to live forever and not have to worry about the everyday mundane shit of just being human.

I chose the number one for something a little less obvious to others but is so very apparent to me, Mookie Wilson. I was ten years old the last time the New York Mets won the World Series and my favorite player of all time is Mookie. He wore number one. I smile every time I think about game six when he hit that little dribbler to Bill Buckner. I still think that even if Buckner makes that play, Mookie beats it out.

I can tell Serene has her away message on. That tends to happen around this time. I know she's home but she might be busy doing other things. I start looking through my notes when I realize that I have to finish up a project that is due in a few days. I'm supposed to compile some numbers on student retention during the Civil Rights era to make a case on how student activism leads to better enrollment and better overall engagement.

Before I get into my work I make sure I go the Star Wars web site for my daily routine of downloading the Episode One trailer. It was Brian who gave me the idea of doing this after we went to see the trailer in the theaters in November. Yes, him and I are those type of people who waited in mall on that long ass line to see *The Phantom Menace* trailer and then leave before the real movie started. It was everything that I needed. In fact, it's everything I still need. If I ever buy a computer I'll make sure to see the trailer at least once a day.

The other thing that I need to do is submit this poem for LUCHA magazine. The deadline for submissions is the Friday before Spring Break, which is basically next week. I've already pondered it and have rewritten it over several times. I'm at a good place with it mentally. I still think it is garbage but it is better than dog shit. I pull up my email and type in Lucy's email. I know she's not the editor of the publication but she will get it to her. I attach the poem, written on Microsoft Word, to the email with a very short message in the body of the email: *Here's my submission, I hope you like it.* I hit send.

I actually feel better about this. Especially after that crazy discussion I just had with Isabel. After I watch the trailer for a second time I close out of Internet Explorer because now I have more important things to do like actual work. I take a page from Naomi's playbook and pull out my CD Walkman. Since I haven't gotten into burning CD's yet, I have to make sure whatever albums I carry with me have to be dope. I don't want to listen to two songs then have to change the disc. I pull out my CD case and flip through my collection. I think I feel like Big Punisher today. I put *Capital Punishment* into my player and put the buds in my ears.

I press play and then pullout my spiral notebook with all my notes from class. I bob my head to the beat of *Beware* and begin my work. About 15 minutes into reading my books and adding up numbers on Excel, a chat window pops up.

SxyEyes315: Hey cutie.

I smile. Maybe this night won't end up in such a disaster. I can probably spend the rest of the night talking to her and it wouldn't even bother me.

El_Jander1: Hello there pretty eyes. Did you have a good day at work?

SxyEyes315: It wasn't bad. Chad had to fire someone today. It was pretty awful.

El_Jander1: Wow, really? I hope it wasn't Jason or Madison.

SxyEyes315: Nope. You know Madison is way too good and Jason doesn't care enough to do something this dumb. It was Dennis.

El_Jander1: Oh snap! I remember him. What he do?

SxyEyes315: He cursed out a customer over the phone. I think he just snapped and lost it. You know Chad was not having any of that nonsense. I thought he was going to physically throw him out of the call center.

El_Jander1: Well that's rough. Too bad I missed that.

SxyEyes315: I know. It's not the same without you. I have no one to beat on a regular basis. It's so lonely at the top. ☺

El_Jander1: Well it shouldn't be too lonely since you'll be seeing me in a few days. Besides I let you win.

SxyEyes315: You know I like you, so please don't flatter yourself. ☺ And, yes, we do get to see each other again. Where are you taking me? Can I order the lobster? heehee

El_Jander1: I'm not sure that The Spaghetti Warehouse has lobster. I mean, I can check but I'm doubting it and technically since you have a car, you're the one taking me. Haha.

SxyEyes315: I can't front though, I love some Spaghetti Warehouse. But, yeah you know, Mr. Master's Degree over here needs a ride.

El_Jander1: Well, I mean… I would never say no to a ride from you. ☺

SxyEyes315: Are you being fresh?? Is that the type of woman you think I am?

El_Jander1: um..

SxyEyes315: Did I make you nervous? Haha

El_Jander1: Well you never know, I'm new at this whole chatting thing.

SxyEyes315: Oh stop you know I'm joking. I like to mess with you.

El_Jander1: I can tell. I'm glad you know how to make me laugh.

SxyEyes315: Well I hope I'm not disturbing you and your work.

El_Jander1: I won't say that. I really do like talking to you but I need to get this project done.

SxyEyes315: I understand. I need to go to bed anyway but listen, if you're lucky maybe you will get that ride.

El_Jander1: Are you being fresh?? ☺ Goodnight hon.

SxyEyes315: Goodnight cutie. ☺

This is what I needed, something to make me smile. I think I can go the rest of night. Nayo looks over to me and she sees me smiling. "It doesn't take much huh?"

I look over to her and say, "Nope not at all. I think I might be able to survive all this."

"Good, see I told you that you're not like Ellis."

"Why because I'm smiling?" I chuckle.

"Well there is that, but I did find out why Ellis was in my room that night."

I stop everything in my tracks and I look over to her. "What? Why would he do that?"

"Because he claimed to be in love with me since Summer Institute. He was so overcome with feelings for me that he just couldn't stand not being in the same room with me. Those are his words by the way."

This is the first time I'm hearing this. I just can't imagine him having the maturity to love someone. But then again, maybe that's the whole point, he just doesn't know how to deal with this. We all think about how much of an asshole he is that maybe we miss the obvious proof of him being a complete emotional wreck. Then I think about it again. I really don't care. "When did he tell you this?"

"He called my house in Brooklyn one day last summer and told my mother. I thought I told you this?"

"What? No. That's crazy."

"Yup. We promptly changed our number. I know you would never go that far. Maybe you are obsessed to a point. You want answers so you can seek closure."

Damn it. She's right. I need closure.

UNRESOLVED ISSUES

She never answered the question. It's been three days and I'm still thinking about this. The consensus between Frank and Naomi is that I need to move on. I need to let this all go; I need to find closure. The constant stressing about this is not good. I think I may have to agree with them.

But, the real problem is that I find myself in a very precarious situation. I went on date number two with Serene tonight and we had a better time than I thought. Unlike the first date where we just went to the dinner and a movie, this date was more sexually charged.

Because money is tight we decided to do dinner at The Spaghetti Warehouse and then hit up a bar in Armory Square. It just so happens that the place we went to played some really good Hip-Hop and R&B. There was a lot of drinking and grinding and at the end of it all I brought her back to my place.

My room is dark and the only light I see is coming from underneath the door to the bathroom. Serene wanted to "freshen up", so I wait in my bed with *Ribbon In The Sky* by Intro playing in the background. I made sure to have the CD/Cassette player on the floor by my bed since I don't have a dresser or night stand. I tried to set the mood as much as I can but I really don't own many R&B albums. There was a time, maybe three years ago, when I borrowed a bunch of R&B CDs and recorded them on tape. Groups like Silk, Boyz II Men, SWV, Blackstreet, and Jodeci were all at my disposal. I made this awesome mixtape because all my boys told me that it is a requirement to have slow jams playing when you're about have sex. This is the third time I've played this tape.

Thank God for dance parties at the Student Union because had that not been happening, Frank would've been home smoking with Madison. Instead, he's at work and she's somewhere that's not here. As soon as we walked in the door, we started kissing. All the sexual tension that was building up from our date was finally being released through heavy kissing and touching. From the door we ended up on the couch with me on top of her. It's been awhile since I've been this hot and heavy over someone, so I knew that I was beginning to lose track of time.

I was able to convince Serene to come to my room because I had a feeling that homeboy would show up if we're not careful. Now I'm lying in my bed waiting for her to come out of the bathroom. I'm definitely nervous. I can't remember the last time I had sex. Actually, that's not even true. I do remember the last time, I just chose to block it out of my mind.

As a matter of fact, it was three years ago. I was in the Bronx and I was just dying to have sex. Enter Ingrid, my first girlfriend. She knew I was down for the summer from SU and she wanted to "hang out." There are many things I remember about that day but one of them was the fact that Ingrid gave me some nude pictures of herself. I thought about how bold that was considering that these weren't Polaroid pictures. These were actual go to a photo booth pictures.

Ingrid laughed about how the guy looked at her when she picked them up at the booth in Bruckner Blvd Plaza. He told her that if there was a next time, she needs to warn the person working about the content of the pictures. She gave them to me for safekeeping, which I thought was foolish considering I might just lose them. But, over the years I managed to keep them out of sight. I remember thinking, at the time, the pictures were so erotic that I was down for whatever. I took her to see *Independence Day* at the Whitestone Multiplex and then afterward to a motel where we had the worst sex of my short adult life.

This was when I learned that not all sex is good. I mean, maybe it's me but I just couldn't feel anything. We were naked and the condom was choking the hell of me. I went inside her and started doing my thing. Apparently she was having a very good time but all I was thinking was, *how can I make this stop?*

I remember getting angry with myself too. Most guys would love to be in this very position banging a girl hard and making her scream. But for some reason I just felt no sensation and no pleasure. At this point so many things made sense in my life, like the reason why guys lie about their sexual conquests. There is no way that every guy I know who has bragged about some chick has not had a bad day. I refuse to believe it. Sex is an awkward act if you have no idea what the hell you're doing. There is just no way that any of these guys from high school or college was always knocking out the pussy like a Ron Jeremy.

I had to really think about how I was going to get out of this situation. So I did the only thing I could do, I *faked* an orgasm. Since I had already had sex a few times, I could easily fake the moans. It really wasn't that hard to do. I had a condom on so she technically couldn't feel it. I got up and got rid of the evidence before she could question it.

As for her, she was in a state of euphoria. I stood there looking at her, she was all smiles and half asleep. I was almost turned off by the wet spot we generated. Thankfully we had to go because our hour was almost up.

I really hope this isn't what happens here. I'm a little older and hopefully a little wiser. Serene is also older and probably knows how to do things that I can only imagine. The last thing I need to be is that two-minute brother women talk about.

The bathroom door opens and I see her silhouette. Serene wanted all the lights out. Despite her obvious beauty, she is still very much a shy person. She's not the type of woman that was going to strip nude for me. Although I can tell from light coming from outside that she is indeed naked. At that moment the song switches to "Freak Like Me" by Adina Howard.

"Are you ready for me?" She asks.

"You bet I am." I say smiling. I might be lying a bit. I should be ready but I'm not. I'm just way too nervous. What if she has all these expectations of me that I cannot meet?

Serene climbs into bed as I lift the covers. I feel her cool body press against mine. Her skin feels so smooth. I put the covers over her as we embrace.

"Hey cutie." She says.

"Hey yourself," I respond. We begin to kiss and then my hands begin to wander. They trace the curvature of her body from her shoulders to her breasts. I'm already excited. Her tits are really big. She releases a slight moan when I pinch her nipples.

We begin to kiss more passionately. I feel her hands start

139

to wander too, between my neck and my chest then down to my abdomen. Together our hands find the spots between our legs. We both smile at our discoveries. This is helping me relax. I can feel myself growing in her hands.

I'm already amazed by the fact that she has no pubic hair. It's completely smooth with no stubble. I smile quite widely. Serene has quite the hold on me.

"What are you smiling about?" She whispers

"I'm smiling because it seems that you expected something to happen tonight."

"You think so, huh? This coming from the guy with the slow jams playing all night."

"I was told to always be prepared."

"So was I."

We begin to kiss and as I to rub my fingers up and down her vagina. She begins to moan again softly. "Oh my, you are so smooth. You must've done this today," I say as I begin to kiss her neck.

"Yes, I did." She says softly.

The thought of all of this is so in tense that I almost forget about the condom that I had under the pillow. I pull it out from under her. "I almost forgot about this," I laugh.

"That would've been bad," Serene laughs right along with me.

We both have a good laugh as I put it on. I get on top of

her and we kiss some more. I'm about to put it in and I notice something's wrong. I'm not hard enough. This absolutely sucks right now. I have a beautiful naked woman in my bed and I can't get it up all the way? What?

"Is everything ok?" She asks cautiously.

I sigh. "No. I don't think I'm ready to do this"

"You're thinking about your ex-girlfriend aren't you?"

I roll over to my back. "Yeah..."

"It's ok Louis. I don't think I can do this either."

I look at her, "What you do mean?"

"Well, I mean that I think we're in the same boat. I thought I was ready tonight, but I'm not either. That is why it took me so long to get out of the bathroom. I can't help but think about my ex too."

We both laugh hysterically. "This is ridiculous." I say.

"We're so pathetic," She replies giggling.

"I was so ready for this. I really thought I could handle this. I'm so sorry."

"You have nothing to be sorry about. Most guys don't even have feelings. They just want to hit it and be done. But, the fact you care enough to not take extreme advantage of the situation says something about your character. Quite frankly, I think this Isabel girl is crazy for letting you go."

I smile because I know that her statement is heartfelt.

Maybe I'm not the crazy one in all of this. There's something to be said about getting a compliment like this from a naked women in my bed that I'm not sleeping with. "I appreciate that but this doesn't explain what's going on with you. I mean you do gloss over this dude when he gets brought up in a conversation."

"Well there's not much to say about Dante. I mean, to keep it real, I do love him. I've loved him for a long time but he's not the one for me. I'm just still going through the motions, ya know?"

"I know, how long has it been since you too split?"

"About five months."

"Wow, that long huh?" I don't want to be feeling the same way I do now in four months. I recall someone telling me that the length of time it takes to get over someone is double that of the length of the relationship. So in my case I would be four years. That cannot be true, I reject that idea. "Do you mind if I ask what happened between you two?"

"I don't mind. Dante has issues that are hard to explain. He's a military veteran who went to the Gulf War."

"Operation Desert Shield, I was in high school when that was going on, how old is he?"

"He's 28. He was sent over there when he was 19 and I think maybe that was part of the problem. I've known him for such a long time before we started dating and I always saw him as such a sweetheart. But then he would go to these dark places sometimes and it really scared me."

"Did something happen?"

"He almost killed someone one night during a road rage incident on Route 481. It was at night and the road was empty, this guy came speeding along behind us with his bright lights. Dante switches lanes after a while and this dude flips him the finger. This enraged him. It was like he saw red. He sped up to follow the guy. I remember pleading with him to stop and all he was saying was that he didn't fight for this country to be treated like an irrelevant negro. Finally the guy gets off at the exit by Great Northern Mall and gets out of the car to confront Dante." Serene pauses for a minute to compose herself for a few seconds. "Dante is big guy and he beat that man's ass. I've never seen anything like it. I was so afraid. Since then I just couldn't trust him to keep his anger in check. I broke it off a few weeks later."

"Oh man, that is terrible. Where is he now?"

"From what I know, he's on active duty in the Middle East again."

"Wow. Didn't we just bomb Iraq a few months ago?"

"Yup, in December. He was there."

"I'm sorry you had to go through all that."

"Thank you. You know, no matter what he's still a good guy and I think that is why it's taking me a while to get through this."

"I understand. I want to believe that Isabel is, at the core, that same decent person I meant a few years ago, but I'm not sure I can do that." Just as I'm speaking, we hear the keys at the main door. Frank is walking in and it sounds like Madison might be with him. The one thing that I can say about these two is that they have no idea what it means to be quiet. She tends to laugh loudly no matter what the occasion is. It must be later than I thought. The dance parties usually end by 2 a.m.

The song switches to "Lots of Lovin" by Pete Rock and C.L Smooth. I then hear Frank shushing her. He must've figured out by the music playing that I'm here and I'm not alone. Serene starts to place her head on my shoulder. "Getting tired?" I whisper. I hear Frank's door close.

"Yeah, it's been a long day and right now, I'm so very comfortable with you."

"Well that's good to know." I start playing with her hair a little bit.

"So tell me handsome, besides being an awesome deejay what do you really want to do in life?"

"What do you mean?" I chuckle.

"You said you're getting your Masters in Higher Education but is that your passion? Is that what you want to do?"

"I didn't realize we were getting all deep tonight," I say. Serene giggles and I continue, "I dunno. I guess I always wanted to be writer."

"Really? That sounds interesting. Do you want to write books or movies?"

"Books, I suppose. I always wanted to write comic books when I was a kid. I still have a notebook of all the characters I've created from eighth grade until the end of high school. I was obsessed with this idea that Latinos can super heroes too. I figure since I don't see any I will just create some."

"So why didn't you write comic books?"

"That's a good question. I remember one day I was sitting in my guidance counselor's office. Mr. Northrup, I will never forget him because he was an asshole. He asked me the same question and I answered the same way I just did. He gave this really funny look and said, 'you know there is no money in comic book writing, you might want to rethink that.' I was so mad."

"He said that? I thought high school guidance counselors were supposed to be encouraging?"

"I guess you can say he encouraged me to do something else. Of course when I told him that I wanted to go to Syracuse he told me that I should aim lower. Needless to say I taped a copy of my acceptance letter on his door."

"That is crazy and what did you major in?"

"English. I guess I never gave up on the idea." I smile.

"I see and now you're still not writing."

"Well that's not true. Aside from writing papers for my classes I write poetry here and there."

"Are you serious? You're a poet too?"

"I wouldn't say all that. Writing poetry doesn't really make me a poet. But when the mood strikes I do write some here and there."

"Maybe you can read me some one of these days."

"Maybe, but they aren't very good. I'm not like these

people who read poetry in front of crowds. Although, I did submit one recently to an on-campus magazine. When it comes out I will show it to you."

"Well, aren't you filled with surprises, Mr. Ortiz." Serene says as she yawns.

"Am I boring you?"

She shakes her head, "No, not at all." Serene is asleep within a few minutes. I can't help but feel bad. I have no idea what this means now between the two of us. We probably shouldn't really date anymore since we just admitted to each other that we are still hung up on our exes. Of course, I feel like I just talked my way out of getting some ass. Damn. I can already hear Ruben telling me to turn in my man card.

I will just have to sleep on this. Besides it can't be all bad. It's not like I'm sleeping in this bed alone tonight. I definitely miss the feeling of having someone in my bed laying next to me and feeling the warmth of their body. She feels really comfortable right now. I have no complaints whatsoever about this.

I want to turn off the tape but I'm way too comfortable as "What's the 411" by Mary J Blige plays. Let me just close my eyes.

Slumber; images of faces swirling around. Haze. Long deep breaths. Feelings of warmth. Pushing and pulling. I'm being pulled. Not moving but something is moving. Hazy images.

I open my eyes and I squint. The brightness of the room fills my vision and there's no music. The sun must be shining through the blinds. Before I can even think about what time it is. I see Serene in all her glory on top of me. Her beautiful chocolate skin is not being covered one bit.

"Good Morning, Sleepy." Serene smiles.

I look down and I see her round black breasts with huge areolas. "You must be a morning person," I mumble softly. She's on top of me and I'm inside of her.

"Well, apparently, you are a morning person too." She laughs as she begins to ride me. Maybe I'm in shock or I haven't woken up as fast as she would like me to. She takes both of my hands and places them on her breasts.

I slowly match her riding with my strokes. She begins to moan. "I thought we weren't ready for this?" I ask.

"We're not. But that doesn't mean we still can't have our fun. All the pretense is gone and I did promise you a ride. Besides, certain part of you was ready so…" She begins to grind harder.

"Wait, what about the condom?" I ask.

"Shhh. You left it on. Don't worry about it. Just enjoy the ride as much as I am." She smiles and flips her head back. I would normally care about the noise but considering I hear my roommates have sex all the damn time, I couldn't really give a shit.

The best part of this right now is watching her. The expressions on her face, the way she looks down at me. I begin to enjoy this even more as her back arches in pleasure. I don't know how this is happening because last night was just not doing it for a certain part of me.

"This is a great way to end our date," I say.

She puts her finger on my lips. "No more talking. The only thing I want to hear is you telling me what position you want me in next."

I look into her eyes with a devilish grin. She pays me back with a little wink. I lightly push her off me and stand up. "What are you doing?" She asks playfully.

I place my finger across my lips and press eject on the tape player. I flip the tape to the other side. "Anything" by SWV and Wu-Tang Clan begins to play. She smiles.

Then I say, "I want you to grab your ankles."

SPRING BREAK

It feels good to be back in New York City. I need this time off from school and my upstate life. I got in a few days ago from a bus ride that always seems way too long. Since then I have just relaxed and enjoyed my dad's cooking.

I don't have any expectations on going out much when I'm home because people tend to be busy, but today is a special day. I'm meeting up with my buddy, Dopeness, for lunch. Of course, that is not his real name but that is what we call him. His name is Ray Mars, which he hates because he always felt that he was too dope for that name. As a matter of fact he's too dope at just about everything he does.

First, the man can dance. Any dance party that we went to he was would be in the center of that floor just killing it. He would do twirls and leg kicks that I could never do in this life. We often talked about how he was a B-Boy who was born in the wrong decade. This man had such great dance skills that they had to let him into the all-black dance troupe on campus called, *Expressions*.

Second, he also has some serious skills when it comes to television production. I first met Dopeness on the set of a campus show called, *The Rhythm*. This was a show that was on campus television that no one really watched, but was also broadcasted to the Syracuse community via public access. The only people who watched our show were townies and we were ok with that. All we really did was play Hip-Hop/R&B music videos along with some interviews and skits. When there were concert on campus, Dopeness would try to get the interview and in most cases he did.

Third, Dopeness is an overall great guy. No one ever had a problem with him. In fact, it was a widely held belief that if you aren't cool with him then something was wrong with you. Dopeness has always been levelheaded with no real ego issues. In fact, he was a member of the *No Ass Crew* for a while. Nobody seemed to understand why he didn't get more play. Was it because he wasn't an athlete? Was it because he wasn't Greek? No one really knew because he was definitely popular with all the extra-curricular activities he was involved in. Plus, all the girls loved him. He would often tell me that he would never take advantage of the situation. Dopeness wanted to do his work, have fun, and smoke a little weed.

Naturally he's working for BET these days because he's that good at what he does. I'm meeting him for lunch in Times Square in a few minutes. Since I know that he's probably going to be late I asked him to meet me at Midtown Comics on 40th and 7th Avenue. I wanted to browse the new comics section because it has been a very long time since I've bought any. I had to give up my comic books habit because I couldn't afford the three to four titles of Spider-Man or Batman that came out every single month. So it was either school or comic books.

There's a buzz around the store today because *The Incredible Hulk* was being cancelled this month at issue #474. This was such a big deal that everything Hulk related was on sale. I'm personally not a fan of a white man changing color when he gets angry. Lord knows that if the Hulk were black they would find ways to get rid of that dude. But that is just my opinion. I'm more into the Uncanny X-Men and The Justice League of America. I used to be into Milestone Comics when they came out in 1993 but I heard they stopped doing comic books when I was an undergrad. I should look for back issues.

As expected, Dopeness walks in about 15 minutes late, which is cool. Every time I see him his dreads are longer. They are a little past his shoulders now. He has this big smile when he sees me and we do the bro hug. As usual, he looks like a superstar with his sunglasses and trendy baggy jeans paired with a nice green jacket.

"What up L? Good to see you, man. How you been?" He says pretty loudly. We both tend to be that way when we're around each other.

"Good to see you too bro! I'm good, you know. Trying to survive grad school."

"That's so crazy that you're still up there. I don't know how you do it man. There's only but so much of that cold I can take. They say black don't crack, but my shit was crackin'." We both laugh.

"How are you doing though?"

"Son, I'm chillin'. They got me working on Rap City right now. It's all good. I can't complain. But, check this out, let's head over to get this food because I really don't have much time." We leave the store and head out into the chaotic madness that is Times Square. The streets are always packed with people. As a New Yorker, dealing with tourists is something I've gotten used to. They walk slow and are everywhere. It takes a real skill to dodge and move past hundreds of people just to navigate three blocks. There's nothing special about today, it's typical Time Square pedestrian traffic.

We decide to go to McDonald's because it's quick and easy. Even though the line is long, we get our food pretty quickly. I get the Quarter Pounder meal and he gets a Big Mac meal. We take our food and go to the second floor where the seating is. Before we start eating, he tells me that he his next meeting is with an up and coming rapper at the Virgin Megastore so we will have head there soon because he wants to get there a little early.

We reminisce a little bit on the good times we had in college and as roommates. I don't think we ever had a real argument, which is a rarity. The only argument we may have gotten into was who was a better rapper, Biggie or Tupac. We both loved Biggie, which is not even a question. Dopeness somehow got an advanced copy of *Ready To Die* on CD that said "promo" on it. Not only was it all the songs from the album there were other songs like *Dreams* on it. Dopeness would put on that album every morning for a month before we headed out to class. But, despite his love for Biggie, he felt Tupac was a better lyricist. I laugh thinking about how mad that made me.

Of course like all my conversations with all my friends the conversations always comes back to one person. "So how you really doing man? You survivin' all this bullshit?" Dopeness asks.

"Things are OK, I guess. I just take things day by day," I answer while I scarf down some French fries.

"I can't imagine how you can concentrate."

"It's not easy. All day I try my best to avoid seeing her when I'm in between classes and work. Then when I'm home Frank is either fucking or smoking or maybe even both depending how baked he is. I thank God for Naomi because without her I'm not even sure I would handle any of this well."

"Nayo is good people for sure. Wait, Frank smokes? When did this happen?"

"I forget you weren't around for this. His girlfriend is a big time weed head and got him into it."

"No shit. I never thought of Frank as a pothead. I mean nothing wrong with that of course, I've been known to dabble." he laughs.

"Yes, I know all too well." I laugh because I remember when he first really got into weed. While he was not as bad as Frank, Dopeness would be the chilliest dude ever when he was high. He would say some of the most incredible shit after smoking. The best were his wannabe deep literary type haikus that made no sense.

If brothers want them drawerz
they must learn to eat mangos
otherwise they ain't shit

The best story was the infamous birthday party we had when he turned 21. When you have a South Campus party you need to make sure all of the special accommodations like liquor, red cups, beer, moving the furniture so people can dance, and getting the D.J. are all taken care of. We had all that handled because we spent time having people buy booze for us and honestly didn't we all have a friend who deejays?

The only issue for me was I had to work until midnight at

the Student Union that night. It was my regular information desk shift. I rarely subbed out any of my shifts because I needed all the money I could get. Before I left for work, everything was set and ready to go. The D.J. had started the music and a few of his smoking buddies started dropping by. I figured by the time I came back, the party would be in full swing. Well, I couldn't have been proven more wrong. I get home about a quarter to one and my apartment is empty except for two of his smoking buddies chilling in the living room playing a game on my Nintendo.

The eerie thing was that not only was there no one else in here, the house was remarkably clean. I couldn't even tell the D.J. had been here. So I ask the guys, who are still here like it's their place, what happened and they proceed to tell me that the party never really happened. Apparently, Dopeness got so wasted that by 11 p.m. he passed out on his bed. When I went up to his room to check on him all I could do was laugh. There he was in his bed wrapped up in his covers like he had no worries in the world.

"So how is your crazy ass cousin, Ruben? If I didn't know better, I would swear I saw him on a subway ad the other day."

"Really? I have to ask him, but he's doing well. Actually he is dating Ingrid. You remember Ingrid, right?"

"What? Ingrid, as in your ex-girlfriend, Ingrid?"

"Yup."

"Yo, I remember her! That is some crazy shit, bro."

"Dope, I keep telling you that my life is never dull."

"Yo... that is so true. Your life is never dull. How do you

feel about all this? Damn man."

"You know what, it's OK. I was taken aback by it at first because I never imagined those two ever getting together but if they're happy with it, then so be it."

"Bro, that could not be me. I'm just saying. Lou, you my boy and you like my brother but if you ever date one of my exes then we might have a problem."

"You know what? I respect that. But the thing is I know you well enough to know that you never had a relationship in which you didn't love someone hard. The thing about Ingrid is that I never loved her. I didn't have that strong of an emotional connection. Don't get me wrong, it's awkward as fuck, but what am I really going to do about it? He's family. No woman is worth losing that."

He nods his head, "You right about that."

We finish up our meals as he looks at his watch. It's time to go. We put our trays on the trash bin as we throw away our wrappers. The walk to the Virgin Megastore should not be very long at all, but with the amount of tourists in this area, one should always add an additional five minutes of crowd dodging to any trip through Times Square.

Dopeness explains to me that he's meeting this new rapper that came on to the scene as a part of a group I had never heard of called The Freestyle Fanatics. Apparently they had one decent song that played locally a few years ago and then they could never really get on the airwaves after that. But this dude, Gumshoe is supposed to be really good.

Walking into the store is like walking into a musical heaven. The first thing that anyone can see are the new releases of music and DVDs. Row upon rows of new merchandise that is around the perimeter of this massive floor. From here I can see the Nintendo games across the way. In the center is an opening where the escalators begin that takes all customers to the lower levels.

Each floor contains different genres of movies and music depending on your tastes. If I wanted Wu-Tang Clan or El Grand Combo then I would go to the second level down. But, if I wanted movies, then I would go the third level down. Dopeness was meeting with Gumshoe and a BET cameraman on the second floor so they can have this interview amongst the CDs for added ambiance.

I knew this is where we would go our separate ways because I certainly do not want to get involved in his work, besides that Nintendo display had my name on it. We do the bro hug and I say, "It was good seeing you man. We should do this more."

"We should, of course, with you still being up in the 'Cuse, its kinda hard to do that."

"I know, I'm working on being here this summer so.."

"That's dope. Well I gotta run... oh shit, I meant to give you this," he reaches into his pockets and hands me two movie tickets.

"What is this?" I take the tickets. They're for a movie playing at Lincoln Square for Friday night . The movie is *Wing Commander.*

"I have a friend who works for 20th Century Fox and she had some of these to give away. Since I have to go out of town tomorrow for a video shoot I figured you might want them,"

Dopeness says smiling.

I start wondering why he's smiling. I have no desire to see this movie. Wait a second. My eyes light up. Is this what I think it is? "Holy shit, this is movie that's playing the new *Phantom Menace* trailer!"

"Yes, it is. I don't know any other nerd as big as you are."

"Wow, man, thank you! I dunno what to say or how to pay you back for this," I say as we bro hug again.

"How about when you finally write that book you used to talk about so much, you sign it for me."

"You can count on that."

"Alright kid, let me bounce. Oh, let me know how good the trailer is." Dopeness goes down the escalator as I stare at these tickets. Friday at 7pm at Lincoln Square. Well, I will be there and I know exactly who's going with me. But first I need to head over to this Nintendo section to see which new games are out.

IT'S COMPLICATED

My life is complicated. My stepmother, Ana, wanted to sit down and talk to me about life. I knew when I came down here for break that this would happen eventually. I've kind of been avoiding her because I'm never ready for this level of conversation. Sometimes she wants to talk about really serious shit I'm not always confortable with. This time around I'm not entirely sure what the topic is, but eventually it will end up getting back to the subject of my mother. I may keep time with my watch to see how long it takes for her to get there.

We are sitting in the dining room listening to "Mi Gente" by Hector Lavoe as my dad cooks his amazing black beans. He tends to make a lot so he can freeze them for later. If I'm lucky, I will take some back with me to Syracuse. The dining room is spacious and there is really no distinction as to where this room ends and the kitchen begins. It just looks like one big room. Ana and I are sitting at this huge wooden table covered by a plastic tablecloth. From my seat I can see the far part of the room covered with plants next to the door that leads out to the porch.

"So I wanted to talk to you about a few things." She chuckles. "I know how much you just love our conversations."

I smile, "I have no idea what you're talking about." The reality is that my stepmother has been in my life for a very long time. I have a very complicated life when it comes to my parents and sometimes I forget how painful it all can be. Even if I had a diagram I'm not sure I would be able to successfully make sense of it.

"I need to get your opinion about this girl that my son is seeing." Ana can be very direct. I know that she has an issue with what's going on. Her tone suggests that she could be more than just annoyed about it.

"You mean Ingrid huh?" I ask with full acknowledgement that I'm playing dumb.

"Yes…her. Wasn't she your girlfriend at one point?" She asks. I feel its important to point out that I'm very glad that this is not an inquisition regarding me because I can almost feel the hot white light glaring down my throat. Ana might as well be the bad cop, which means my dad will probably play the good cop. This isn't my first rodeo.

"Well, yeah. But that was in high school, so about four years ago. Papí met her a few times," I point over to him.

"That's right I did meet her. She's a nice girl." My dad randomly blurts out as he's cutting cilantro on this huge cutting board next to the sink. He doesn't look up when he says this and it's a good thing too because he never sees the dirty looks she tosses his way.

"Did I meet her?" She asks while rolling her eyes back over to me.

I think about it for a bit. "No, I don't think you did. We didn't date for very long."

Which is true, it must've been a few months. Ingrid and I go all the way back to grammar school. We went to Holy Cross right off Soundview and Randall Avenues. As little kids we would tease each other, but when I saw her years later at a high school dance, everything changed.

I went to an all boys Catholic school so things were not particularly fun for me. For my first three years, I didn't have a girlfriend. Shit, girls barely looked at me. But it wasn't just that. Even if a girl did talk to me I wouldn't even know what to say. I remember when I lived with my mother in Riverdale when I was a freshman at Saint Raymond's High School for Boys. I would take the BX12 bus across Fordham Road where I would run into all types of kids my age. I was with some friends when this girl from St. Catharine's Academy said hi to me. To this day I have no idea why I couldn't speak back. Was I shy? Did I lose my voice? The funny thing was a couple of years later I had the opposite reaction. I would see Ingrid on the bus after I moved into my dad's after my parent's divorce was settled. I would always smile and say hi because I knew her. I guess familiarity made it easy for me to speak.

Needless to say my lack of self-confidence played a huge role in my high school life (as it still does now to some extent). By the time my senior year came around, I was tired of my own shit. I was tired of not being able to talk to girls and having my classmates wonder if I was secretly in the closet. So when the my school had a dance, I was very surprised and excited to see a very good looking trigueña with a long black pony tail walk up to me and say hi. Could this be the same Ingrid I used to tease as a child? Indeed it was the same girl, all grown up in all the right places.

I remember how attractive her smile was. Her brown skin exuded a sensuality that I hadn't seen from her before. There was liveliness in her that seemed to be held back when wearing a Catholic school uniform. When I finally responded back with a hello I did everything I could for her not to catch me looking at her chest, which seemed to barely be contained by her black tank top. Her jacket was tied around her thin waist and covered most of her acid washed jeans that were tucked into her black Doc Marten boots. We talked and caught up but when she told me she had to get back to her friends, I was disappointed in myself for not taking that extra step.

I must have spent 20 minutes beating myself up but then something inside of me just said, fuck it. I found her through the crowd and I started to dance with her. She was receptive and (later she would tell me) relieved that I finally made a move. It turned out that she was someone's date and he turned out to be a flake. He was a junior at my school and I really didn't know him. I was just happy to walk away with her number at the end of the night.

The rest is history I suppose. Ingrid was the first girl I ever slept with so I guess that should mean something. Maybe that's why I should be a little more bothered by all this than I currently am. Now I have my stepmother asking about this girl because clearly she doesn't care for Ruben's current situation. This is complicated because Ruben is my cousin, son of my mother's brother and kind of my brother because his mom is my stepmother. This is when that diagram would come in handy.

If anyone wanted to keep score, my parents got a divorce when I was in high school, around the same time that Ruben's parents got theirs. There was constant speculation that our parents were cheating with each other once news got out that they were a couple. All the talk about this, got to the point where Ruben and I confronted our parents about the rumors. We needed to hear directly from them what the truth was. My dad and Ana have always denied any involvement with each other while they were married. I suppose if you ask anyone from my mother's side of the family they would tell you that the jury is still out on that.

All this leads to my strained relationship with my mother. Everything about their divorce was horrible. The beginning, the middle, and especially the end were all dreadful. I never went to the court proceedings. Honestly, I really didn't need to because I could sense how this breakup was affecting them both. They were both fighting for custody and being pulled from either side was not fun. My mother threw herself into her work and my dad drank a little too much. They were both angry with each other and would lash out through me. I would hear stories about how this whole situation was both of their faults respectively. What I learned from them was that all this anger and venom being tossed back and forth is just not worth it. I've always told myself that if I am lucky enough to get married, I will make sure to work things out with my wife so I would never get a divorce.

Also, I was never one of these kids that blamed themselves for this divorce, I blamed both of them. I was told so many times, by family members, how spoiled I was. I had all these toys, ThunderCats, Transformers, and G.I. Joe. Then there were the video games. I remember my Atari and Nintendo Entertainment System. My mother would buy me comic books so I could read. It all looked very awesome. But you know what? I told my dad that I would've gladly given up all of that for just one family vacation. Just one trip to Disney World, shit I would've settled for Six Flags. Was it too much to ask to have some memories of when I went somewhere with my parents? I never got any of that. I don't know if it was the general disdain for each other, or the constant excuse of work being too busy that allowed them to hardly be in the same room together. What I do know is this, I used to sit on the stoop of the house as I watched, with a touch of sadness, other families go out and spend time together. I guess shouldn't complain because I did go on a trip to Puerto Rico with my aunt and a trip to Orlando with my cousins. I suppose I have those memories to cherish.

Somewhere in the middle of all this fighting was me trying to be a teenager who wanted to talk to girls and make friends. But the constant moving my mom did to make sure she could afford rent for the both of us did put a bit of a strain on what I considered to be a meek social life. My brother was already too old to care, he was already attending Hofstra and doing his own thing. He would come and go as he pleased because he lived the campus life.

It came to a head when I hit 16 and I had to make the ultimate choice. "What parent are you going to choose, kid?" The judge didn't say it like that but he might as well have. How can anyone put a 16 year-old boy who reads comic books, plays role-playing games, and masturbates to stolen Playboy magazines through that kind of torture? For the record, I did know all my options. I could live with either parent of my choosing or I could do six months with one and then go live six months with the other. I mean, is there a right choice? No matter which parent I chose to live with, the other would be heartbroken. The six month living was not an option I cared to go with, but I did it anyway. It felt so disingenuous to have to live two different lives every year. I decided to do the first six months with my dad because I lived with my mother for so long, it was only right that I go to him first.

About three months into staying with him, I choose to live with my father permanently. I cried over this decision. I didn't want my mother to think that I didn't love her. I just felt that I needed learn how to become a man. It was probably the hardest breakup I ever had. Maybe that is why I'm having such a hard time with Isabel. Maybe it's because I feel the need to fix the situation with my mother and I don't know how. I did see her last Christmas and it was awkward. To this day, it's hard to have a very meaningful conversation with my mother. God, my life is complicated.

"Well, you know I don't like her." Ana says bringing me back to reality.

I smile, "I kinda figured that. Did Ingrid do something wrong. I've never known her to be disrespectful."

"It's not that I find her disrespectful. Let me be honest here. My son hasn't really bothered to formally introduce me to her and yet I see her over at my apartment all the time." Ana is still very protective of her apartment in Parkchester. She rents a small 2-bedroom apartment right over Zaro's Bakery. This is a prime location because the 6 train is right across the street. Since my dad and her had gotten serious over the last few years, she has spent more of her time in this house in Clason Point than in her place in Parkchester. This, of course, allows Ruben to make it a little more of his bachelor pad. He pays for most of the bills but Ana maintains all her rights as his mother and the prime renter of the apartment.

"So she's there a lot then?" I ask this already knowing the answer. I was over to see Ruben a few days ago and Ingrid was there. It is such a different feeling seeing her now. Where I was once very much attracted to her, I now feel as if I don't quite understand what I saw in her. Maybe I was attracted to the fact that she liked me. Her physical appearance hasn't changed but she looks different to me.

"It seems like that girl is there all the time. I'm almost convinced she lives there and I told him I don't what any of his women claiming they live there. There is only one alpha female in that apartment." My dad laughs and we both look at him.

He's having a good ole time cooking and dancing to his salsa music. Ana laughs at him, "...and what is so funny to you?"

My dad looks into this big pot of beans that has been cooking for at least an hour. He's been steadily adding ingredients like onions, cilantro, and garlic. He closes the pot and he places the hand towel around his neck. "I'm laughing because I don't think she's that bad. I mean, okay, Ruben didn't do the right thing but I don't think you should take that out on her. She's a young girl and she probably doesn't know any better."

"Well, if she's such a nice girl, who is respectable, why not just properly introduce me instead of waiting until I discover her half-naked coming out of my shower? Are you saying that she doesn't know any better than that?"

"Yeah, I can't defend that!' He laughs.

"I'm telling you that I don't trust her. I think she has some ulterior motive. Why would she date someone who's related to you? Were there any problems between you when you broke up?"

"Nope. I mean, again, we weren't together long enough for there to be a real problem. But that is my opinion."

"Maybe she wants a threesome!" My dad says laughing which just makes me burst out in laughter.

"No. No, don't laugh at his jokes. They are not funny. Qué sinvergüenza!" She manages to smile.

"I doubt that's what she wants," I say still snickering.

"Did she tell you that?" My dad responds.

"Well, no, but this is a little weird right? Ruben and I are close and we share some things, but this?"

"¡Mira! We are not talking about this," Ana laughs.

I've had this conversation with my dad before. Clearly, he finds this whole thing to be a little more than humorous. His theory is that she's a young girl possibly looking for fun. Maybe it turned a little serious but he's always told me to never underestimate women. They're capable of doing and wanting the same things that men want.

"I don't know what else to say. I've known her for a long time and, I will admit that I've always felt that she's made questionable decisions. But those are her choices."

"Really. What do you mean?"

"Ah, I really shouldn't get into it. You don't like her enough as it is," I scoff as I say this because this is true. I've learned to just keep certain things to myself when it comes to telling parents about the people I date. You never really know if they are going to be out of your life forever or come back in some way.

I hate to be the kind of person to call a girl a ho because that word is so overused. No one calls men hoes, and that's a shame. From what she's told me, after we broke up, she's had a string of guys. Some she dated and some she slept with. Ingrid is the sweet talking type that will tell me that even though she was with this guy or that guy, she really wanted to get me in bed. She's even mentioned this several times to me when I was with Isabel. I was always surprised that she never got pregnant like many of her friends over the years. She would tell me the Castle Hill section of the Bronx was slowly become a giant baby nursery.

One day last year, before her and Ruben got together, she called me crying. I always seem to get those calls for her either crying or distressed. Ingrid would tell me that I was the only person that she could talk to that would never judge her. I suppose that is true. She was my first girlfriend and I, at least, owe her that respect. It was during this call that she told me she had yet another abortion. At that time, I did not know she had more than the one she was telling me about.

Ingrid was always afraid of her parents. While I didn't know them very well, her dad was super strict (I would not rule out abuse) and her mom was one of those religious types with the seven day candles everywhere in the house that would scare the shit out of me. The one thing she didn't want to do was disappoint them. Technically she wasn't even allowed to have a boyfriend until she was 17, so I have no idea how she was able to date. She learned the art of hiding things from her parents to the point that she never told them about the two other pregnancies. She called me because she was ashamed of herself for being so careless. After this third abortion she told me that she didn't feel right. There were some complications that may mean she can never have a child again. I promised never to breathe a word of this to anyone.

Ana decides to back off with the inquisition. "Fine, but we are not done with this subject," she says and just when I thought that I might be in the clear she asks the question that we all knew was coming. "When was the last time you spoke to your mom?"

I can't really confirm this happened because my dad's back is to us, but I would bet anyone money that he rolled his eyes. The divorce ended about six years ago and I know there are hard feelings on both sides. Ana is not the type of person to skirt these issues. She feels that despite the deep freeze that my mother and I share, she thinks that it is my responsibility to nurture and thaw out the relationship.

I check my watch, a little over 10 minutes have passed since I started timing her. I shrug my shoulder, "I don't know."

"What do you mean, 'you don't know?' Please tell me that Christmas was not the last time you spoke your mother."

I remain silent.

"Louis! Really? That's your mother! No matter what happens, she will always BE your mother."

"Time moves quickly when you're in school with all the work I have to do. I just lost track of time I guess."

"Are you, at least, trying to see your mother since you are down here?"

I remain silent again.

"¡Ay Dios Mio! You can't be serious! It's Thursday, don't you leave Sunday?

"Yeah…" What I really want to say is, "Look, I'm really uncomfortable with all this. My mother and I haven't spoken in over six months and while a lot of that is on me, I can't just roll up there and say hi." I keep that thought inside because it's going to come out and angry and sarcastic. So I just stay quiet.

"Déjalo, Ana. Just leave it alone. If he doesn't want to call his mother then let him deal with it. Besides, I don't see her calling him," my father says. He takes a swing of Budweiser then continues chopping the onions that are making my eyes water from where I'm sitting.

Ana turns to look at him and says, "Abe, that's not the point. I think they both should be trying to communicate with each other."

"No, that's exactly the point. The door swings both ways and frankly it seems like she shut it." My dad responds sharply.

They are about to get into this argument, again, in front of me about who's right and who's wrong. Before I can interrupt, the door bell rings. "Saved by the bell folks. Look, this is really more of my issue. There is really no point in both of you arguing about this." I get up from my chair in the kitchen and walk down a small hallway passed the living to open the front door.

Ruben is standing there smiling. He's looking very trendy with a slim tan sports coat over a blue-collared shirt and dark blue jeans. He's also carrying a messenger bag with the strap slung over his left shoulder. The man has brown shoes on and it makes him look like he stepped out of a J.Crew catalog. "Well look who finally decided to show up," I say.

He walks in and says, "I know. It's almost like I own the place."

"Shouldn't you have a key?" I ask sarcastically.

"You would think."

Before he walks in the kitchen, I stop him. "Hey, I got something you might want to see."

He looks me up and down. "You know I'm not into guys right?"

"Asshole, look." I pull out the tickets that Dopeness gave

me yesterday

"Holy shit!"

"Please tell me you're down."

"Of course I am, but I found out something even better than this."

"What could be better than these tickets."

"Lucasfilm released the trailer on QuickTime."

"What?? Dammit. I don't have a computer!"

"But, I do. I already downloaded the trailer." Ruben taps his messenger bag. Before I can protest he continues, "Don't worry, I haven't seen it yet. After dinner, we will watch this bad boy at least 10 times."

He walks into the kitchen and greets his mom and my dad. I stay behind thinking about something Ana said. Maybe I really do need to take some more responsibility about my situation. This whole thing with Isabel has clearly thrown me for a loop and through all of it, I've constantly beaten myself up about it. In fact, I have all but taken the blame for this breakup. The truth is, maybe I should've seen the signs. Perhaps I was so desperate for love and affection that I took the first thing I could find.

I quietly go upstairs. They won't miss me for a few minutes. Ruben will go through his own inquisition with Ana, he doesn't need me there for that. I walk into my room and open my book bag. I brought something all the way down from Syracuse that I plan on leaving here with hopes of destroying it when I'm ready to.

I pull out a large manila envelope with all the letters that Isabel ever wrote me. At one point I thought that this was all the proof I needed to show that maybe at one point Isabel loved me. But, I'm beginning to realize that this is all false hope and that I'm grasping at straws. I brought these letters here so that I don't have the temptation of looking at them when I go back to school.

Something tells me to open the envelope just to give the contents one last look. I pull out the letters and a picture falls to the floor. I flip through these hand-written letters on loose leaf and I realize this is all too much. These are all words written at a different time. They were written when I spent the summer in Syracuse taking classes. We both thought it was a cute thing to do to keep in touch with each other outside of the long-distance phone calls. I always thought these letters were something I could look back on with fondness. I imagined pulling them out to show our children that we had love letters that we used to send each other.

Then I think about the box of things that she left at my apartment a few weeks ago. She truly gave me back just about everything I've ever given her. I can only imagine what she's done with the letters I wrote to her. I'm sure she threw them out the first chance she got or maybe she had the time of her life with Felipe reading my heartfelt words and laughing at my expense.

I put the letters back in the envelope. I bend down to pick up the photo that fell on the floor. It landed with the back facing up. I stand up and turn it over in my hand. It's a picture of Isabel in a flowery sundress. I remember this dress. It was my favorite. She took this picture for me when she went to Shea Stadium with her brother. That dress reminds me of the good times we shared. I have done such a poor job of reminding myself that I did fall in love with her for a reason.

The Isabel I remember was a sweetheart. She was fun-loving, passionate, and had a great sense of humor.

I remember that dress because she wore it on the day I told I loved her on a warm day in Central Park. We decided to have a picnic, just the two of us. I thought it sounded kind of cheesy when I suggested it, but she loved the idea. Since I lived in the Bronx and she lived in Queens, we just had to meet each somewhere in the middle. We surprised each other with food we thought the other would like. Of course, she was the one thoughtful enough to bring the beach towel.

Her long dark brown hair was flowing that day. There was a slight wind and it made me smile when her hair partially covered her face. We had just laid down the towel and pulled out the food when I gave her a loving look. Isabel asked me why I was looking at her like that. I almost didn't know what to say. I've never told anyone that I loved them before. I kissed gently on her soft lips and told her that I loved her so much. It was then that I saw the love in her eyes as she returned the sentiment.

But that was in the past. I thought about putting the photo back into the envelope before I closed it. But I will the take it back up to school with me as a reminder that she may not be as bad as I've portrayed her to be. I look around for a good place to put this repository of old memories. I certainly don't want to leave them out in the open so the top of my dresser or on my nightstand is not the best option.

I begin to pace around my room thinking about hiding places. I have all these boxes of comic books, but I don't want to put them in there either. The last thing I want to do is look through my back issues of *The Fury of Firestorm: The Nuclear Man* or *Static* and find her letters. I open my closet and I find a perfect spot for this envelope. On the top shelf is where I have all my old Dungeons and Dragons books and modules. I slide the envelope behind them just to make it harder for me to reach. This way if it's meant for me to read them at some point I will find them when I'm ready.

I sit down on my bed and I grab the cordless house phone on my nightstand. I can hear the raised voices downstairs and laughter. Ruben has always been a charmer. Ana may be mad but he has a way with words. My stomach begins turning from hunger as the aroma of dinner fills the house. I need to make this phone call. I dial the numbers slowly. I'm amazed that I can even remember the numbers at all. I put the phone to my ear thinking that perhaps I'm making a huge mistake right now.

The phone rings three times. I guess she's not home. I'm about to hang up when I hear her voice, "Hello."

I'm nervous to say these words, "Hi ma. How are you?"

Memorial Sloan Kettering
December 19, 2015
12:10 pm

I spend most of the morning watching her read while I type on my laptop. Every so often Naomi will put the book down to drink some water and other times she will shut her eyes. Just when I think she's about to nod off, she opens her eyes and continues to read.

I continue my editing process by fixing mistakes that have been pointed out to me by the various proofers I have. It continues to surprise me the amount of typos that a book can contain and while some people catch the same ones, there are usually a few that I catch on my own that no one else sees. Lately, I've been so unsatisfied with my own work. I question myself everyday if I should even be doing this.

This is something that I've never done before. I thought that I was a blogger at heart because that's what I seem to do best. If someone doesn't like what I wrote or disagrees with my point then they can engage me on Facebook, Twitter or on my blog itself. I get to know instantly what someone thinks. But this endeavor here? This is a book and it could suck really badly. It's one thing to have a blog that is bad because it's free and people don't have to read it, but if they buy my book and it's bad then that's something I'm not sure I can deal with.

The nurse comes in with a tray of food and places it on the overbed table next to her. Naomi puts down the book and sits up as the nurse rolls the table in front of her. She smiles at the nurse and thanks her for bringing her lunch. I close my laptop because lunch is not a bad idea. I didn't want to just leave to get food when I know she hasn't really eaten.

"What you got there?" I ask as she opens the lid.

"Well, I really wanted a ham and Swiss sandwich and it looks like I got exactly what I asked for," Naomi answers. She uncovers a medium-sized ham sandwich that is cut into two pieces with a pickle and chips on the side.

"Really, so you order whatever you want? That's pretty cool."

"Yeah, well they want to make sure they give a dying woman what she wants," Naomi says chuckling in such a manner that it almost slaps me in the face. When she's in her bed reading she doesn't look like she's dying. I know that she's very sick, but I have such a hard time coming to terms with the fact that she may be passing away before my eyes. She takes a huge bite of her sandwich before she notices the awkward silence. After a few bites she says, "I'm sorry, I'm being morbid. You can tell me to shut the hell up when I do that."

"No. It's not your fault. I'm just not ready."

"The surgery may be successful, I just say these things without thinking about it."

"It's fine, Naomi," I say not trying to think about this.

"How about I change the subject?"

"Sure, let's do that." I answer.

"What's next with you? I know that this book just can't be it. What's your plan?"

"I'm glad you brought that up. I've been meaning to get into my future plans at some point."

"Good. You can tell me all about it while I eat," Nayo says as she continues to eat her sandwich.

"Right now, I'm just trying to make this self-imposed deadline I set for myself. I want to have all of this done by mid-January so I can self-publish by the end of March."

"I know I've asked you this, but have you thought about looking for a publisher?"

"I did think of that, but most publishers will only deal with you if you have an agent and I certainly don't have one. I can't afford it, not on my salary. I already have too many things going on. I won't even get started on the house Frank still lives in."

"So how's that going? I thought he had roommates."

"He did have roommates but they're gone now. I don't know why but all of a sudden I got some emails a few months ago saying they're moving out."

"From both of them?"

"Yup. Strange, right?"

"That is strange. Is he still seeing that girl? What's her name?" Naomi snaps her fingers trying to remember.

"Paula? Nah, that's over. I knew it wasn't going to last long. She's not his type."

"Wow, because she's not a white girl?" She grins.

"No, because she's too smart for him. She got accepted to the Ross Business School over at the University of Michigan and she pretty much bounced."

"Wow. She really is smart. How did he handle that breakup?"

"He didn't seem too broken up about it, like it wasn't that big of a deal to him. I always thought that it was more a fling anyway."

"I don't understand. So he's all alone in that house? How's he paying for the mortgage and the bills?"

"I really don't want to get into that right now." The truth of the matter is that Frank and I are having issues. It's one thing to live with him, but it is another to have him as a tenant. He's been missing payments and avoiding my phone calls.

This is not the first time he's missed payments. Even when I had the other tenants, he had a tendency to be late with his payments, which bothered me a great deal. I didn't want to let something like this affect our friendship so when I went to Syracuse in October for homecoming I took him to lunch at Pastabilities so we can go over our issues. I spoke candidly about how I didn't want money to get in the way of our friendship and if he was having issues because of the divorce all he had to do was tell me. I also hid the fact that Paula had texted me a few times about the issues she's had with him. So I knew that things were not going well and all I wanted to do was help.

A year and half ago Frank left his wife and moved in with me before I left Syracuse. His wife, Lidia was not taking any of this sitting down so she was going to make sure that she put his ass through the damn ringer. After what happened with Annette, I was unsure if Frank would ever date anyone again, but Paula was there to pick up the pieces. I did think it was odd that they got together, but I don't judge.

Honestly what was on my mind this morning is that Paula texted me last night insinuating that Frank may have been seeing someone else and had possibly cheated on her. I'm unclear of the timeline as of yet, but this breakup was not all that recent. I know Frank pretty well and he doesn't seem like the type to cheat, but how well do we really know anyone? When I asked her if she had any idea with whom he might be having a relationship with, she only mentioned one name. Lidia. If that is true, and Frank really is dating his ex-wife again, then it's a real big problem. There is way too much history that I'm not willing to get into right now.

"Ok. So, no publishing company…" Naomi changes the subject pretty effortlessly.

"Yeah, you know. I really did think about that but I'm just tired of the rejection letters. I constantly think about being rejected from MFA programs I applied to at Sarah Lawrence and Columbia. I'm still mad about the rejection from that writer's workshop at NYU. It fucks with me because it starts making me think that I'm just not that good."

"You know Hitchcock never won an Oscar," Nayo says from the corner of her mouth. She seems to do this from time to time when she wants to make a point, particularly when I'm on a self-loathing rant.

"Yeah, I know but ever since that NYU rejection I've been jaded. I spent so much time writing blog entries for years and writing short stories on my own that when I finally want to do something substantial, I get curved."

"*The Alchemist* was a failure when it was first published."

"Here we go…" I put my hands up. I already know where she's going with this.

"Now it's been on the bestseller's list for years"

"You've been watching Oprah too much on that TV."

"Paulo Coelho wasn't a success until he was in his 50s. Did you know that?" Nayo is smiling because she's busting my balls.

"Yes. I know all of this." I say mockingly.

"So then why are you afraid about getting your work out there?"

"Because!" I say as I raise my voice a bit. I immediately feel embarrassed. I know I'm being extremely defensive right now but for some reason I just can't help it. "I'm sorry, that letter from NYU made me realize something terrible. It made me realize that even though it was just another rejection, I've become so used it. I'm really used to hearing this word, no."

"Please don't say it like that." Naomi regards me with a serious look. Perhaps I am being too hard on myself.

"It's true though. I know it sounds like I haven't moved on but I really have. This book that I wrote, that you have on your lap, I sent them the first two chapters when it was completely raw. I mean, I did edit it for typos and stuff like that, but I figured this would be a good way to get some help. Maybe I can get some guidance on the publishing process or maybe I can be a part of this illustrious writing community that I hear so much about. But when they declined me, I knew that my dream of writing a book can only come from one source and that's me."

Naomi wipes her mouth with the napkin and looks at the cover again. "You know, you're right. I think that things happened the way they were supposed to and this rejection gave you the motivation you needed to finish this. I'm really proud of you. I don't think you're a failure or that you're even a bad writer. I think that you should look at things in a different way. We've always talked about how everything happens for a reason. Maybe it's not meant for you to be like other writers. Maybe it's not meant for you to be in a MFA program at the moment, I mean you do know how white-washed many of those programs are, right?"

I always nod my head when she starts speaking truths. "Yeah, I know."

"So it may not be your time to do theses things at this moment, but that doesn't mean it will never happen for you. As far as the workshop, just think about when you lose $20 in the street and when you find $20 in the street. There are times when I've lost money and my mother would tell me that God meant it for someone else who needed it more than me. Then one day I find money and I know that somehow that this is the work of the universe giving me a little something for what I've lost."

"You've been reading *The Alchemist* again haven't you?" I say with a smile.

"Actually I just finished it again last night."

Naomi is right. Her wisdom has gotten that much better the closer she's gotten to...I can't finish that sentence. I just know that I need to finish the final touches on this book so I can finally hit submit on the website I'm using to self-publish. But first, I need to grab something to eat.

THE BANQUET

I already know I'm going to regret this night. It has been on my radar since Lucy mentioned it to me awhile back. Tonight is the annual LSA Banquet and just about every Latino on campus is going to be here. More importantly, Isabel is going to be here.

It's hard to imagine that it's been a little more than three months since that night. I keep telling myself that I need to just survive until she graduates. Once she walks across that stage, I will never have to see her ever again. As much as that sounds horrible and painful, it's the light at the end of the tunnel. I will welcome this because then maybe I can finally let myself heal without wondering if I will see her around campus.

I know it shouldn't matter to me. I've had this casual thing going on with Serene that's lasted longer than I thought. The sex has been great and it has certainly been a welcome distraction, but I know at some point it will end. I'm just not able to give my heart to anyone right now. As much as Serene will tell me she understands, I know that eventually this whole arrangement will become unfair to her.

Frank and I set ourselves up behind the small stage in the

largest room inside of Drumlins. This place is really a golf resort owned by the university, which also serves as a location for student organizations to hold their events. The only real problem is that it is roughly a mile past South Campus. In order for students to show up they need to take a car or the less appealing Centro bus. However, Lucy had her shit together and arranged for shuttle busses to pick up students from both South and North Campus. It made students feel like they were being accommodated.

Frank and I have been here since noon. He dealt with sound check while I focused the lights and programmed the cues. The good thing is we loaded and installed all the equipment last night. This is the part of events most people never see. When they come into the room they just see the finished product of speakers stacked in the front of the stage and light bars hanging from the ceiling. When the doors open at 7pm we will be ready.

The sound position was on stage right while I was on stage left. Despite my usual location backstage and out of the way, I have a very good view of the room. In fact, we both can see everything that's happening. Of course, we have to have this type of view in order to get our cues correct. Not all the performances are taking place on the stage as we found out in rehearsal earlier.

The room is set up banquet style with large round tables draped in black with red napkins covering the silverware. On each plate is a program for tonight. The tiny booklet that has few pages highlighting the night's performances, as well as the acknowledgements. We both have a copy for show order purposes. In front of the stage lays a huge hardwood dance floor that will double as a performance area for the dance troupes.

Various members of the LSA executive board were here during rehearsals to decorate the room. I could tell early on that Lucy had complete control of the situation. She also let Naomi come in early to take pictures of the room for a class project. Nayo has been hard at work this entire semester putting together a magazine to present for her final project. In order to get everything she needed, she took a photography elective so she could take all the pictures for the project herself without having to rely on anyone.

People began filling in the seats a little after 7pm. Frank started playing Latin jazz right before the doors open to set the ambiance. The catered food was set up on the buffet stations with the servers behind them. The food smells amazing. They were able to cater the event with authentic Puerto Rican food and I have to admit my mouth is watering. I'm not sure of the last time I had maduros.

Right now the only thing we're waiting for are the banquet hosts to come up on stage and give the customary welcome address. It's a really easy cue, Lucy and her co-host, Carolina, will come onto the stage and invite people to start eating. All I have to do is just raise the levels of the par cans on either side of the light bars when they are ready to speak.

Just as I begin to scan the room looking for Lucy, I see Isabel walk in. For a moment, everything else stops. She's wearing an open back black dress with a hem that hits a bit above her knees with dark high heels. Her jet-black hair is done up in a way I've never seen before. Clearly, she dyed her hair but it looks almost wavy in the front. But the one thing that really gets my attention is the deep red lipstick she's rocking. She's definitively a sight to behold. I would really love to talk to her, but then I see she's not alone.

Let me tell you about Felipe. This little pothole face dude

has emerged in her life as if he's always been there. I first met this fucker when I was in the Student Government Association when he joined the Public Affairs committee. Since I was the Vice President of Public Affairs in my senior year, one of my jobs was to oversee this committee. He was just a committee member that joined student government as an assembly member. It seemed like he wasn't all that serious about being in SGA because for any project we needed to get done he either never showed up or he half-assed his part.

In the end, it turned out I was right about his dedication. Felipe used his "experience" as an assembly member as a springboard to pledge one of the new Latino fraternities that came to campus in the spring of 1998. He crossed last December and has been a new man ever since. The moment Isabel broke up with me I kept hearing these rumors about this vulture swooping in. It made me think it was his intention all along to disrespect my relationship with Isabel.

Frank seems to think that this is all in my head. The truth is, Isabel is not mine. She is not my property but I still feel a certain way about Felipe being that dude waiting next in line. I'm not sure I'm used to being this jealous, but I do know this sucks. I continue to look at them and then I notice that Felipe gets Naomi's attention so she can take a picture of them. Nayo puts on the faux smile like she's happy to do it. I hope the picture comes out blurry.

Before I can do anything else I see something fly by my head. I look back and see a small ball of gaff tape. I look towards Frank and he's motioning for me to turn up the spotlights. Both women are on stage glaring at me. Oh shit! I raise the lights and Lucy begins her announcement:

"¡Bienvenidos! I want to welcome you all to the Latino Student Association's 10th anniversary banquet! Please take your seats as the wait staff will be going around to let you know when you can go and get some of the delicious food." Lucy then moves over slightly so Carolina can speak. "We will start our program in about 20 minutes. Thank you all for your support. ¡Buen provecho!" She has a slight South American accent. With my luck she's probably Colombian too.

They both leave the stage but not before Carolina gives me a dirty look. Frank looks at me shakes his head. I can already hear him say to me, "Good job."

I look back into the crowd and I only pray that she hasn't chosen a table that's in my direct view. At first I don't see her but then a portion of the crowd that was waiting on the food line shifts and she appears in my line of sight sitting at the center table. I have no clue if she can see me but given our recent interactions, I will assume she cannot. Knowing her, if she could see me she would move, but instead I get a full view of her sitting next to fucking Felipe.

Before the program is about to start, Lucy allows us to get food and I took that opportunity to avoid Isabel the best way I could. I exit the stage quickly and head toward the back of the room in search of Lucy.

"Hey, Lucy."

She turns around, "Hey Lou, what's up?"

"Sorry about what happened earlier. I got distracted."

"Oh please, don't even worry yourself about it," Lucy waves her hand in dismissal.

"Hey, I was wondering if you had any copies of the LUCHA Magazine that came out a few weeks ago."

"You know what? I don't. You didn't get a copy?"

"No, I've been so busy with class that I neglected to get one."

"Damn! I will see if I can find one. I really liked your poem."

"Thank you."

I rush over to the food line.

While I'm happy about the positive feedback, I would really like a copy of the magazine for myself. I will have to search elsewhere. Usually when the magazine comes out they scatter them across the campus. I will have to check the library when I get a chance. I get my food and go back to my post. The only problem is that somehow I've lost my appetite. This always seems to happen when I see Isabel. Sure, the breakup was three long months ago, but I still have a hard time dealing with the not knowing. It's annoying actually, I can't imagine how many meals I've skipped because I can't keep my emotions in check. Despite this, I still made sure to stock up on maduros because eventually I will get hungry. I put my plate of food by the lighting board and pick at it every so often.

I watch Lucy and Carolina walk over to Frank to give him the signal that the show is about to begin. In these situations I defer to him because he's been doing this a lot longer than I have. He's technically the manager on this gig. As the three of them speak I can't help but notice how sexy Carolina is. She's wearing a knee-length red dress with thin straps. Of course, she's wearing heels because it seems as though all the girls are wearing them at this event. Lucy looks amazing too, but she is more conservatively dressed. Her black dress is much longer and elegant.

I've known Lucy for a few years and I never seen her as anything more than a good friend that I occasionally debate over politics. Carolina turns around and starts walking toward me. She brushes her light-brown hair to the side as she hands me a sheet of paper. "Here's a copy of the show order. We wrote in some updates and crossed off this group," she says as she points to what she's referring to.

"Thanks a lot," I respond.

"No problem. Maybe you will pay better attention this time." I couldn't tell if she was joking at first, but she isn't smiling. I just nod my head in acknowledgement. I just watch her leave the stage. I really have a knack for disappointing women.

The shows goes on without a hitch. A few poets, a few dance routines from Tempo (the Latino dance troupe), an award presentation, and finally the Keynote Speaker who is that chair of the newly formed The Latino-Latin American Studies program. All of that pales in comparison to the performance by Felipe and his fraternity brothers. Now, I did witness this during rehearsal earlier in the day. But I'm caught totally off guard by the surprise ending.

The five brothers come out to "La La La" by La Banda Loca. On the other side of the dance floor, five women join them at the center of the dance floor. They practiced this routine during rehearsals for at least 20 minutes. What they did not practice was the last minute change toward the end of the routine. All 10 dancers went to grab people from the audience to join in. Since this is a short song it had to be done quickly and correctly. After a few seconds, Felipe had Isabel on the dance floor, twirling and whipping her around. Of course she loves it. If rolling my eyes were my superpower, I would be fighting crime right now.

The heat rising in my chest was less about jealousy or even envy, but more about pure anger. In the two years we dated she never danced with me once. Isabel told me that she never cared to dance. I always felt bad going to these LSA banquets with her only to dance with her friends. Now here she was, dancing it up with fucking Felipe.

As the case is with every LSA banquet, when the program ends, the co-hosts thank everyone for coming. After that, the DJ takes over with a few hours of salsa and merengue to close the night out. I programmed the light board with a set of random lighting cues to simulate a club feel. I sit in my chair trying to not let all this bother me. Lucy and Carolina say thank you to the both of us and then fade in to the crowd of dancing students.

"You ok?" Naomi asks as she walks over to me.

"Man, I don't get paid enough for this," I respond.

"You know Felipe's whack right?"

"That's not what she thinks," I say as I look out on the dance floor. I see the two of them dancing.

Naomi follows my gazes and sees them as well, "Yeah, but that doesn't matter. He's a scrub. When TLC made that song they were talking about dudes like him. Trust me, I've seen his type. You can tell he's a follower."

"You think so huh?"

She turns back to face me and says, "Absolutely. Have you ever seen him do anything that didn't involve impressing a woman or his fraternity brothers?"

Her question snaps me out of my gaze and I respond, "I wouldn't know. I try not to pay attention to him."

"It's not a matter of you paying attention to what he does. I mean I don't care for him either, but I can tell that he's the type guy that needs constant validation."

"I see. You got all that just by taking a picture of the lovely couple?"

"Actually, that is exactly what I got from their picture. He was very insistent on getting a picture with her but she seemed like she didn't care all that much."

"Well, she can be kinda flaky when it comes to pictures. I've always felt that way when she was with me."

"…and what does that tell you?" Naomi smiles then points her camera at me. I don't even smile. I'm so not in the mood for this. She laughs and snaps a picture.

We both look out into the dance floor filled with students well-dressed and dancing to "Suavemente" by Elvis Crespo. As she heads out into the dance floor to take more pictures, I start thinking about how I really don't want to be here. Not just in this place or at this moment, but at this school. I made this decision to pursue my master's degree at Syracuse because I thought it was a smart decision at the time. I know the area and the school, plus it all made sense as it pertained to my relationship goals. Now look at me with my shattered relationship and barely acceptable grades.

As the DJ continues to spin, I can see Frank at his post checking sound levels before he walks off to the exit. He motions to me that he will be back in 10 minutes. At this point in the night there's not much for him to do but monitor sound levels. I just hope nothing happens in relation to the sound. All this DJ needs to do is turn up the dial on his output looking for more volume and the whole EQ gets knocked out of whack.

I have very little experience in how to fix such a problem like that, but for some reason I would rather deal with that than with the knots in my stomach. The good thing is that I cannot see her in the crowd anymore. I made sure that it is pretty dark on the dance floor. My mind begins to wander. Maybe it's the lack of sleep because I'm taken by surprise when I see Carolina walk up to me again. She must need Frank. Maybe the volume needs to be adjusted.

"Is Frank around?" She asks.

"He stepped out for a few minutes. Is there something I can help you with?"

"The president of Tempo wants her CD back."

"I can try to find it for you." I say as I get up from my seat.

"Could you?" She asks. I'm still not sure if she's being sarcastic.

I walk over to Frank's area. I'm not sure where to start looking but it has to be around here somewhere. At first glance, I don't see anything but the lighting is poor so I turn on my little flashlight and start looking around. I may not be a sound guy but I know what the CD player looks like. I press eject from the player labeled, ONE, in bold written in silver permanent marker. A CD pops out of the player and I put my finger through the hole and lift it up. I look at her and ask, "Is this it?"

"Yes it is, I think it came in a case too."

Now I have to find that. I begin looking under the multi-channel soundboard. "I hope I can find it."

"Can I ask you a question while you look?"

"Sure." I duck my head under the table where he put some of the empty road cases.

"You're Isabel's ex-boyfriend, right?"

I pop my head up quickly and look at her. "Yeah, why?" I ask very suspiciously. I don't know Carolina that well. In fact, this is most we've ever talked.

"You're Puerto Rican too, right?"

I want to use my super-powered eye roll just for the simple fact that she answered my question with a question. I thought she was going to ask just one? Not to mention that she asked the ethnic question. It's almost as if Latinos need to verify the country or island of origin question in order to approach each other. Let's see how this plays out. "Yeah, I guess you can say I'm Puerto Rican with a dash of Ecuadorian."

"OK, so you dance salsa?" There it is. What if I was Dominican? Would she ask me if I strictly dance merengue? Also, what's up with the 40 questions? I need to find this case. I will have to look under the chair.

I nod my head, "Yes." I find the case under the chair and I pick it up. "Here you go. Why are you asking?" I give her the case. She grabs it from me and places the CD inside.

"Well, I remember last year's banquet. There was this guy

that looked a lot like you who was dancing with all the girls except for his girlfriend. I was always curious as to why that was. He was a really good salsero and I never did get to dance with him that night."

I've never been one to brag about my dancing skills. I don't think that I'm particularly great because if I was, I'm sure someone from Tempo would have tried to get me to dance in one of their shows. However, after going to more than my share of LSA events, I've picked up a few moves here and there. "I'm sorry we didn't get to dance. I remember last year. I was tired by the end of the night."

"So how come you're not dancing tonight then? Is your job preventing you from any having fun?" Carolina begins to smile. I would almost find it creepy considering that she practically scolded me a few hours ago but she has a great smile so I dismiss it.

I look down and chuckle then look back up at her. "Yes, that is the reason. I mean, there is no rule against dancing but it would be frowned upon I'm sure. Also, I'm not even dressed the part." This is true. I have on a black collard staff shirt with dark blue jeans and black Timberlands. None of this screams out salsa partner.

"Oh Really? Who's gonna tell your supervisor? Unless Frank is your boss."

"I tell you what. When the right song comes on, I will find you. Deal?"

"How will I know that song?"

"You'll know." I smile.

Frank walks up asking if everything is ok. Carolina tells him that she came by for the CD she's holding. She thanks us both for all the A/V work for the evening and then she walks offstage. I watch her ass as she walks away. Tonight just got interesting.

"What was that all about?" Frank asks almost accusingly as if I'm going to take her home with me tonight.

"Nothing." I say as I walk off the stage smiling.

"Where you going?" Frank asks because he knows that I'm up to something. I say nothing.

Because the stage is pretty small with no room for any real set up, the DJ is located a few feet off of stage right. I walk up to him and wait for a few minutes for him to look and then I ask, "Do you have 'Pedro Navaja'?" He nods and gives me a thumbs up. I wink and point to him then I walk back to my post. I take off my staff shirt because underneath is a gray V-neck that will make it less awkward of a sight as I get into this.

"Why do I have a bad feeling you're up something?" Frank says when he reaches my location. If I didn't know better I would say that he went out for a little smoke.

"I have no idea what you are talking about. How was your smoke?" I smirk at him as I begin to re-tie my boots. I will not enjoy dancing in these. I feel that salsa is meant for shoes. Frank looks at me and smiles.

"Pedro Navaja" is an old-school salsa song by Ruben Blades that I absolutely love. Songs like this come from a generation of musicians that my parents played all the time when I was growing up. I loved these songs and mimicked my dad's dance moves until I had moves of my own. I remember dancing with mother in the basement of our house anytime we had a family gathering. For the most part my sense of rhythm was instilled in me at a young age.

I picked this song because it's a long ass song that requires some serious stamina to dance all the way through. If Carolina really wants to dance then I was going to pick one where she gets to see all my moves. I also picked it because Isabel knows that this is my song. This is the song I closed down banquets with.

I play with the lights a little by making slight adjustments to the cues on the dance floor. These aren't the best lights for this sort of thing. Par cans are not really meant to be party lights. They are meant to spread light within large areas for theatrical performances. My goal is make it just a little brighter until... the beat drops.

This is a song that separates the dancers from the non-dancers. If you know this song then you know the pace begins slow and builds up, gradually getting faster as it reaches the chorus. Most people who are not used to this will just leave the floor. Most of them probably think that this song is way too old. But you cannot mess with a classic. Frank and I look at each other and he immediately knows what's about to happen. His slow blunted look is hilarious as he gestures for me to go to the dance floor.

I start walking off the stage and Carolina catches my eye. She knows its about to go down. The drumbeats are very pronounced. I can also see Frank, from the corner of my eye, shaking his head. The lyrics start:

Por la esquina del viejo barrio lo vi pasar, con el tumba'o que tienen los guapos al caminar.

I walk toward the center of the dance floor. By the time I reach it, there's hardly anyone there because people are clearing out. I hear some cheers because some people, like Lucy, know that this is my song. There was a time when I was nervous to dance in front of people because I was worried I would never get the footwork correct. Tonight, I will not worry about that.

Las manos siempre en los bolsillos de su gabán, pa' que no sepan en cuál de ellas lleva el puñal.

Carolina now joins me and we stare at each other. I begin to hear people clapping. She has a very serious look but I can tell she is already starting to enjoy this. She grins slightly.

Usa un sombrero de ala ancha de medio la'o, y zapatillas por si hay problemas salir vola'o.

I start to circle around her and she stands in on place, she follows my movement with her head, our eyes are locked. At this point people have gathered around the outskirts of the dance floor. I can see flashes from Naomi's camera from the corner of my eye. I think she's going to have some good pictures of this.

Lentes oscuros pa'que no sepan qué está mirando, y un diente de oro que cuando ríe se ve brillando.

Then I stop in front of her and she begins to walk around me. Our eyes never break from each other. It's not often that you can find a dance partner who is in sync with my movements. Once the beat hits, I will see how good she really is.

Como a tres (beat drops again) *cuadras de aquella esquina una mujer. Va recorriendo la acera entera por quinta vez.*

When the beat drops we lock bodies and begin the dance. She follows my lead as we make this a production. A brilliant spectacle filled with twists and turns. Her footwork is good and matches mine perfectly. I have to make slight adjustments because I'm wearing boots and I hope it does not throw me off too much.

Each move is crisp and tight. I turn her hard so that her skirt spins in the air. Our rhythm is completely in sync. I can tell that she lets the music move her body. We almost become a blur of her dress and my dark jeans. I love this song and I almost surrender myself to it. The only thing I regret at this moment is not being dressed the part.

I'm angry and I dance like it. She wanted to dance with me and I picked one of the longest songs to work out all of my frustrations. She is going to have to earn this dance. I'm going to make her dance her ass off. In my mind, I dedicate this last dance to Isabel. She never had the pleasure of dancing to anything with me and I plan to let everyone know that this dance, to this song, is something she can never have nor can she ever take away from me.

I give her all the credit in the world. Carolina is into this. There was no doubt in my mind that she could dance, but she does it with such style that I feel a sexual energy coming from her. At one point I caught her biting her lip after coming out of a twirl. We hover extra close like two heavenly bodies caught in each other's gravitational pull. My hand runs down her sides and I can feel her curves and her sweat. Then I spin her again and bring her back to me.

After 4 minutes of this, we're still going and in true Latino fashion, we're not the only ones on the dance floor. I look around and three other couples have joined in. Just when I thought that Naomi might have run out of film, I see the flashes come the other side of the dance floor. The song continues:

La vida te da sorpresas
Sorpresas te da la vida, ¡ay, Dios!
Pedro navajas matón de esquina
Quien a hierro mata, a hierro termina

The song kicks it up another gear and now I have to admit to myself that I'm getting tired. My legs are starting to burn a little bit. I wink at her and Carolina winks back. I take that as proof that she's in this until the end of the song.

The final chorus hits and the song stops. We both look at each other exhausted. I clap slowly and bow, *"Muchas gracias."*

Carolina returns the sentiment. "That was pretty amazing." We begin to walk off the dance floor toward the stage as the DJ plays another song. "Thank you so much. I just needed to dance with someone who knows what they are doing." She says softly in my ear. Naomi stops in front of us and she takes a few pictures of us before moving on to someone else.

We both happen to be facing the center tables where I see Isabel looking at me as she puts on her coat. She does not look happy. She turns around and walks out. I look over to her and before I can say anything Carolina says, "Fuck that bitch!"

I give her a confused look.

"Did something happen between you two?"

"Felipe is my ex-boyfriend. I just can't stand that bitch."

Oh. My. Goodness.

FUCKING FELIPE

The last day of class marks the end of a 15-week journey. I feel like this semester has been a total fucking mess. I have no idea what my grade point average is going to look like at the end of this semester. The worst part about that is I haven't event partied all that much. In fact, all I do is work and schoolwork, but somehow all the distractions in my life have taken a hold of me.

Even though this breakup has affected me in some of the worst ways, I've been able to get through my classes. First, I was fortunate enough to land a practicum assignment in the Diversity Engagement Office for next semester. Secondly, my research paper on examining Latino student retention rates in predominately white institutions that I wrote last semester, is going to be published in the Chronicle of Higher Education. I can't even to begin to express how happy this makes me. Lastly, I was able to go to my first Student Affairs Conference where I met and networked with many people in this field. The only thing that is left for me to do is to get a summer practicum in the city.

So despite my issues with Isabel, I'm still having a decent semester. I'm not seeing Serene anymore. We both agreed that

199

our issues make it difficult for us to be anymore than just friends. I think this is the right move since I would like to spend the summer back home. It also seems like Carolina is interested in me too. I don't know how all this happened but when I talk to Frank about it he is convinced it was our erotic Latin dance. It must've stirred up something. I would be lying to myself if I said I wasn't interested, but it's just weird that she's Felipe's ex-girlfriend. I'm not sure how I feel about that.

In either case, I've been too busy to mess with either girl. I've either been at the library or at the computer cluster over that last several weeks trying to gain a foothold on all the papers that are due during finals period. Technically I should be used to this. All those years as an English major have prepared me to do all this writing. I used to brag to the rest of the crew that while they had to stress out and study for finals, all I had to do was write four or five papers and I was done. While the prospect of writing seemed worse than finals to some of them, I relished in it.

However, this is graduate level work and the bar has been raised significantly. Each paper I have to write is more than 15 pages long, including a bibliography. Sure, I could bullshit my way through the standard English class with a six page long glorified book report, but I can't do that in any of these master's level courses.

I'm currently at the main computer cluster in Kimmel Hall where I've been typing away since noon. Kimmel is the type of place where everyone goes to get their papers done. The room is huge and has at least 35 computer workstations all setup next to each other in rows. It's the only place on campus that is open for 24-hour student use. This includes a help desk that we can go to in case we have trouble printing to one of the many printers set up around the room. It's an elaborate set-up for one of the most packed places on this campus. To top it all off, this place is a lot quieter than the library.

Naomi is at the computer next to me working on her final project. I tend to forget that her program lasts only one year, which means she graduates next week. Nayo has been my rock this past semester and I'm not sure how I'm going to deal with any other bullshit that comes up. I know there will be phone calls, emails, and instant messenger but it's not the same as staying up and working on projects then getting a bite to eat or having drinks. Truth be told, she has been my crutch. I've leaned on her so much since the breakup that sometimes I just randomly thank her for just being there. That's something I can't do with Frank because he's not in school. Besides, even if he could come to hang out, he's always going to bring Madison and that just never stops being awkward.

Luckily for us, we managed to get here early enough to get open workstations. When I say we, I really mean her. Nayo is the one gets here first and saves me a seat. At times like this I'm glad we're doing our work together because we have a way of motivating each other. We edit each other's work and in turn push each other to better results. I don't know jack shit about magazine layouts, but apparently she values my opinion when I tell her what I think looks good.

Tonight we're planning on doing something we've not done all semester. We're all going to a happy hour. This is something that Frank noticed about a week ago. We don't hang out anymore. The things we used to do together as undergrads (like drinking), we have unknowingly given up since we're all wrapped up in our daily grinds. In response, the three of us have decided to go the bar at the Sheraton to have a few drinks, some chicken wings, and pizza. I was surprised when he said "three" of us because I assumed that he was going to bring Madison, but he insisted that he wanted time away from her to hang out with his friends.

Happy Hour started at 5 p.m. and we are already 10 minutes late. I'm very conscious about being on time to this because when free food is available, I don't want to miss out. The other hungry students outnumber us and I refuse to be left with pizza crust and hot wing sauce. Frank said he would meet us there but sometimes he can be late and my stomach cannot afford these setbacks.

I did all the work on this paper that I'm going to do tonight. I save all my work to my 3½-inch floppy disc and print out what I've done so far. I'll review the hard copy later and make some edits to it when I'm doing laundry tomorrow. Nayo, on the other hand, seems to be in a bit of groove with her project. She doesn't seem like she's ready to leave any time soon. The last thing you want to do is disturb anyone working on their magazine layout project. I value my life, but right now my stomach's needs trump everything else.

"Are you almost finished?" I ask as I pack my book bag.

Naomi continues typing. "I think you should go on ahead without me. I will be there in a little while."

"You sure? I can always stay."

"Just go. Your stomach has been speaking to the both of us for the last hour." She chuckles.

"Alright. I will save you some food."

"You better."

I sling my book bag over my right shoulder and then I put the other strap over my left. I head out of the computer cluster and realize how packed it is. Finals are in full swing and waiting students are like vultures when a computer becomes available.

As soon as I get to the exit I see someone already taking my seat. I head toward the Student Union because I really want to drop this bag off. Since I have a key to the light booth in the auditorium, I can store my stuff there. The last thing I need is to lose my work during a night of drinking.

This walk also gives me some time to really reflect on what I want to do this summer. Do I go home or do I stay up here to work? As much as I would like to go home, I'm a little hesitant. It would be great to see my dad and hang out with Ruben, but can I do that all summer without a job of some sort? Truth is, I grew to be very independent as an undergrad and even more so now in graduate school. Going back home would mean staying with my dad and living under his rules like I was a teenager. I'm not sure I'm willing to do that. However, I think a week or so down in the Bronx might help me clear out some of the cobwebs in my head. Ruben did tell me that he got us tickets to see *The Phantom Menace* already and I'm excited about that. I just hope to hear back from some last minute inquiries I've made to some schools down there about a practicum position.

I find my way into the lighting booth and it's dark in here. I know my way around so I really don't need to turn on the lights. I drop off my bag in front of the lighting console and lock the door behind me. The good thing about working backstage at a lot of these shows is that I know my way around so I can leave through the back exit and avoid seeing people I may not want to see.

I decide to walk through the balcony so I can leave through the exit that leaves me out by the loading dock. I find myself remembering several shows I worked over this past year, but as I enter the stairwell I think about how I ran into Busta Rhymes a few months ago before he went on stage. I was on my way down these very stairs to switch out some batteries to the stage manager's clearcom headset. That is when I saw him looking high as hell. He was waiting in the little vestibule while his DJ was playing and his hype man was doing his thing.

He just gave me a nod and a *"wassup"*. We did the bro hug thing and then I went backstage to change out the batteries. Not that we would've had a conversation, but my job was to reconnect the stage manager and return to my post as the spot light operator. It's memories like this that make me love my job right now. No stress and if I'm lucky, I get to meet a hip-hop artist.

The Sheraton is across the street so it takes me no time to walk there. As I guessed, this place is getting busy and of course, there is line for the complimentary wings and pizza. Lucky for me, Frank is in line and he waves me over. I jump in front of him. "What happened to 5 o'clock?" he asks.

"Things happen. Unlike you, I have school work to do."

"Where is Nayo?"

"She decided to stay back. Her work is not done yet. I told her we would save her some food."

"Well I would say she's got about an hour, but if people keep rushing the food, they may run out sooner than that."

We finally get to the food after a few minutes and I fill one tiny plate with little chicken wings and another plate with pizza. The best part about this is that they have bowls of Sassy Sauce from Sal's Birdland. This is a local treasure up here and it's worth the wait. We walk back to the table and start eating as if no one feeds us at home. We order drinks as we really begin to let go and enjoy happy hour.

Frank held seats at the back of the bar, which is pretty big. He figured this a good way to be far enough away from the commotion of the undergrads and be closer to the TVs and pool table. It's not even 6pm yet but Sportscenter is on and it is nothing but NBA playoff hype. The Knicks play tomorrow and I'm just way too excited about that. I don't think they stand a chance but I'm still bitter about that John Starks game in '95.

Naomi does eventually show up close to an hour later. We managed to save her some food after multiple trips to fill our bellies. It was as good thing too because by the time she showed up the food was gone. The three of us sit and talk for what seems like hours. We didn't care, draft beer is like $2 and tomorrow is Saturday. We have nowhere to be. The feeling is mutual because the later we stay the more crowded it gets and the music changes. In almost a blink of an eye we go from hearing *Hotel California* to this new song called *Bitch Please*.

By the time the hip-hop starts playing Frank and I manage to shoot some pool with some people from my cohort. I'm feeling pretty good as we are doing exceptionally well playing nine ball and killing the competition. Good thing for all of them that we don't play for money. I'm not the gambling type and I really believe with my luck we will run into a ringer and lose it all. I look over and see Naomi is talking to some guy that has been trying to pick her up for the last 40 minutes. As Frank hits the winning shot again, I decide to get another drink. "I'll be right back. I need to get another beer," I say to Frank.

"Hurry up. We got another match," Frank says and I wave him off. I shouldn't be too long. I have a tab open and all I really want is another Corona. I walk up to the bar and there are a few guys in front of me paying for some drinks they ordered. One guy grabs his drink and leaves and I slip into the gap he leaves and wait for the bartender to see me. When I look over to my left I see Isabel and she seems to be sitting alone in front of a half empty glass of something that looks like hard liquor on the rocks. She's a bit more causally dressed from the last time I saw her. From here I can tell that she looks a little down. She stares down at her drink and takes a sip. Isabel looks up and begins to scan the room. I turn my back to her before she can recognize me. I think this bar is packed enough for me to go unnoticed for now.

Just fucking great, the one time I go out with my friends and it happens to be the night that Isabel is here. This is not good. I'm inebriated and all I'm thinking in my head is maybe I can finally talk to her. I have no idea why I do this to myself but she does seem to be alone. But I know better. I take a few glimpses around the bar looking for Felipe. There's no way she is here without him. Of course, Lucy could be around here too.

The bartender sees me and I order my beer. Let's keep it real here, Isabel is about to graduate in a week and I will probably never see her again. The possibility of this is more than likely. I should, at the very least, offer to buy her a drink. This will be my final send off to her. We can let bygones be bygones and we'll never have to deal with each other again. Yeah, that sounds like a good idea. I grab my beer and I head over to her. She has her back to me but I know her from anywhere. The seat next to her is empty so I need to be quick with this.

"Can I buy you a drink, you know, since you are graduating?" I ask. This time I have different approach. I'm smiling and being friendly, none of the typical lost puppy eyes bullshit. She looks up almost startled to see me, but then her expression changes to a not to so pleasant to see me look. I can tell that she might be a little drunk. That is another thing I'm going to try not to complain about to myself. Isabel has never been a drinker. She never cared for it because she always thought her father did too much of it. Come to think about it, it's a total surprise for her to be here.

"No, thank you." She says politely, which is a surprise for sure. What if she's like this when she's drunk? Is she a nice person once you put alcohol in her? Isabel turns away from me and goes back to her drink. So much for that theory.

"You sure?" I know I'm reaching now.

I take a swig of beer.

"Yes, I'm sure. I see you still find it hard to take no for an answer," she says very calmly as if nothing is bothering her. I'm also trying to ignore the fact that she still looks beautiful to me. I was hoping that there would come a time in which I wouldn't find her attractive.

I lean in closer as if I may sit on the empty chair, "Well, considering it's a free drink and you never did any of this when we were together, I thought you might want to reconsider." I say with a smile that probably came across very sarcastically.

She turns her head to me and says, "Hmm. No. I owe you nothing. Not now and not ever. How about you get your new friend a drink?"

"Carolina? Is that jealousy coming from you?"

"Don't flatter yourself. I see it very clearly that you chose that whore to get me upset. Which means you still can't take the hint of letting all this go."

I want to protest so badly. Before I can find the words someone bumps into me and I almost spill my beer. I look over and it's fucking Felipe. "Hey, look it's the poet!" I give my full attention to this prick. "I read your poem, it was just the sort of rambling that I would expect from such a poor lost soul. You know last time I asked you if you a had problem, you never answered me? But now I'm feeling that you don't need to answer because I know what your problem is."

"Really, how would you know that?" I begin to notice that he's not alone. There are quite a few of his fraternity brothers around. I know some of them and while they don't look too suspicious yet, I don't trust this. Some of them are laughing at his dismal attempts at a joke.

"Because every time I see you trying to talk to her, she's always telling you to go away. So, I'm thinking that your problem is a lack of hearing." I see lips moving. I find him to be an ugly guy as far as I can tell. A light-skinned Latino who lost his teenage battle with acne. I can see the potholes in his face as he seems to get closer to me as he speaks. "...so I'm going to say this real slow for you. She wants nothing to do with you bro."

I just look at him. There is a silence between us. I envision smashing this bottle across his face because I won't make the same mistake I did with Ellis and awkwardly punch him in his ear. This would be done with slow-motion precision. I grab the Corona bottle by the neck and turn it over. I would take a baseball swing and crack it over his face. There would be glass and beer everywhere. He would scream like a little bitch while I stomp his motherfucking ass into the ground. But then I start to think about how much I lose if I do this. Imagine me, of all people, going to jail for attempted murder? That's what it would be, I want to release a semester's worth of frustrations, anger, sadness, and rage onto his broken body.

I start to laugh in his face. I can't believe I'm in this

hilarious situation right now. Me getting into a fight over a woman who doesn't even want me. She doesn't even give me the time of day. All I want to do is find out what went so wrong and I keep running into this guy who constantly defends her honor. It's like *Karate Kid II* but I'm Chozen. What's worse is that he doesn't even know me! But you know what is really funny? Even if I could get one good punch in, which I would love to do, his fraternity brothers would pummel me. No one is worth any of this, not him and certainly not her.

I start laughing so much I almost double over. Felipe and Isabel are looking at me like I've lost my mind. Some people do join in my laughter because it is genuine. I even see Isabel crack a small smile. Felipe is not amused, "What the fuck is so funny?"

I try to get the words out. I take a deep breath. "Wooo, I need a minute." I take a nice deep breath. "I just realized something, you poor bastard. You're just like me but like two years ago." I start laughing hard again. Felipe is completely confused. "The thing is I don't see a label on her anywhere that has your name on it and since we all know you're the rebound guy, it makes me realize that the problem in all this is really you." I stop laughing and look him in his eyes.

Felipe becomes irate I think he's going to hit me and I'm ready. "What the fuck did you say, nigga? I will fucking end you right now." The commotion begins and we just stare at each other. I can hear people saying *yo, chill!*

Then I feel someone push me aside. "Lou, let's go." I look over and it's Jason.

Felipe looks up at Jason. "This is your boy?" Jason looks at him as he steps in front of me. I see Frank walk over and I want to laugh again because he's taller than everyone else.

Words are exchanged between him and Jason that I can't hear. I look over to Isabel and she's talking to her roommate, Sasha. The next thing I know Frank is shuffling me back over to the pool table.

"What the hell happened? I leave you alone for two minutes and you're breaking the place up?" Frank says.

"Man, fuck that dude," I say.

Naomi gets up and asks, "What's happening?"

"I was just trying to buy her a drink and her guard dog shows up," I answer.

Naomi looks at Frank. "Should I even bother to ask who he was trying to buy a drink for?"

"You can ask, but you know it's Isabel." Frank says with pursed lips.

Naomi shakes her head and sits back down. I keep staring in the direction of Felipe, but Frank blocks me from doing something as stupid as going over there and starting a fight. "We were having such a good time today." Frank says.

Jason walks over shaking his head. He has two bottles of beer in his hands. He gives me one. Apparently those two know each other. I had no idea, but I guess since Isabel is probably seeing him it would only makes sense that he has been over to the apartment. "That kid is so mad right now. I don't know what you said but he's some kind of upset right now," he says smiling.

"Fuck that dude," I say again. Jason and Frank just laugh. "Nah man, I'm serious. He can eat a fat one. Since when are you two buddies? He come over a lot?"

Jason still laughing, "You're so bitter bro, is that what you think? That he's hitting that? I think you got it all wrong."

"What are you saying? Of course I think that way. He has been all over her since we broke up, but please, enlighten me."

"Man, sit your angry ass down. I gotta story to tell you and I want to preface this by saying that I'm sorry I haven't been around. You know The Direct Club is not an easy gig."

"That's right. I forgot you still work there," Frank says as I have a seat near the pool table.

"Used to work there," Jason looks at Frank.

"Oh shit, when did that happen?" Frank replies.

"I gave them my two weeks notice about, well two weeks ago. Yesterday was my last day. I told Sasha, that once finals season started, I'm out. This way I can help her pack and we can leave this soul crushing place together."

I'm starting to get impatient waiting for this story. But I can't help but feel happy for him. Jason is living the life I wish I had. He stayed up here because he loves Sasha and wanted to be with her during her last year. He absolutely hated The Direct Club but he was making that necessary sacrifice for the relationship.

Frank continues this damn conversation, "That is so dope. So what's the plan? When you two going back to New York"

"Yo! What the fuck?" I interrupt. I think they do this on purpose. They both start laugh.

"My bad man, you know you my boy. We just had to mess with you," Jason says. I really believe that if my life were a cartoon strip, there would be dialogue balloon over my head right now with a ball of squiggly lines like you see in *Peanuts*.

Alright so this is the real story about Felipe as told by Jason:

So check this out. Ever since the night you two broke up Sasha and I have been worried about Isabel. Not that we were never worried about you, but you live with Frank. He's gonna make sure you don't jump in front of a bus. We noticed that first week she was sad and lazy. She still went to class but she wasn't herself.

Then, sorta out of the blue, Felipe starts showing up. He's dropping her off and picking her up. This is like week two and I'm like, "did this chick really play my boy like that?" So I had to confront her about it. She was all nice and apologetic saying that he was just a friend and there is nothing going on because she doesn't want a boyfriend. "No disrespect to Louis, but I just want to be free."

I have to admit that she seemed sincere. She still kept hanging with this dude so I asked Sasha about this because, you know, they live together and I know they talk. Of course, I never told you any of this, but she said that Felipe has been up her ass for about a year.

Sit yo ass down, I'm not done.

She never did anything with him, in fact, I'm pretty sure that she's stringing him along. According to Sasha, he's never spent the night. Sure, he's come by and we chilled a few times watching the basketball game but it really ain't that deep, homie. If anything, he's playing a role. He's probably intimidated that you might actually get back with her. So he plays that role and she lets him apparently.

I thought it would be a better story than that. I just take a few more swigs of this beer. I hate when I'm right. I just knew that he was hard up for her. "So wait, what did Sasha say exactly when it came to Felipe sweating her for a year?" I ask Jason very directly. "No more games. I need answers."

"Sasha wasn't very specific, just that he would try to flirt with her when he knew she was going out with you."

This makes my blood boil. This makes sense when you put some context to this. Carolina explained to me after our dance that she's Felipe's ex. She went into this story about how he was a jerk (no surprises there) and that the only thing he cared about was getting those letters across his chest. She supported him through the pledging process by bringing him food, providing him with a place to hide and sleep (because he was a skater), and even lending him money during the rough times. Her reward for all that? He broke up with her the day he crossed. She had a feeling that he had his eye on someone but she couldn't narrow it down to anyone, until she saw them hanging out all the time.

The reason why Carolina cannot stand Isabel is because she feels she's using Felipe. She also thinks that they had something going on last semester while we were still together. I assured her that was not the case. When I think about it now, I almost laugh at the stupidity and the confidence that emanated from that statement.

"Fuck this." I get up and start to walk over to Felipe. I hear Naomi asking what I'm doing but I ignore her. I just want to settle this. His frat brothers may fuck me up but all I need is one shot right to the face and all is good with world.

I take like two steps and Frank gets right in front of me. It's not even fair how big he is sometimes. "Where do you think you're going?"

"Come on, Frank move out the way!"

He just laughs. I can hear Jason telling me to chill out and something about how Felipe isn't worth it but I don't want to hear any of it. "Get out my way Frank! I don't want to have to move you!" Ok, I admit that this may not go well but I need to at least try. I'm just so tired of being angry. He cannot take this away from me.

Frank again laughs and starts eating bar nuts! Ugh! "You're welcome to try. Maybe the effort will burn off some of that negative energy from you."

I'm sure that I will look back at this day and laugh but the beer and the overall agitation was just too much that I actually try to move him. My friends laugh at me and I can hear them telling me to just sit down but now, I'm embarrassed. I have no idea what to do.

"I want to go home then." I groan.

"Really? It's like 10:30." Naomi says.

I turn around and say, "It's fine, y'all stay here. I can catch the bus."

"Come on man, I don't hang out very often." Jason says. He is right though. But I need to not be here right now.

"Look, I will walk you outside. Go get some fresh air and come back in 10 minutes. I will wait in the lobby for you so you don't do anything stupid," Frank says. I guess I don't have a choice. I really don't want to ruin the night for my friends. They were certainly having fun before my little bullshit antics.

"Ok. I will be right back." I say as Frank walks with me

out the bar and into the lobby. We walk on the opposite side of the bar so that there are no further altercations. Frank watched me leave the hotel because he simply doesn't trust me in my current state of mind.

I'm sure they all think I'm drunk but I'm really not. In fact, I'm completely sober and in control. I'm just angry. I walk towards the Student Union. Maybe I can just take a few paces across campus. It's a pretty decent night so I decide to walk towards the library to finally check to see if there are any issues of LUCHA magazine left. I'm sure there won't be but the walk may help me calm down.

This reminds me of when I was so pissed at Ellis that I just had to leave his apartment and walk home. We were playing Coach K College Basketball on his Sega Genesis when we got into an argument. He had one job and that was to set up a study group with this girl Jennifer who was in the same math class that we were both doing poorly in. We had noticed that she aced every test and I was tired of failing so I suggested that we try and form a study group.

I really didn't want to explain to my dad why my math grades were so poor. Ellis agreed and he went to speak with her after class. About a week later, I'm at his house playing this game while waiting for her to show up. Once he beats me (because it was his game) he tells me that she's not coming because after he fucked her, he forgot to call her. We got into a huge shouting match and I left.

That was just another instance where if I had a little bit more confidence in myself, I would have been able to talk to her. Of course, had I done that then I would have been able to get a much better grade than a C-. Because I knew Ellis, I was guilty by association, which always pisses me off when you have such an asshole for a friend. I guess it was for the best because Jennifer was the one woman he couldn't control and because of that he was slightly afraid of her. He would tell us that she was a stalker who would do crazy shit. I'm starting to think it was the other way around.

I stop in front of the parking lot in front of the library because something catches my eye. This car looks familiar to me. A silver Honda Accord with a fraternity tiki hanging from the rearview mirror. Yes, this is Felipe's car. I've seen him drive by the bus stop on College Place several times. I would love to piss on it right now but I'm in the middle of campus and that wouldn't be a good idea. Although, I do have my keys. I could key his car right now as I walk by and no one would notice.

I take out my keys. I have two sets, one for home and one for work. The work keys are actually the sharper ones. I could scratch the fuck out his car and not even feel remotely bad about it. I begin to whistle as I walk by the passenger side of the car, scratching it up when I hear a woman's voice, "Excuse me? What are you doing?" I close my eyes. Fuck. What if this is not his car?

I turn around and it's Carolina. "Hey there! How are you?"

She gives me this disapproving look. "That's Felipe's car you're scratching up. Did you think no one would see you?"

Damn.

"That was the plan."

"Well you fucked up because that's not how you get his attention."

"What?" I'm confused by her statement.

She goes into her purse and pulls out a huge pocketknife. "This is how you get that motherfucker's attention."

I back away slowly with my hands up saying, "oh shit," as she begins to jab the knife several times into his front passenger tire. I look around to see if anyone's watching. I start hearing a hissing noise coming from the tire and I am wide-eyed.

She stands back up smiling a very crazed, yet attractive smile. "Well, that was fun, you want to try?" Carolina asks as she passes me the knife.

I look at it in my hand and I look at her. "Fuck yeah!" I go to the back passenger tire and stab it until I hear the hissing sound as she looks out for anyone. I stand up totally satisfied. I feel a complete wave of adrenaline rush through me. She looks at me in the same way she did when were dancing a few weeks ago. "That felt really good!" I say.

"I know! We're so bad. We need to get out of here before someone see us," she says. Of course, at the moment a Public Safety car starts coming down the street and I, the dark-skinned Puerto Rican, have a knife in my hand. Carolina acts quickly by putting her arms around me like we're hugging. I drop the knife back in her purse as the car rolls by. We just look at each other and she kisses me. I return the kiss and we make out for a few seconds. She pulls away and says, "We must do this again."

We walk in opposite directions. I'm not gonna think about this. I walk back toward the hotel and she walks toward the bus stop. I try not to walk fast but I can't help it. When I look back I can see the car is slightly lopsided. It's obvious now that he has two flat tires.

I'm not gonna think about this or the fact that I'm totally aroused by what just happened. I walk into the Sheraton and I see Frank sitting on one of couches in the Lobby. I tell myself that I'm not gonna think about this.

He sees me and gets up, "How was your walk?"

I stop in front of him and pat him on his shoulder. "It was stimulating. The next round is on me."

COMMENCEMENT

This is going to be a long day. I find it hard to complain about this because at about $11 an hour, working 26 – 30 hours over a three day stretch makes this whole weekend worth it. Saturday is the anchor leg for me. The auditorium in the Student Union hosts three individual school convocations and the only thing I'm responsible for is the lights.

Overall A/V comes with the job description, so if the slide projector starts acting up then all I would really need to do is replace the bulb. Brian takes care of the sound, which makes his job just as easy as mine. I turned on the lights, adjusted the spotlights and I was fine. I already did the pre-work of focusing the lights last night when the room was set up. All Brian has to do is run some cables from the podium microphones to the audio check in the floor. He tapes them down and he's good. So, this morning, I turned on the lights and he did the sound check. After that, we just sit here until the program ends.

Once everyone exits, we get ready for the next school. Sometimes there's a minor adjustment to the podium or I have to create a lighting special to highlight faculty in the background, but all in all it was a cushy job for me. Brian had a little bit more work to do with sound levels and adjusting the microphones. All things that I don't get into because he's good at what he does and I'm good at what I do. In fact, I think that Brian might be better at this than Frank. After all, he is a theater major.

Of course, all this free time gives me too much time to think. This morning I got to see a few people that I know finally graduate. Doing enough events in this building combined with about five years of being a student means that I still know quite a few people. But all the speeches and name calling doesn't really do much for my habit of overthinking.

I'm relieved that at this moment, across campus at the Carrier Dome, my ex-girlfriend is graduating. which means her family is up here. They are the last people I want to see. I don't want to deal with the inevitable awkwardness because I can only imagine what she may have told them about me and the breakup in general. She never seemed like the type to tell her mother everything, but I do know she is close to her younger brother, Fabian.

Fabian is a freshman at St. John's University who came out of the closet to his parents about a year ago. I wasn't there when he did this, but I do remember Isabel talking about how unhappy her father was about it. Her mother was and still is very supportive of everything Fabian does. I remember how close the three of them were and I just can't imagine seeing them again.

Their parents have been separated for years. I'm not sure why they don't divorce but I'm guessing it has something to do with religion and/or some sort of "cultura". They met and married in Colombia before immigrating to this country. While I have no clear reason as to why they are separated, I would venture to guess that her father's temper was an issue. He was never really around as much as Isabel wanted. There were times she would call me disappointed and in tears because, once again, her father didn't show up to the house when they had plans. I always felt that I needed to tread lightly when it came to the subject of her dad. I never got the impression that he cares for me too much. I was always quite respectful but sometimes you just know when your presence is not wanted.

I often wondered if our relationship was affected by her parents' relationship. Isabel had no control over anything her father did or didn't do. I can only assume that she felt the need to control what she could in other aspects her life. She was very guarded when I met her and even when we first started dating. This all makes me wonder if she ever really dropped her guard with me.

I wonder if she ever dropped her guard with Felipe. I shake my head because I still can't believe what happened last week. Jason would later tell me that he was really angry about the tires and he was convinced it was me. Jason is a good friend and an incredible liar. He told Felipe that I never left the bar so how could I have done anything? Felipe had no choice but to believe that fantasy. I want to die laughing just thinking about it.

Then there is Carolina. What is up with her and why did she have a knife in her purse? Granted, the average number of campus rapes have been on the rise so I can understand the concern, but this was like a *Crocodile Dundee* knife. I want to remind myself not to mess with her, but damn that girl's so fine and apparently interested. I know there's a general man rule not to mess with crazy women but unfortunately I'm incredibly attracted to them. This is not a good thing, I'm just going to point that out right now.

The other problem I have is that at a little past noon I

have to dip out to the Carrier Dome to see Nayo graduate. I promised her I would go and I want to make sure that I get there. Her school's graduation begins at 12:30 p.m., which means I will have to try to navigate this campus without seeing Isabel and her family. Brian is cool with me slipping out because there are no lighting cues for this event. Once I turn on the lights, I'm good to go.

Speaking of women, I haven't seen Serene in a few weeks. We had that one morning of great sex but after that we had been slacking off. I think we both needed a release and some time to just be with someone but now that it's done, I guess there is no reason to go out on dates. She's still on my AIM buddy list so I'm sure she won't mind if I hit her up. Seems like dating may not be in the cards anymore. To be honest, I'm ok with that. I don't really want to go down that road. I guess my slow jam tape will have to go back into the shoebox.

The auditorium begins to fill up with all the people who've come to see the Information Science & Technology school graduation. The first six rows on either side of floor are blocked off for graduates. According to the schedule given to me, the procession should start in about 15 minutes. I walk out of the booth onto the top of the balcony where a few people are seated. This area holds about another 500 seats and I'm sure before this ceremony starts, it will be full. I look around to pass the time. I should've brought a book or something else to read.

I turn around to go back to the lighting booth and I see Lucy in her graduation cap and gown walk in though the balcony entrance. I totally forgot that she is an IST major. "Louis! Hey!" She obviously looks very happy.

"Lucy! Congratulations!' We hug and I spin her around. "I'm so happy for you." I put her down.

"Thank you! I knew you would be here. I wanted to drop by to say hello and thank you so much for everything you did for LSA."

"There's really no need to thank me. I just simply did my job, which was to turn on the lights." Lucy and I have seen each other since the banquet but never really had time to talk for one reason or another. She was either hanging around Isabel or I was in the computer cluster with Naomi. This would be the first time since then that we've had a chance to really talk by ourselves.

"You say that, but in actuality you danced so well that Carolina can't seem to stop talking about it. I think you better watch yourself with her. Esa Loca," She says laughing.

"I will make sure to be careful."

"Good. So what are you doing with yourself this summer? Are you stuck up here?"

"No, actually, I'm not. I applied to a summer practicum at City College and I got accepted."

"Oh my God! That is awesome! When do you start?"

"I start June 1st. What are you doing after all this? Did you land a job somewhere?

"I did. I got hired as a Y2K project manager at Deutsche Bank in midtown."

"Wow, first, I've never even heard of that bank and second, I heard about this Y2K thing what is it?"

"Well, you know the year 2000 is coming up fairly quickly

so all the corporations are freaking out because all their computer dates end in two digits like 99 for the year 1999. Some say when the clock hits midnight on January 1st of next year this massive failure is going to occur because those digits will reach double zeros."

"That's insane, so what does that mean you'll be doing exactly?"

She chuckles a bit, "I will be one of a few people in charge of a large team of people that will search through hundreds maybe even thousands of lines of code to fix this two-digit bug. This is happening worldwide by the way."

"Wow that is interesting. I could never do it but it sounds like you might actually enjoy this."

"It is! It's a very good time for information technology jobs. But listen, I wanted to give you something," Lucy goes into her medium-sized purse and pulls out a small booklet. "This is our last copy of LUCHA Magazine."

"Oh my God!" I say wide-eyed. "Thank you. I really thought I would never find a copy!"

"I know how much it meant to you and when I found one I had to hide it until I saw you."

"Wow," I say as I open it. There's a post it note on the page where my poem is listed. It has her number and her AOL Screen name, PRd1va99.

"Hit me up on AIM. There are a few things that I need to tell you but I can't do it right now."

"Can I get a hint?"

She chuckles, "No, just remember that we're friends and when everything is said and done, I would like to remain so. I have to go. I have to drop this bag off to my mom downstairs before the ceremony begins." We hug again before she leaves.

I walk back into the lighting booth and sit down on the stool in front of the board. I look at the cover, which is a collage of different South American and Latin American flags that celebrate the 10th anniversary of LSA. I turn to the back over and it is filled with thanks you and acknowledgements. This is the first time since I've been in Syracuse that I decided to write anything for LUCHA. I open the magazine again and reread the poem I wrote:

We all have roles to play
you play yours
and I will play mine
and in the end
neither of us
will get an award.

Every action
has a reaction
every actor
has their script
every singer
has their lyrics

We all conform
in our ways
and we all perform
on other days
we transform
but real life never pays
in wages
for our roles

so while you give
an inspiring performance
on how you may not care
your role has been recast
because the audience
is not believing it

I stare at the page. This may the first time I've ever seen my work in print that wasn't corrected by a professor. There's something about reading this right now and knowing that I put this out there for the world to see is comforting. Maybe I need to put my feelings about this whole thing out there in order to gain some type of closure.

I start to wonder if Isabel read it, but I have a feeling she probably did. Just because she didn't say anything doesn't mean she didn't read it. I know Felipe read it since he called me a poet in the most sarcastic of ways. I hope it got under his skin.

I see the light on the Clear-Com headset blinking. It must be Brian telling me that we're about to start. I put the booklet down and put on the headset. I click the answer button, "What up?"

"The processional is about to start," Brian says dryly. Sometimes you can never tell if he's in a good mood or not. With his quiet demeanor, I suppose anything is possible.

The music begins and everyone quiets down. From my vantage point I see the faculty walk through the center aisle of the auditorium and then onto the stage taking their seats. Then the graduates follow behind filling up those six rows in front of the stage.

I wait for the dean of the college to step in front of the

podium before I turn on his spotlight. I have a very good feeling coming over me. I'm starting to see that light at the end of the tunnel all I have to do is get there.

The dean steps up and I turn on the lights.

I rushed so quickly out of the booth that I almost forgot to tell Brian that I'm headed to the Carrier Dome to see Naomi graduate. I rush out of the open doors of the auditorium entrance into a sea of people in the atrium that oddly reminds me of Times Square. I fight my way through the crowd until I exit via the east entrance.

It takes me less than 10 minutes to cross the Quad. I do my best to avoid all major walkways because I know that with my terrible luck I will run into Isabel and her family. I keep my eyes peeled for any sign of her and I breathe a sigh a relief by the time I get to the gate I'm looking for. The Carrier Dome is a huge football stadium that's right in the middle of campus. There is barely a place around here where you cannot see it. All the entrances and gates leading into the stadium are open. If there were a game I would be standing on line right now but since there are no tickets for this non-sporting event, I can walk right in.

Of course, I rushed for no reason. The graduates haven't even walked as yet. This may be my chance to actually talk to her before she takes her seat. I vaguely remember where the graduates lined up from when I had to do this last year. I will have to rush the other side of the place and then find her near the field level.

I finally get to where the graduates are lining up. The only thing going for me right now is that because she is getting her master's degree, her robes will be black but that also means that she will be heading out first. I fight my way through the numerous amounts of undergrads when I hear someone telling the all the graduates to quickly start lining up. I only have a few minutes before they go out.

As they begin to scramble I finally see the black robes. One of the things I remember her telling me was that she was one of few black master's students. So on that account it is not hard to find her. I call out to her, "Naomi!"

She turns around with a typical Brooklyn look like, *who the hell is calling me by my government?* I start dying of laughter and she looks at me and smiles, "Why are you always laughing at me?"

I take in the vision of Naomi in her black robes and Kente cloth stole. Her high heels make her look even taller than she already is. "I'm not always laughing at you, I'm laughing with you because you looked like you did years ago when we started Summer Institute."

Naomi waves her hand, "People always think I have an attitude, but you did call me by my government in a crowded place so I had make sure it was someone I knew."

"Of course. By the way you look great. I wanted to say congratulations now because I have to run back to the student union right after your name is called." We hug and I continue, "I'm so proud of you Nayo. I'm really not sure what I would've done this semester without you."

We pull away from our embrace and she says, "Oh stop it Louis, this is what friends do. You were there for me so many more times than I can count. You got me through my issues with Brandon and you kept me from killing Ellis. I'm just glad you kept me sane."

Someone yells out that they are about to begin and Naomi

passes me her camera. "Take a quick picture of me. I haven't been able to get anyone I trust to take one since I've been down here."

I stand back and take a few shots of her with her mini Kodak camera. She's smiling which is a rare sight because I do remember the rough times she's had over the last five years. Brandon was one of her ex-boyfriends that really screwed her over during our freshman and sophomore years. He was that dude that didn't really want to be with her outside of just sex, but didn't want anyone else to be with her either. It was all kinds of ridiculous shit that lead to a lot of pain for her. I still wonder if she will ever love another guy.

As for Ellis, well he's the biggest asshole of them all. He started a series of rumors about her that she's had to deal with. According to him, Naomi asked him over on that fateful night where they shared a bubble bath together. When that was done, they went into her room where she performed numerous lewd and lascivious acts. According to Ellis, they had rough sex and it was so loud that her roommate thought Naomi was being raped, which is why she busted in with a bat. In this version of the story he barely manages to get away with his life.

While this may sound ridiculous to some of the people who actually knew her, for the rest of the male population, this was just the type of story they needed to hear about her. Naomi was one of those girls who kept to herself and because of that, there were no rumors about her. That changed during senior year and it took a toll on her. I give her back her camera and smile.

"Thank you!" She says, "I need to go. My mother and brother are sitting in section 116." Naomi takes her place in line and I slowly move out of the way as the ceremony begins and the line moves.

Sometimes we are blessed with some of the best friends in our lives. I find myself feeling very fortunate that I have such good friends at such a young age. They say college is where you find the best friends of your life and that they will stay with you until the end.

I thank the Lord that I have four such great friends, Naomi, Frank, Dopeness, and my cousin Ruben. I'm with them until the end.

Memorial Sloan Kettering
December 19, 2015
1:56 p.m.

There is nothing like a New York City hot dog. I'm sure there's some dietician or vegetarian somewhere writing a blog or taking a survey about how people shouldn't be eating processed meat, especially from a street vendor. I couldn't care less about that right now. The truth of the matter is that I'm hungry and I'm depressed.

The doctor's decided to run some more tests on Nayo and I took that as my opportunity to get some lunch. I find that a hot dog stand on the street is much more cost effective than eating at the hospital food court or walking to any of the places on First Avenue. Besides, I needed to get some fresh air and some time to think. I couldn't do too much of my overthinking in the sterilized atmosphere of Naomi's room.

I'm upset because I feel like a complete failure. I didn't want to tell her this because it seems ridiculous at this point. I've set some pretty high standards for myself when it comes to writing and there are times I even wonder if any of this is worth it. There is no guarantee that anyone is going to buy this stupid novel. Not all hard work equals success, which means that I have to prepare myself to be disappointed.

Self-publishing seems to be every bit as isolating as it sounds. It sounds great at first. The freedom of writing a book the way I want and creating the vision of how I want it to look. Then there are the royalty payments that are supposed to be higher because the overhead costs are so low. Sure, it sounds wonderful. But then it really gets all kinds of frightening when I start thinking about the fact that this entire process rests on my shoulders. The editing, the proofing, the cover layout, and the dreaded biography that I cannot stand.

Publishers do all of this for their clients. The big authors like Stephen King or Toni Morrison never have to worry about margins. All of this is scary because I feel like I have one shot at this and if I'm not successful do I really want to try this again? Sometimes all I can think about is how I will deal with that first negative review. I honestly don't know how any author or artist can deal with negative reviews of their work, especially now with Twitter. People will tell you directly that you suck accompanied by the appropriate hashtag and GIFs.

All of this just gets to me because I think about missed opportunities like that NYU writer's workshop. It was my goal to get accepted so that I can learn from proven writers and hone my craft to the level of my own expectations. But instead, I feel like a failure and I know that sounds crazy considering that I'm about to do the one thing I've always want to do. I'm this close to putting out my first novel and all I really want to do is delete the whole thing. How am I ever going to be taken seriously in this field if I can't get into a simple workshop?

I shake my head shuffling through the the music on my iPhone. With all the songs in my library and I cannot find a song that I really want to listen to. This is a classic symptom of me overanalyzing this workshop rejection.

I remember being notified over email:

Dear Louis,

Thank you so much for your application to the New York University Diverse Writing Community Workshops. This year we received an extremely large amount of applications from across the country and unfortunately, we are unable to offer you a seat in our workshops. Please do not view this as a criticism on the quality of your writing. We can only accommodate a specific number of applicants with the space that is available.

Keep writing and always stay positive.

From…whomever the fuck.

I just remember being hurt and angry. I was angry because it seemed like a scripted answer that was copied and pasted to all those who didn't get in. I'm sure that everything that was said was true. Maybe it had nothing to do with my writing and it really was a space issue. I just didn't buy it. I guess it was the competitive person in me that strives to always be first in things like Mario Kart. It could also be that I don't like my shit sugar-coated. Was my work good or not? More importantly, what are the criteria that allowed them to waitlist some people and not others? Was that a space issue as well?

So many questions and too little answers from such a short email. I thought about responding to this email and asking all my questions but how would that have made me look? No matter how petty and childish I feel about this, it is more important to maintain composure in the face of rejection. In the end, I just expected more of myself because no matter what anyone tells me, it will always be about the quality of my work. If I were them, and had a chance to choose between gold and dog shit, I would choose gold every time.

This happened several months ago and the workshop

occurred last week so I'm still bitter. It took a special kind of patience to observe all the pictures and videos on social media. I wanted to know what I was missing. I wanted to see what kind of community is being built while I go to work. It took a lot of swallowed pride to admit that the experience these writers were having seemed unique and life-changing. Perhaps I just never belonged.

I will admit, that sounds crazy because Zenia had to set me straight. The letter did say to stay positive and I was allowing something that I had no control over to dictate my attitude. In actuality what this rejection has done, much like the ones before it, is given me the drive to keep going. What my visit with Naomi continues to do is prove to me that giving up is not an option because as bad I think I have it, someone may have it worse.

I finish two hot dogs thinking about how much of a fool I must be to hold this inside. But I do have a burning desire to be better than what I am now and to definitely be better than the person I was. This is why I wrote this novel because I need to remind myself of what I used to be. The mistakes that I've made.

It's starting to rain again. I should get back inside. Thankfully the hot dog stand was about a half a block from the entrance to the hospital. I check the time on my phone and it's about 12:30 p.m.. I have a Facebook message from Zenia telling me that she misses her cuddle buddy. I smile because there are very few things she loves more than sleep. I text her as I begin my walk back to the hospital.

Me: Hi honey, I'm miss you too. Are you finally awake?

Zenia: Yep, I am. Been up for 2 hours now actually, had breakfast too. lol

Me: I see. I just finished having lunch.

Zenia: Anything good?

Me: Two Hotdogs! You?

Zenia: I went to Starbucks for some café and a croissant, smh. We need to take advantage of this warm weather. We should start running again and eating better.

She's right, we spent a great deal of time this past summer running and getting our lives together. But, of course, when the holidays come around we always seem to go back to bad eating habits. I can almost smell the large amounts of pernil and chicken that will be served with a healthy serving of coquito. As I stand out here texting her with the touchscreen gloves she got me last year, I still can't believe that Christmas is next week.

Me: Yeah, I suppose we should go to the gym...

Zenia: Are you ok?

Me: Is it that obvious over text?

Zenia: Yes. Is Naomi ok?

Me: She's as good as can be expected.

Zenia: How is she liking the book?

Me: I think she's really digging it. Seems like she likes it better than I do. lol

Zenia: Hun, are you beating yourself up again? The book is fine. I've read it and I like it...even though you pretty much wrote a book about one of your skank ex-girlfriends. ☺

I start laughing because this is something she says to lighten my moods. I know that all of this stems from fear, but I'm not sure if I'm afraid of failure or afraid of success. I spend so much time wondering about what to do if people hate what I write, that I never bother to think about what I would do if people actually love it. That possibility is just as scary.

Me: You know how I am. I'm always seeing flaws in my writing. It makes me angry and sad all at the same time. lol

Zenia: That's the reason why you are becoming so good at it. You never give up and it's one of the things that I admire about you.

Every time I think about overcoming my failures, I think about her. The woman in my life that I changed me and made me see things for what they were. I'm lucky to be able to face all these challenges with her by my side. I just need one of my oldest friends to make it through the next few days.

Me: Thank you sweetheart. I'm not sure I could've done any of this without you.

Zenia: I love you. I will be here when you get home.

I do have to leave soon. Naomi is not going to finish this book today. I will wait for mom to show up before I head home.

PICTURES SAY THOUSANDS

Today was the first day that I could really relax. I finally had time to reflect and put some of these issues that I had with Isabel behind me. It's ok to miss her with the understanding that we were never meant for each other. While I still may be a little somber, I've come to not regret being with her.

Something tells me that this is an experience I may come to rely on. Although the thought of something like this defining me absolutely sucks, I'm not sure I have any choice in the matter. I'm just grateful to be where I am…sitting here kicking some serious ass in Mario Kart. This has been our thing, our nerd tradition of doing nothing all afternoon playing one of the greatest games of all time.

See, Brian thinks he's slick. He has been practicing way too much by finding all these little short cuts though the game to piss me off. His explanation is simple, "if the game let's you do it then it can't be cheating." Fuck that, I got something for his ass this time.

The four of us have been playing all afternoon. After graduation, there isn't much event work to do for about a week. We thought Frank would have some free, non-weeded out time but Madison, who usually works during the day, took today off. Luckily, to make the rest of us happy in our blissful, nerdy state she just agreed to be our fourth player. As for Brian, he's always down for a few rounds of Kart no matter when or where. He's the type of person to set-up the Nintendo 64 in the auditorium so we can play on the huge wall across from the balcony.

We're in the living room, sitting on the couch with our specialized Nintendo 64 controllers. I say special because Brian has a clear one, Frank has a Buffalo Bills sticker on his, and Madison bought a GoldenEye 007 controller because she loved the movie. As for me, well, mine is a conglomeration of all the controllers I've broken and put back together. No judgments, they still work.

The way we play is real simple. We race all the courses in all the cups and in the end, the game keeps tally of all the results. Right now, I just crossed the finished line of Sherbet Land virtually leaving these three in my dust. Not that it matters because Brian is still winning in overall points. In the center of the coffee table is a big bag of potato chip crumbs and the remnants of the subs we got from Sabatino's.

"I own this shit right here." I say as stand up with my arms spread. I walk away as they battle it out for second place. I already know Frank is going to lose. I walk into the kitchen to grab another can of Pepsi when there's a knock at the door.

"You expecting company?" Frank asks.

"No. Maybe it's our favorite neighbor from upstairs," I reply. We seem to have this effect on the guy who lives above us. If I didn't any know better I guess he's from Yemen or somewhere in that region. But in either case, I call him Thunderfoot. Sure, he hates when we play Mario Kart at night and he certainly complains about it, but when he walks around his apartment, it sounds like God is bowling.

"Why would it be, it's like 2:30 in the afternoon?" Frank says as he puts his controller down. He lost. Madison rubs his knee to console him.

"Well, I suppose we disturbed his nap." I walk to the door and I open it. On the other side is a person I didn't think I would see. Ruben is standing in the doorway with Ingrid standing behind him. I'm happy to see him and yet, somewhat stunned. The last time we talked was a few days ago. He made no mention of coming by.

"Hey, mind if we come in?" Ruben asks.

"Of course," I move out the way and hold the door open as they both enter. I can tell there's something wrong. He's not his jovial self. Ingrid looks like she's seen better days. It's always weird to see them together. While it's true I only dated her for a little while in high school, she's still my first girlfriend. There's no love lost since, but we can only manage a nod of acknowledgement between us.

"What's up everyone?" Ruben nods over to Frank, Madison, and Brian. They both nod back.

"So what's going on? I didn't expect to see you." I ask.

"I need the pictures," Ruben says directly.

"Pictures? What are you talking about?"

"The pictures I gave you three years ago," Ingrid interjects.

Oh, *those* pictures. I almost forgot that years before Ingrid got together with Ruben, she had shared some pictures that someone took of her completely naked. That was such a long time ago. Why would any of this matter right now? "Did you really just drive all the way up from NYC?" I ask.

"Yes. Because I want the pictures," Ruben says dryly.

"Ok…what's going on?"

"You really have no clue do you?"

"That is why I asked…"

"Your fucking friend Ellis is what's going on," Ruben says accusingly. His sudden raised tone startles me.

I turn my head to look at Frank who is now very interested in what's being said. "Wait, what did Ellis do?" I ask.

"He called me and told me that you showed him the pictures you have and he also told me that you gave him my phone number." Ingrid says accusingly.

"What? That's bullshit. I never did that."

"You sure? Because you showing off her pictures sounds like something you would do." Ruben says very angrily. I have to try not to be defensive because Ruben is absolutely correct. Showing Ingrid's pictures is something that I would do and he would know because at one time, I showed them to him before the whole idea of dating my ex-girlfriend popped into his head. But, the idea that I would have given Ellis her phone number is something that I would never do because he's insane. Right now I'm having a little trouble trying to figure out how all this happened.

"I don't understand. You really think I would give him Ingrid's phone number?"

"Anything is possible. Can we just get the pictures please so we can get out of here?" Ruben's posture and stance is very cold and closed off. I can immediately tell that anything I say will not matter.

This is so disturbing. Ruben is family. Him and I go way back to the days when G.I. Joe action figures didn't have swivel arms. He and I used to go to Preston High School dances together where we learned first hand that girls had no time for us. Ruben was the first person I called when Biggie died. How did it come to this?

"Fine. I will get them." I head back to my room and I hear Ruben say "Thank you." I remember where I put them, in a shoebox behind my binders of basketball cards in my walk-in closet. I pull out the shoebox that is filled with junk like UNO cards, role-playing dice, pens, and some of the old Ninja Turtle toys that I've been saving for God knows what reason.

I pull out the envelope with the pictures and put the box back. I walk out into the living room and I hand them to Ruben. He takes them and hands them to her. He looks at me and says to her, "Count them." I roll my eyes. I don't even know how many pictures were in there. I suppose common sense would say that it could be 12 or 24 pictures in a roll. There was no way there are 36 pictures in that envelope.

"Some pictures are definitely missing." Ingrid says.

"How many?" Ruben responds with his icy glare still fixed on me.

"I dunno, two or three I guess," she says as she looks even

more disappointed than she did before. It's almost as if those missing pictures provided some sort of evidence that I was guilty. The room goes completely silent. You could hear a pin drop.

Ruben just stares at me and then breaks the silence, "Really Lou? So what am I suppose to think of this?"

"Dude, you really can't be serious. Obviously, Ellis stole those pictures. You cannot really think that I would give those to him. They were taken three years ago. Why would I show them to him now after all this time. I barely remember having them!"

He looks back at her and she just shrugs and says, "I just want to go back home. This is all too much for me. He keeps calling me and harassing me. I've had to change my number and to think he has my address too, where else do you think he would have gotten that from?"

"Look I understand how this looks and I understand he may have told you whatever, but why would you believe him over me? He is fucking nuts. Ask any one of these guys, they can tell you how crazy he is." I point to Frank and Brian.

"That dude is nucking futs," Brian says. I slump over in place. I want to slap him right now for being so damn silly at the wrong moment.

"Frank please help me out here," I plead.

"Louis is right. You cannot believe anything that comes out of the mouth of Ellis. At this point he's not trustworthy at all."

"See?" I look at Ruben and Ingrid.

"So then how is it possible that he got his hands on these pictures. Let's just say that I buy the idea you didn't show him these pictures, then how did he get them? Did he break in? When was the last time Ellis was here?"

Shit. I haven't seen Ellis in a few weeks. It seems no one really has an answer for this. Then Madison says, "I let him in." We all look at her.

Frank says, "What are you talking about?"

Madison gets all red. She can feel all the eyes on her. "Well, he came by a few weeks ago, when you'll were on spring break," she says nervously.

"What?" I say. I look at Frank, "Did you know this?"

"Yeah, actually I forgot," he responds.

Of course he forgot, all he does is work and fucking smoke! This is insane. I can feel my pulse race. "Well, what the hell did he want?" I ask.

"He said he was friend of yours and he needed a place to stay," Madison answers.

"...and you believed that?"

"Not at first, but then I called Frank and he said he knew him and if I felt safe then it should be ok."

"Should be OK? What the holy fuck is wrong with you people?" I then look at Frank, "A few weeks ago, you are all upset about me not beating his ass and you let him stay here?"

"I mean I wasn't with it at first but I guess Madison

convinced me that he seemed to be in need of a place," Frank says. I can't believe I'm hearing this. I live with a bunch of idiots.

Ruben abruptly interrupts, "Look, It doesn't matter. The point is whether you gave it to him or whether he stole it, Ellis still has the pictures of Ingrid. I mean don't understand why the fuck you would still have them anyway?"

I'm truly at a loss for words. There's a moment where he gives me a look to let me know that he's waiting for an answer. Truth be told, I forgot I even had them until recently. Ingrid's not really a thought in my life. "I just had them for safekeeping. It's not like I ever look at them."

Ruben looks at me. This man knows me better than I know myself. There is no way in the world that I could ever bullshit him. I can tell from the way he's looking at me right now that he is analyzing my answer and trying to figure out if what I'm saying is the truth. We've been through a lot together. We've seen our parent's split and we've seen our families suffer because of lies and deceit. He's going to have to make a decision right now if he believes me or not.

"Fine. Maybe you didn't show him these pictures and maybe he did go through your shit and miraculously find them. I just can't be here right now thinking about all of this. We need to go." Ruben turns to Ingrid and she opens the door so they can both walk out.

"Wait! You're driving back? You just got there," I say as I follow them outside.

"Yeah, we're driving back. We got what we came for. No reason to sit here with you douchebags."

I watch them get into her car. Ruben gets into the driver's seat. Ingrid looks very distant and defeated. I guess I'm in a bit of shock that they would make that drive all the way here only to go back so soon. There must be a level of anger that I'm not understanding. After he puts his seatbelt on, Ruben rolls down the window and then puts the car into reverse.

"You can't seriously blame me for this." I say as they begin to back away.

"Yes I can actually. I don't think you really understand the gravity of the situation. Ingrid is my girlfriend and when something like this happens, it makes me very angry," Ruben says with contempt through his gritted teeth.

"...and irrational," I finish his sentence softly but loud enough for him to hear me and hopefully get the point.

Ruben pauses for a bit before he backs out to think about what I just said. He frowns and nods his head. "Maybe, but I'm okay with that." He continues to back out and then drives away as Ingrid looks at me.

I put my hands on my waist wondering what the hell just happened.

BLAME IT ON THE GOOD TIMES

All I can say is that this is not what I wanted. The last thing in this world that I want is for my relationship with Ruben to be damaged. We've been through the wars together, the family crises, the funerals, and the breakups. Now, I feel that our "brotherhood" of sorts is in danger. This is not about losing a friend, this is about losing a family member.

I decided to take a walk today to clear my head. I just couldn't make sense of everything that happened yesterday. Things fell apart so quickly and everything came crashing down. I just wandered in circles for what seemed like forever and finally gave up trying to untangle this holy mess I was entangled in.

I walked into the apartment and had a serious discussion with the Ganja Twins. Ultimately they both apologized, but we really had to figure out some way to contain the damage. I called Ellis in Queens several times but he was never home. His mother, of course he lives with her, informed me that she wasn't sure where he was but will make sure to give him the urgent message to call me back. I have to get to the bottom of this. I need to find his ass and make sure he gives me back those pictures. The problem is that I know he will not give them back easily. Nothing is ever easy when it comes to him.

To make matters worse, it turns out that Ingrid wasn't the only person he called. Ellis went through my address book and took Naomi's number. He also called her a few times as well. When she called and shared this information, I was stunned. However she was nowhere near as upset with me as Ruben was. Clearly she knows what he's capable of and dealt with him accordingly.

When I asked her what Ellis wanted she responded by saying that he really needed to express his love to her.

"What?" I said so surprisingly. I almost had the urge to stare at my phone.

"Yup, he's still in love with me apparently." I could hear her complete disgust over this idea through the phone.

"That's all he wanted? He didn't say anything else?"

"He was yammering about all he wanted to do was anoint me with some African oils because I was his queen and I needed to be worshipped accordingly." I started howling in laughter on the phone. I couldn't help myself because I've never heard such nonsense.

Naomi was not amused by my response. "Let me know when you're finished."

I calmed down and apologized. "I wasn't expecting this. How do you feel about all this?"

"There's nothing to feel. He's an asshole, a liar, and a full-blown stalker now. I don't believe this little bullshit story of him being in love with me when it was him that started a smear campaign against me. All those fucked up rumors about how was I a dick tease and how I asked him to come over. Fuck him. There's no way, at all, that I would ever take anything he says seriously. I also warned him that if he called me again. I would file for a restraining order."

"Wow, do you think he will call again?

"Doesn't matter. I've already changed my house number." That was pretty much the end of the conversation. She wasn't going to deal with the foolishness and for his sake I hope he doesn't show up near her side of Brooklyn. We had to keep the conversation short anyway because MCI will charge an arm and a leg for long distance rates.

After my failed attempts to reach Ellis by phone, I decided to check my room to see if there was anything else he might have taken. I began to realize fairly quickly that perhaps I may not have many things that he would consider valuable. At the same time, it may be possible that there were a few things missing from my room that he could've taken or that I simply lost or left back home in the Bronx. It's hard to tell at this point.

But now I have to really think about what I want to do. I'm already spending this summer in New York City doing this practicum so I will be in close proximity to Ruben. Perhaps I will have a chance to fix all of this. That will also require me finding out Ellis' whereabouts and to be quite honest, he can be anywhere.

I'm just so tired of all this. I had hoped that when I put him on a bus out of Syracuse a few months ago that I would be rid of him. Now, it seems like he has embedded himself within the fabric of my family life. He is the main culprit for the strain between Ruben and me. I know I'm going to have to fight hard to keep a fraction of the relationship we had as kids.

There was a point in time where Ruben and I did everything together. Especially when we were in high school. Sure, I had my Dungeons & Dragons friends, but hanging out with Ruben meant a greater chance of meeting girls. I always viewed him to be so confident in himself and I wanted so bad to be that way. We went to every Preston High School dance together and he never ceased to impress me with the amount of girls he knew.

On weekends we would spend time in my house playing Contra for hours with our ham & cheese heroes and grape juice. Playing Contra was probably the single most important thing we did back then because it was our time together. It was a two-player game on the Nintendo Entertainment System. We would put in the code to get 30 men (up, up, down, down, left, right, left, right, A, B, A, B, then press start) and kept beating the game over and over again. The levels did get harder but we were a great team. This was when we would talk about everything from his limited sexual encounters to my dream girlfriend.

Every so often we would get the chance to really hangout outside of my neighborhood. Those were the times when Desi was around. Since Desi was older, we could do things we couldn't usually do like buy alcohol. As long as we were near him, we could just drink until we passed out. He was the responsible one and made sure we always got home unscathed.

I remember making the mistake of revealing at one of these parties that Desi let us come to that I was a virgin. I quickly learned that this was taboo. You never tell another man that you're a virgin unless you are asking for help. See, that is the thing, I wasn't asking for help. I was scared shitless by women with their curvy bodies and multiple orgasms. I never mentioned anything about actually being scared, so when Desi comes by randomly one night with a friend to take us out, I didn't protest.

My dad frequently worked weekend nights so I felt that as long as I was home when he checked in on me, I should be good. Desi showed up at about 1 a.m. to take us "bitches" out for a night on the town. That was code word for them going to a high-end strip club in Queens while the two of us wait in the car. At the time I never understood why we just never went to the strip clubs in the Bronx. But after going to some a few years ago, I understood.

After Desi and his friend returned to the car from watching nude women, a question was asked, "Who wants to get their dick sucked tonight?" I felt all the blood from my face drain. They can't be serious can they? I was afraid to ask what that meant, but before I could say a word Desi's friend continued, "Boys, we are about to find us some hookers to top off our evening."

Scared. Shitless.

Ruben seems to be down with this idea and for the most part I had to play this role as well. I had to play it cool because that is what men do right? We go out and search for prostitutes. Whatever the proper procedure is, I'd better learn it fast.

At some point we end up on the West Side of Manhattan near the Javits Center. It was late and the streets were dirty with litter and we were in the middle of a block with warehouses. But these streets were not empty. I saw a few cars and a plethora of women in tight short skirts. These women came in all different shapes and sizes. I felt a twinge of disappointment because I always had this vision that all hookers looked like Jaime Lee Curtis in *Trading Places*.

A couple of women come up to the car and look inside. Desi's friend is in the driver's seat. Desi, in the passenger seat, rolls down his window and a discussion begins. It felt more like negotiations that both guys were having and it went very similar to this:

"Hey handsome, what you got for us?"

"How much you charging?"

"It's $20 for a blow and $40 for a fuck and don't ask me if I blow without a bag because I don't." Since I sat behind the driver I heard this conversation and I can only assume that Desi was having a similar conversation. The only thing I remember thinking was, what is a bag?

Before I can try to figure out the answer to this question, I hear Desi saying, "Well, there are four of us. So get two to blow in the car and me and my buddy just need one."

I just started think about what's going to really happen. I never even had a girl touch my dick before. This is not how I thought this would happen. That is when I saw Ruben look over to me and say, "Dude, just relax. It's not that big of a deal. All you have to do is just let her do the work."

Strangely enough, his words were a little comforting. After pulling over to the sidewalk, I was told by Desi to get in the front-seat and Ruben will stay in the back. He gives me twenty bucks and a smile before walking away. "Where are you going?" I ask.

He turns around, "Don't worry yourself about that. I'm sure you'll be done before me. Have fun." He laughs as he walks toward the sidewalk. I get into the driver's seat.

Two prostitutes approach the car. The light-skinned girl goes to the back seat with Ruben and they start talking. The black girl opens the passenger seat door and sits down. I can already tell that she has on too much make up. She smiles at me, "Hey baby. You look pretty young, is this your first time?"

I struggle to get the words out, so I just nod. I hear Ruben's zipper go down. "Aww, don't even worry about it. Just take it out and I will do the rest," she says very sweetly. I can feel my heart racing. A part of me wants this and part of me does not. The reason why I'm so hesitant is because I'm not ready!

I unzip my pants and pull it out. I'm so embarrassed by how limp it is. All I'm thinking is how this wouldn't be an issue for a real man. All those damn magazines and porn tapes I watched should have prepared me for this. I was always up and ready for those, but now that I have an actual woman willing to do the one thing I've been wanting to do, my penis gets stage fright. To add to my sheer horror is her reaction. "Are you nervous? It's okay baby. Just try to calm down." I close my eyes and I try breathing deeply. I can feel her put a condom on me and then that's when it hit me. Bag must be a condom, duh. I watch her go down on me.

Very few things can really describe this moment. I learned that as much as I tried to will my penis to be erect, it just will not happen. I think there were overwhelming factors that stopped me from this. Clearly there was my fear of anything with a vagina. I was also trying to block out the moans coming from the backseat. Every so often Ruben would say something like, "a little to the left," or "Yeah girl, jerk it a little. Just like that." There was no way I was going to be able to focus.

I looked down and I just don't know what's going on down there. There is tugging and I feel teeth. I think I want this to be over. She eventually looks up a me and she says, "Well, there is nothing I can do for you, but just know I still get my $20 whether you finish or not."

Her words were very blunt and real and at this point it would not have mattered if Sharon Stone from *Basic Instinct* showed up. This was totally not how I pictured my first blowjob happening. Before I know it, she stops and pulls off the condom. "I'm sorry but I don't have time for this," she says as she holds out her hand.

I put myself back in my pants and zip up then reach into my back pocket to give her the $20. I handed it to her as she smiles, "Come back when you have some life experience, kid." She gets out of the car and I sit there wondering where I went wrong in life. It was at the moment Ruben finished. I heard him and I just put my head in my hands and just start laughing.

I find myself smiling about it now as I think about how horrible and hysterical that entire night was. I was sure that Ruben was going to tell this story to his brother and then I would never live it down. It turned out that Desi purposely did this to make men out of us. All they did was walk around the block. So I anticipated Ruben telling his brother that I owe him $20 for the worst blowjob every purchased, but, Ruben kept my secret and we never really talked about it.

I've been walking along Comstock Avenue, which is this long road that connects Main Campus with South Campus. It's a pretty long walk, but it's something I do to clear my head. I have been making this walk for the last few weeks since finals ended. I turn left onto Stratford Street. My destination is close.

I shake my head because the only question that I have for

253

myself is, what happened to the good times? It wasn't always about video games and hookers. Ruben was the reason I went to Syracuse in the first place. He's a year older than me, so naturally he did the college thing first. When he left I remembered feeling a small sense of emptiness in my life. I had to find other people to hang out with or simply deal with my Dungeons and Dragons friends. Ultimately I didn't have an issue with this by having an after school job, but there was still a void.

I wasn't sold on the idea of going to Syracuse at first. It seemed so far away from home, but there was this nagging feeling that I needed to get out of the Bronx and away from family. The divorce was still lingering in the air. I took some time to visit him on campus during the fall of 1993 and I absolutely loved it. When Ruben invited me up to see him, he didn't tell me that he had gotten tickets to see Black Moon in concert. Everything was so live and the parties were dope. I had so much fun that I knew I had to apply.

I arrive at a two-family house on Sumner Street and I ring the number two bell. I look around. This street is pretty much empty. This is a typical Wednesday afternoon in May. With classes being over at the university, things have died down pretty drastically. The door opens and Carolina's in the doorway wearing a black ribbed tank top and tan shorts. We've been seeing each other for a little bit after our crazy tire slashing adventure.

The truth is that Carolina has been everything I needed. I've come over to her apartment several times over the last several weeks and all we have done is talk, watch movies, and make out. What I'm really enjoying is the fact that there are no expectations for anything. I'm not even sure what to call what is happening right now, but one thing is for sure, it doesn't matter.

After a quick kiss we head up the stairs. She lives on the top floor of this duplex. She lives in a three-bedroom apartment with a huge living room overlooking a balcony. Carolina does have two other roommates for the summer that have not moved in yet. Summer Session one starts in a few days so we have the apartment to ourselves. The ceiling fan is spinning in the living room and the television is on. I sit on the couch that is placed in front of the window so that it's perfectly angled to receive a cross breeze from the balcony and the fan. She grabs the remote and cuddles up next to me.

This perfectly represents what we have. I think that we are using each other for fun and company. It almost reminds me of Serene and what we should have had if we dated at another time. Carolina turned out to be a lot sweeter than I thought. While we jointly did something crazy together, we kept it to ourselves. Felipe did confront her on what happened to his car but she denied it. Although I have no proof, I think she could be too good of a liar, but even that doesn't matter. We are not looking for anything more. This is something that I would have loved to have during the past semester.

Carolina flips a few channels before stopping at MTV. *The Real World* is on. This has become routine for us because it really does not matter what is on television, in a few minutes we are going to be making out and enjoying each other's company. She shifts her weight, then gets up and asks, "¿Tú quieres agua?"

I love when she speaks Spanish even if she's just asking if I want some water. It sounds so proper coming from her. I nod my head and watch her walk into the kitchen. I'm going to miss this. I know that going to New York in a week is going to be a good thing for me, but I highly doubt that I will be having as much fun as I'm having right now.

I just need to make sure that I take care of a few things this summer. Saving my relationship with Ruben is my utmost priority. I also need to put whatever issues I may have with Ingrid behind me and just be there for him. Doing well in my practicum is obviously a no-brainer. I can't wait to apply my classroom education to an actual job.

Carolina comes back with a carrying tray that has two glasses of water and a bowl of grapes. She has such a great smile. "I figured we should also have a snack." She puts the tray down on the coffee table and resumes her snuggle position next to me.

I lean over and take a quick sip of water. When I lay back we look at each other. "What's on your mind?" I ask her.

"Nothing really, just relaxing. It's too bad you won't be here for the summer."

"I know. I wonder if this is something we can continue to do when I get back."

She smiles, "It almost sounds like a relationship…almost."

"It does almost sound like that, right? Good thing we don't do such things," I chuckle.

"It is a good thing. When do you come back again?"

"Two weeks before class begins."

"I guess we will have to see what the future brings."

We both lean in and kiss and enjoy the right now.

EPISODE ONE

Today is that day. It's no secret that I've been waiting for *Star Wars Episode One: The Phantom Menace* to come out for quite some time now. I've treated this like a once in a lifetime event. I was barely old enough to remember seeing *Return of the Jedi* in the theater and thanks to the creation of the VCR, I will always be able watch the trilogy. This new sequel and its thrillingly beautiful trailers have teased my imagination. It makes me want to forget all my issues, even if it's only for two hours.

Unfortunately, just like anything else in my life, this night is going to be a bit awkward. Despite our issues, Ruben did manage to get three tickets to this movie at Ziegfeld Theatre on West 54th Street. This is one of those classic old theaters that has a single screen and has maintained its popularity due to nostalgia. The last time I remember going there was when they had a movie marathon of all three parts of *Back to the Future* series. That was a fun day. A bunch of my cousins and I decided to get together for an entire day and revisit these films.

Today, it will be the three of us, including Ingrid because she wants to see this latest installment as well. I want to rebuff the idea of Ruben bringing her because let's be real, this is "Christmas in May" for all nerds. I envisioned this screening as a time for just the two of us so we can talk about the movie and analyze it freely. We need to be the nerds we were always meant to be. I'm not even sure Ingrid has even seen the original *Star Wars*.

Ruben got tickets for the 7 p.m. showing so we knew we had to be at the theater at by at least 5 p.m. The lines are expected to be outrageous with overzealous fans dressed up in all types of *Star Wars* outfits. I asked Brian if he was going to go dressed as Boba Fett when he sees the movie in Syracuse, but he said no. He's the geekiest nerd I know when it come to *Star Wars*. If he's not the type to dress up at these events, then I know those who do are out of their minds. Anyway, the plan was to meet in Parkchester at about 3 p.m. This would give us enough of a cushion to actually get into Manhattan on time.

During this time of day, the 6 train rarely goes express heading downtown. Since we're getting closer to rush hour, we would have to catch the express 4 or 5 train at 125th Street. From there, we'd continue our journey to Grand Central Station and transfer to the 7 train that gets us to West 53st. Just another day for average New Yorkers navigating the vast transit system.

I did my part and got to Parkchester by 2 p.m. I was hungry, so I ate lunch at The Step In Restaurant next to Zaro's. Once I was done I went Ruben's apartment on the fourth floor. I rang the doorbell and waited. I can hear "Believe" by Cher blasting from the stereo. The door opens and it's Ingrid who answers. We share pleasantries and kiss each on the cheek as I walk in to the small, yet well-appointed apartment. She seems ready to go dressed in her black Nine Inch Nails t-shirt, baggy jeans, a pair of Doc Martens and a sweater wrapped around her waist.

Her Nine Inch Nails t-shirt automatically reminds me of

Vivienne. I did manage to get in a couple of lap dances a few weeks ago. I wasn't sure of the next time I was going to be in a strip club, much less in Syracuse. I will have to make time to go back there when the school year starts. If I'm lucky, Carolina's crazy ass might come with me. "Isn't it May?" I ask her.

Ingrid looks down at her sweater and replies, "You know it's going to be cold in that theater. I just want to make sure I'm prepared."

I nod my head in agreement. "Is he ready yet?" I ask this question because despite his tough exterior of wittiness and sarcasm, Ruben is a total diva. I know how long it takes for him to get ready because I've had to sit and wait for him on numerous occasions.

"No, actually, he's not. He's still in the shower."

"Are you serious?" I look at my watch and its 10 minutes to three. So much for being on time. A part of me wants to just walk in the bathroom and say something, but that will do no good. I've been through this routine before.

"He's worse now since he's been getting these modeling gigs," she chuckles a bit. I can tell she's still a little bit uncomfortable around me. I wish I could convince her that I had nothing to do with Ellis or his whacked out behavior.

"Really? But is he ever late to any of those auditions or photo shoots?"

"Not really."

"Yeah, that' s what I thought," I say as I shake my head. I look around. I can still see Ana's influence in this apartment. Everything is nice and neat. The couch sits nicely in front of the entertainment center that houses the television and the stereo. There are a lot of pictures on the shelves as well. Some of Ruben, Desi, me, and my dad.

The song changes to "Livin' la Vida Loca" by Ricky Martin. I'm beginning to feel awkward since we're not talking much so I ask, "How are things going?" I turn around and she's sitting on the couch filing her nails.

"I'm doing well, I guess. I had to change my phone number the other day since I now have a stalker who wonders when he can cum on my face," she continues to file her nails without looking up.

That's awkward. I should've just kept my mouth shut. "I'm really sorry about all this."

"I don't blame you for this. Well, maybe I blame you for some of it, but clearly this 'friend' of yours has issues. I consider it to be one of many lessons that I've had to learn over the years." Ingrid never looks up. I would've almost mistaken her attitude for impertinence if I didn't know better. This act is her way of feigning anger, at least, that is how I interpret it.

"Wait, what part of this do you blame me for exactly?"

"The part where you would befriend someone like this to begin with."

"But not the part where I would ever date someone who is reckless?"

"Are you talking about me or the Colombian?" Now Ingrid looks at me. Her eyes suggest that my assessment of her feigning anger is wrong.

I hear the bathroom door open. I peek down the hallway and I see Ruben emerge with a towel wrapped about his waist. All I want to know is when does this man have the time to work out? I've always felt he was one of those guys that never gets fat. He just remains slim without a lick of ab work.

"Hey dude, I will be ready in a few minutes," he smiles and nods.

"I thought you said three."

"Yeah, I did, but I guess we all can't get what we want." He disappears into the bedroom so he can get ready. I took it as a good sign that he asked me to see *The Phantom Menace* with him. I still think this whole thing will eventually blow over, but I can still sense some tension there.

I turn back around to Ingrid because there's no way I'm going to ignore her comment about Isabel. There's a clear difference between these two women and while things have gone quite astray with the latter, I would never consider Isabel to be reckless. "You know damn well that I'm referring to you."

Ingrid stops filing her nails and looks at me, "I'm reckless? Why? Because I gave you those pictures for safekeeping? Excuse me for thinking you could keep them in a place where no one could get to them."

A radio commercial plays and I look over to the stereo, "Do you mind if I change the station?"

"Sure, go ahead." She shrugs.

Clearly they have the radio on a pop station and right now I need something a little more urban. The problem is that I want to have this discussion without alerting Ruben. I notice that she gets up to go the kitchen as I switch stations. I don't find anything I want to hear, but not to worry. I have Nas' *I Am* in my CD Walkman and I've been rocking it since April. I pull out the device from my pocket and open it up.

I hear the water running in the kitchen as I put the CD into the stereo. It sounds like Ingrid is doing dishes. I guess Ana was right to assume that she lived here. I let the CD load before I skip the intro and press play. The smooth jazz like beat of *NY State Of Mind, Pt. II* fills the room. This album became a part of me from the moment I first heard it. I was really stressing Isabel and all my schoolwork. I had several albums in rotation but when I found out that Nas came out with another album, I dragged Nayo to Carousel Mall to get it.

There are a lot of artists that speak to me on a personal level. While my parents did a great job in making sure that I never lived that street life, I connected with people like Nas, Wu-Tang Clan, EPMD, Redman, Big Daddy Kane, Rakim, Public Enemy, and A Tribe Called Quest. I suppose it could be their overwhelming talent to rhyme words with such passion and ferocity. It could also be that there is a spirit within me that hates being told what to do and while I live this life with rules, the music I love to listen to has none.

There is also something that I fundamentally love about hip-hop. I feel like I've seen some the greatest emcees during their prime. I don't know where this music is going to go, but I do know that there will never be another year like 1993. I know there will never be another Biggie. I know there will never be another Public Enemy. I should always remember this music for what it has given me, which is the ability to step outside of myself and question everything.

I walk into the kitchen as Ingrid is drying her hands with a dishtowel. "Yes, what makes you so damn reckless was giving me those pictures in the first place."

"You weren't complaining about it when I gave them to you."

"That was years ago and therefore not the point."

"So what is the point then? That you have no fault in all this? That you are playing the innocent ex-boyfriend in all this?" Ingrid slams down the dishtowel on the counter.

"See, that's the thing, you can't say shit to me about that when your currently dating my cousin, which by the way, is another reason why you are reckless."

Ingrid gives me a sharp look. "Is this truly about, the fact that I'm dating your cousin? I had a feeling you had a problem with this."

I laugh a little bit. "Hardly. I really don't care who you date, but it becomes a problem when it effects my relationship with Ruben."

Ruben walks in the living room after about 15 minutes like he's all of a sudden in a hurry. "Y'all ready to go?"

"Uh, yeah. Waiting on you." I say as I walk in.

"Well, let's go then."

I stop the music and press the eject button for the CD. Ruben pulls out a small bottle of lotion from the entertainment center. I put the CD back into my Walkman and I watch him lotion up his hands.

"What?" Ruben asks.

"Who are you?"

"You've never moisturized your hands before?"

"Not before a *Star Wars* movie but, whatever you are into man, it's your life," I smile.

Ingrid walks into the room chiming in, "He has to take care of his skin because you never know who may want his picture now that he's model."

"..actor." He interrupts her.

"Excuuuse me," She says as she makes a face. "I have to use the bathroom before we go."

"I'm saying. There's a difference. Most of my auditions are for acting. I just got lucky with the TiVo ad."

"I don't even know what that is," I say.

"Don't worry, you will."

"I hope so because it sounds fake." I laugh because this is not what I thought I would be seeing while waiting for him to get out of the bathroom. Is it possible that Ruben is a snob now or was he always that way and I didn't notice?

I'm hoping to continue my conversation with Ingrid but I'm doubting it will be any time soon. I get why she may blame me for something that is not entirely my fault, but what she doesn't seem to understand is that dating Ruben just makes things difficult in general.

I'm also sensing some tension between the both of them as well, which I always thought should be expected. I know both of them personally and Ruben is a straight shooter who likes order in his life. Ingrid, is his polar opposite. She's not orderly and is clearly chaotic in terms of how she lives her life. Not that either of them is particularly good or bad, but put the two together and it's like mixing oil and water.

We finally leave about 40 minutes after I get there. I want to be annoyed by it but I'm just happy to finally be on our way. The excitement of seeing this movie is far more important than whatever tension is going on. The train ride is peaceful and filled with conversations about the past. The three of us have known each other for such a long time that we can actually have fun together if we wanted to.

When we get to the Ziegfeld, it is exactly what we thought it would be, a huge line of Star Wars fanatics. It would almost be laughable if it wasn't for the fact that we are now at the end of that line. I want to be upset about this because we had a plan and the actor/model in my life picked this day to flaunt his new fly lifestyle. I just shake my head to myself.

"What is it?" Ruben asks.

"Nothing man." I respond as I try my best to pretend to be really interested in some storm troopers a few feet away from us.

"Really? Cause you have a face."

"I do not have a face." In actuality, I do.

"Yes you do," Ingrid chimes in. I am beginning to have this overwhelming feeling that this is how shit is going to be from now on. Not only do I have to deal with Ruben "The

Diva", but now I have to deal with my ex-girlfriend who shouldn't even be here right now.

"You know what? Fuck this. Can I have my ticket?" I say to Ruben as I hold out my hand.

"What is your problem dude? You've been acting like you have a bug up your ass." Ruben says as he hands me the ticket.

"You're right, I do have a bug up my ass. I'm not digging being a third wheel to Tomax and Xamot. All I want to do is enjoy this fucking movie and not have to deal with this." I start to walk away.

"Where the hell are you going?" I hear Ruben ask.

All I want to do is my best rendition of John Bender from the Breakfast Club saying, *I don't think that I need to sit here with you fuckin' dildos anymore!* I turn around and give them both the finger.

I just have to walk. I'm pissed off for too many reasons. I feel like I don't have any control of the current situation, which is basically the story of my life. There is no reason for these things that keep happening to me. I must be in some way responsible for all the calamity.

Let's really think about this. I may never find out what happened with Isabel but I can take a guess that she grew tired of me and why is that? Am I this macho prick that wanted to just have sex with her? Maybe she wasn't happy because I wasn't the person she thought I was because, after all, she was saving herself for that special person. All of the stress of this semester that revolved around this breakup could've been avoided if I just took it like a man. I should have just bottled all this shit up and hit off a couple of hoes and I would've been just like every other guy, right?

I don't even want to think about how I fucked up things with Serene. She was such a sweet woman and I wrecked it because I was too emotionally unstable to get an erection. How is that even possible? Sure, we ended up having sex a few times after that but it wasn't the same after that night. Maybe she looked at me differently or maybe I just acted differently. I realize that there was little actual dating and mainly emotionless intercourse. It was bound to end, I'm just glad that it wasn't on bad terms.

I don't even want to think about Ellis. I just don't.

Then there is Frank and Madison and that whole relationship just makes me uneasy. I thought I could deal with living with those two jackrabbits, but I just find myself being bitter about not having a love life. It's a stupid thing to be bitter because had I decided to sleep with her, they wouldn't be a couple right now. There would've been a good possibility that it would have been me screwing her all this time and not Frank. This doesn't make me jealous, but it does make me feel uncomfortable. realizing how few degrees separate me, Ingrid, and Ruben. I need to re-evaluate my life and everything in it.

I get to 6th Avenue and look around. I needed to walk away from the those two just for a few minutes. This is something that I need to do more often. Learn to walk away from a situation instead of trying to fight a losing battle. I stand in a short line that has formed in front of a hot dog stand. It's better to get a hot dog here for $1 than to pay $3 in the movie theater.

I order my usual hot dog with mustard and onions and a can of soda. This will probably make me feel better which is a welcome change from a few months ago when I could barely eat. I pay the guy and take a huge bite. I look over as I'm chewing and Ruben is standing right behind me. He has the angriest scowl I've ever seen on his face. The problem is that I don't know if he is serious or "acting."

"You done?" Ruben asks as I open my can of soda. I can't answer him right away because I've scarfed down half of this hot dog in just one bite.

Once I open it, I bite down and grab the rest of the hot dog with my hand. I obnoxiously chew slowly while looking at him and then swallow. "Maybe," I say before I take another swig of my soda.

"What's your issue? Seriously, I know this cannot be about Isabel. I know this is not about Ellis. So what is it? Is there a problem with Ingrid?"

I slowly chew on the rest of the hot dog just to piss him off. This is my way of making him wait now. I swallow and say, "Why does it matter? That's your girlfriend and I'm not going to say anything that's going to deepen the rift between us."

"That's bullshit. I would expect you, of all people, to be honest with me when it comes to her."

"You mean like how honest you were with Isabel?"

"What are you talking about?"

I smile and I take another long sip from my soda. I love the way it burns as it goes down. I take a huge gulp and then burp. Another obnoxious gesture of course and then I say, "How about when you told her that she had a stick up her ass when she was bitching about our trip to Dreamgirls."

The scowl he had going slowly dissipates. He wants to smile and he fights hard not to. "That is fair. I will give you that, but are you saying that Ingrid has a stick up her ass?"

I find this conversation to be a bit amusing now. "No, but what why does there always have to be a stick involved. I never understood this."

"I guess it's less offensive than a dick in her ass."

"But is that really offensive though? I mean, some women like that sorta thing."

"Some guys too..." Ruben interjects.

"That is a good point!" I point to him then continue, "I would just assume that a stick would really hurt."

"Of course it would, that is why if you had one up your ass, you would be in a terrible mood."

"So what was the question again?" I smile as I ask him.

His scowl returns, "I thought you were done."

I sigh, "I never said I was done. Look, I don't think that Ingrid has a stick up her ass. She's nothing like Isabel. I just feel that you can do much better than her. Ruben, there are reasons that it never worked between her and I."

"You don't think I know this? The truth is that I'm probably not going to marry this girl, but you know she's good to me and I'm not going to breakup with her for no reason."

That was the answer I was afraid of. This is what happens when guys get too complacent. I'm sensing some emotional attachment here. What happened is that these two got together at a time when they were both lonely and things just clicked? What I'm afraid of is that he's going to feel obligated to stay with her when things get stale. "I understand and I'm not suggesting you breakup with her at all. I just don't want to get into a situation where I don't want to hang out with you because I don't want to be around my ex-girlfriend."

Ruben ponders my statement for a few seconds then says, "You're right. I can see how this may be a little awkward. How about we put that aside for the night and watch this movie we've been waiting our entire childhood for?"

"I think I can do that."

We continue to debate the plausibility of a stick in someone's backside as we head toward the theatre. I think I can deal with this now that I've finally gotten how I feel off my chest. I just hope that this ends well…meaning the movie.

REVELATIONS

I started my practicum about a week ago. The best part about this is having the luxury of living in the Bronx with my dad (rent free!) for the remainder of the summer until I have to go back to school in the fall. This works out well for me because I can try to make some extra money doing some camera work for Dopeness on his freelance projects. The sweetest part of the deal is that Madison is now splitting rent with Frank in the apartment in Syracuse. Things could not have worked out better for me.

I spent the first week learning the ins and outs in the Office of Student Life at City College. I found myself in awe of their Harlem campus. Maybe it's because I'm in New York City but everything seems to be brighter and look newer. I would never come to think of my alma mater as nothing less than great, but I'm starting to think that five straight years in Central New York must be getting to my head.

I report to the Assistant Director of Student Leadership. My task is to help her redesign the student leadership initiative that is the landmark program of the office. I chose to apply for this particular program because I think at some point I'm going to want to run a program similar to this. I need to know how to do it from the ground up. I also knew going into this was going to be a lot of work.

Because this is a practicum, I don't get paid at all for this. I've had to convince my dad that his is how it works and that this is very similar to an internship that some other people have. It is required in order for me to graduate. I explained all this to him because he's the type of man that expects me to be working if I'm not in school. Since this was for school, he let me slide on the "are you looking for a part-time job" banter.

My hours are pretty simple. I work a 20 hour week and I worked it out with my supervisor that I get Friday off. So every Monday through Thursday I'm there from 10 a.m. to 3 p.m. plugging away. I find it very refreshing to have a schedule like this because I'm able to avoid much of the traffic coming to and leaving from work. Also, many people start to party in bars on Thursday nights so when I do decide to go out, with whatever money I do have, I can hang out and not worry about work in the morning.

This also means that I don't have time for lunch. So if I wanted to meet someone during the day, I would have to either meet them for dinner or wait until Friday and have lunch with them then. This is what Lucy and I planned on. I hit her up last week on AIM to let her know that I'm still down to have that discussion. Of course, once I got acclimated to the computer I was using, I made sure to download AOL Instant Messenger. I don't have a computer at home so this was the only way I was going to communicate with anyone outside of using a telephone.

I waited outside of her job on 52nd Street between Fifth and Sixth Avenues. I was earlier than I thought I would be which turned out to be a good thing because I spent a good 25 minutes in the NBA store on Fifth Avenue. The Deutsche

Bank building is huge. From out here I can see parts of the lobby through the glass. The rest of the lobby is hidden behind Roman-styled pillars that jut out of the top of what I think is the second floor. It just seems like an unusual building, but what do I know about architecture? I sit on the bench that overlooks the pathway that runs into 53rd Street. In the middle of the pathway is a phallic sculpture clearly designed to attract the artsy people to the Museum of Modern Art, which is right around the corner.

I laugh to myself because it wasn't too long ago that I was in this neighborhood seeing *The Phantom Menace*. It's not difficult to reminisce about a film that I've now seen about three times. I'm so obsessed with it that I had to buy the soundtrack. However, I do realize that this movie wasn't as good as it should've been, but I don't care because Darth Maul is my new favorite character.

Lucy finally comes out looking very casual wearing a pair of jeans, flats and a lightweight summer blouse. She's one of the lucky few that benefits from these casual Fridays I hear about in corporate America. She greets me with a 'Hey there" and we hug and trade pleasantries. Lucy explains that she has a place picked out called Yips. It's a fast food Chinese restaurant where we can order whatever we want and then we'll go eat on a bench somewhere since it's such a gorgeous summer day.

Yips is packed but the line moves quickly. I have never heard of this place until today and I have a feeling that I won't be disappointed. I order the chicken and broccoli meal and she gets the lo mein. We engage in some small talk about our jobs. Lucy loves what she's doing although she figures this will be a temporary position. Assuming all goes well and this Y2K bug is fixed, there won't be much to do after that. There may be some code checking after the New Year, but there's no reason for the team to do that. Lucy is getting as much experience as possible so she can secure a tech position elsewhere.

We leave Yips and find some benches near her building. I'm anxious to hear whatever it is that she wants to tell me, but I decide to play it cool and continue with the small talk. I didn't want Lucy to think that the only reason why I met her today was to specifically talk about Isabel. I consider her a friend and it would be rude to simply ask her to spill the beans even thought I really want her to.

Once we sat down and started eating, she really didn't wait very long. "So I know that you're somewhat anxious to hear what I've got to say about your ex-girlfriend," she says as she smiles. Lucy is a very pretty girl and even if I was interested, I really can't go there. It may not be an official rule, but I would feel like I betrayed Isabel in some way.

"I figured you would get to it eventually," I say calmly.

"Well, as you know, Isabel is one of my closest friends. We agree on just about everything. The one thing that I feel she was wrong about was how she treated you. I also consider you a good friend as well so I wanted to give you some piece of mind and help you get some closure if that's possible." Lucy speaks very gently. I can feel the compassion in her words.

"I do appreciate that. It was a very difficult semester, but I got through it."

"Good. So to make this easier on the both of us, I think it would be best if you ask me the questions that you really want answers to and I will respond to the best of my ability. Keep in mind, I only have an hour for lunch." She laughs.

I don't hesitate, "Did she meet someone in Colombia?" I almost feel embarrassed as to how quickly that question came out. But there's nothing I can do about it now.

"Yes. She met this guy named Ernesto during the first week there."

"Really? Ellis told me..."

"Let me stop you right there. Isabel told me about that little spat you had in the game room and I must say that was not one of your finer moments. You know better than to believe anything that he tells you. I know he's your boy, but come on. You know better than that."

She was right. I allowed him to play with my emotions. "I know. I let my emotions ruin my better judgment. Can you at least tell me why this guy was so important to her that she decided to end our relationship?"

"Well that's a little complicated. She told me she fell in love with him and that this love made her question everything that she's ever felt for anyone."

Had I heard this information months ago, it would have been like a dagger to my psyche. It still bothers me to hear something like this because I want to internally question what was wrong with me, but I'm too focused on the very next question, "Did she sleep with him?"

There's a pause in the discussion as she eats. I think she is using this to buy time. Perhaps she's weighing her options on whether or not she should divulge that information to me. Lucy takes a deep breath and replies, "Yes, she did."

Bang

I knew it. I didn't want to admit it to myself. I didn't want to think that my father was right this entire time. I can feel the pain and the anger boiling up but I choke it down. This is not the time or place to explode over all this. "I'm sorry, you're just gonna have to give me a moment to process all this."

"I understand, Louis. I just want to be clear that Isabel is a very proud girl, you know that. She feels terrible about all this, but she also didn't want to get vilified for it. So she kept this from you. She would rather you hate her."

"But that doesn't make any sense. Why not just come clean? Admit that she was in the wrong? It would've made my life so much simpler."

"I think her reasoning was that you would try to forgive her and still try to find a way to move past this as a couple. She did tell me that she felt you were both unhappy and just going through the motions. Ernesto was just at the right place, at the right time."

The right place and the right time. How many times have I heard that? Is that what fate is all about? Was I just a placeholder so she could find her purpose? I chew on my food slowly trying to contemplate all of this. I feel a sharp, familiar pain developing in that part of my chest I can't physically touch. It's a muscle soreness within my soul. It doesn't quite hurt as much as it did before, but it feels like too much pressure will make it hurt more.

"So, that's it? She just met another dude and it all ends? No discussion, just me in search of closure and answers."

My words just hang out there in the air. She takes a minute or so to respond. "I know this is hard. But that is why I wanted to give you this opportunity to get the answers."

Lucy is being kind and yet there's a part of me that wants to be crass and sarcastic. I want to ask about how in the world can she be a friend to someone like that. Why not just tell me sooner instead of letting me go through all this. But I take some deep breaths because I already know these answers. None of this would have helped me. I would have only gotten angry and irrational like Ruben.

"So is this why she never dated Felipe? I heard how despite his protective nature, she wasn't really interested." I air quote protective because I'm trying my best to be nice.

"Felipe is a fool. She considered him a friend even though she knew he may have wanted more. I think he got carried away with some of the things he's done. She enabled him because it bothered you so much. But to answer your question, she never dated Ernesto. It turns out that he's not her type."

"What? I don't understand," I say. Is there more to this than I originally thought?

Lucy shifts in her seat. She seems a little more uncomfortable. She even laughs a little nervously as she says, "I feel like I'm your informant and this is an episode of *Law & Order*." I say nothing as she pauses for a minute. "I trust you, so please understand that everything I say has to stay between you and me. I know you're not like your friend, Ellis, but I would really hate to hear rumors about this. So you need to promise me that you will not repeat this information."

I look at her and straighten up. This may be some serious shit I'm about to hear. "I promise to not tell anyone."

Lucy finishes chewing as she puts the plastic cover over her to go plate. She places her phone down beside her and then gives me her full attention, "OK. So during spring break,

Isabel went home. Ernesto and his family had flown in from Colombia with hopes of immigrating since they have family in Kew Gardens. I'm not sure what day this happened but she came home from shopping and saw Ernesto giving Fabian head on the couch."

"What?!!?!" I almost choked. I reach for my bottle of water.

"Yup. Apparently, Ernesto came over to hang out with her but she wasn't there or maybe he really came over to see Fabian. But it turns out the he's gay or bisexual. I'm not even sure how that works."

"Holy shit. But, I don't understand. Did this guy like both of them?"

"Again, I'm not clear on specifics. She called me hysterically crying when it happened. This has put a bit of a wedge between her and her brother. From what I gathered, Ernesto wanted his family to believe that he liked girls. I guess there were always suspicions that he may be gay. It turns out that him and her brother really were into each other."

"So Fabian knew then?"

"Well, of course. I think it went so far as him being jealous of this new relationship between Ernesto and Isabel. I guess they had an argument when they were alone and then made up."

"Wow. I don't know what to say." I'm genuinely shocked by this news. I think I almost feel sorry for her.

"She was devastated. It took her the rest of semester to really get over that." There are so many feelings to sort through. A part of me wants to scream out for joy because all of this has to be karma. But then I think about the pain I've been though, coupled with all the guilt and self-loathing. Why should I really celebrate someone's pain especially when I still feel my own?

But then again, I think back and it makes me angry. "So it took her the rest of the semester to get over him? I wonder how long it took her to get over me, the length of her time in Colombia? Maybe that is why she was so cold."

"Louis, I…" Lucy tries to interrupt.

"No. It all makes sense now. She never really loved me. Don't get me wrong. She liked me, she liked the idea of having me around, but that real love that makes you miss someone when they are gone? Nah, she didn't have that." I can feel the anger burning in that part of my chest that was once sore.

"Louis, I never said any of that. That's not what I mean. I'm sure she loves you, just not the way you wanted."

I have heard that before where someone's feelings are justified to explain a gap or a lack of understanding. The problem is I have these letters from her where she goes into her deep feelings of love. Letters that I now want to burn. I laugh. Lucy is going to think I've lost my mind. "You know what? Maybe you're right, maybe she believes in some way that she loves me, but guess what? Love can be fleeting. The moment someone who embodies the kind of person she really wants shows up, it exposed the farce that our relationship was."

"Look, I'm sorry, maybe I shouldn't have told you any of this."

"No. Don't do that, Lucy. You did the right thing. You set me free from my own bullshit by making me see the truth in all this. I really think you have done more to help me get closure than any girl I see or sleep with." I close the lid to my food because I'm just not hungry any more. The food was good, but I'm done. "Let me just tell you about this dream I had with her. We're basically on a train to nowhere and she's the conductor. I need to find a seat and she was going to help me find one. I follow her from car to car until we get to the end. She directs me to a car filled with empty seats. I turn around to thank her and guess what? She pulled the pin from my car. She basically disconnects me as she speeds off into this nothingness we are headed to. Meanwhile my train car plummets into some ravine. I dreamed this when she was in Colombia."

Lucy looks at me stunned, "Are you serious?"

"Oh yes. I should've known right then and there that my subconscious was trying to tell me something. Did you know I suffer from migraines from time to time? Well our bodies are equipped to warn us when a migraine is going to occur. This allows you time to deal with it before it gets bad. I should've seen this coming."

"There's no way you could've known."

"You're right. But I will tell you right now. There is no way I will let this happen to me again…ever." I mean every word I say. If there is ever a time I'm in another relationship and I have a chance to get mine without getting caught, I am taking it.

Memorial Sloan Kettering
December 19, 2015
3:31 p.m.

I've been waiting out in the hallway for a good 20 minutes. When I came back from my lunch break outside I was told by one of the nurses to wait out here until they are done with her. I found a seat in the hallway that will allow me to continue working on the book if I chose. It was her idea for me to take my laptop with me in case I couldn't get back into the room for some reason. Clearly she's a pro at this by now.

Unfortunately, I'm not in the mood to pull out my laptop especially since I don't know how long I'm going to be out here. It could be another 10 minutes, which is not enough time. When I edit the book, I need to set aside large amounts of time to get into the story and gauge the flow of things. I could do that in Naomi's room because she was reading the book quietly as I was editing. We can both feel the rhythm of the stories without any real distractions.

At this point I just scan through my Twitter and Facebook feeds from my phone until I get bored enough to move to Instagram. I try to keep my patience in check because this is a highly rated hospital, but as with any other place, waiting is universal.

After a few minutes, the nurse walks out and gives the signal to walk back into the room. I gather my things and enter. The television is still on and Naomi is lying on her back staring at the screen with no real sign of interest.

"How you feeling, Nayo?" I ask because I'm getting the feeling that she's not doing too well at the moment.

"I hate everything about this right now." I sit down next to her and hold her hand and it feels cold. She looks at me and continues, "There are times where I just want to give up. All the blood tests and the needles take so much out of me. I can barely stand it." Tears roll down her face and I fight everything in me not to cry as well.

"Did something change when I was away?" Probably not the best question, but I really don't know what to ask her. I have trouble dealing with tears from friends, which is strange when I've seen enough tears from the women I've been involved with over the years. Nevertheless, this is different. Sometimes I have this inherent need to fix things and yet this is the one thing I cannot come close to fixing.

"Nothing has changed. I still have cancer and I still might die."

Another phrase, another slap in the face. I should really start getting used to this, but considering the number of things we've gone through together since we met freshman year, I'm not willing to give up as easily as someone else would. "Naomi…" I begin to say

"I know Louis, but I really don't want to hear your positivity about my survival. I know what my chances are and I'm dealing with it the best way I can, but I'm not going to fool myself into believing that everything will be all puppies and rainbows." I stay quiet. Maybe she's right, perhaps I need to start making my peace with the fact that I may lose one of my best friends to cancer. Then Naomi says, "I'm sorry Louis. There's no reason to snap at you, it's just that I'm so angry about all this."

"I know. I would be angry too."

"Do you remember that famous photograph of that black lady from 9/11, that was covered in ash?"

"Of course, I do."

"You know she died a few months ago from cancer."

"That's right, I do remember that."

"Well this is part of the reason why I'm so angry. A few years after all this went down, I was invited to be a part of this health survey of 9/11 survivors who were being tracked. See, I didn't think I needed be a part of this. I thought it was just another way for the government to track people. I would've never pegged myself as one of those people whose health would be at risk. I was never covered with dust." She shakes her head.

I will never forget that day. I truly believe the world ended on September 11th, 2001. Naomi worked in Two World Trade Center as a communications officer at a financial firm on the 72nd floor. When the first plane hit Tower One, she immediately headed for the exit. She always commented on the fact that she never felt comfortable that morning. Tuesdays were always a special day because that was the day Farmer's Market would set up in front of the World Trade Center. For some reason it was canceled that day and she felt uneasy about it. Once the shit hit the fan she wanted to be out.

Her job, at that moment, consisted of trying to send an emergency message to everyone about what was happening since they had offices on several floors in Tower One. Naomi's instincts got the better of her as she and her staff debated in less than five minutes on who should stay and who should go. Naomi's supervisor told everyone to go. That was the last time she saw him.

Naomi had just gotten off the elevator in the lobby when the second plane hit her building. She often described this moment as the moment when all of our lives changed forever. The paradigm shifted our lives from one reality to another. She went outside only to see the horror of both buildings in smoke and flames. She ran and never looked back until she got to Brooklyn. We both felt that God was looking out for her on that day.

"When that lady died I asked my doctor could that horrible day be the reason why I got cancer. He said to me that it could be a very good possibility. I'm angry because I really feel like I got out alive and that I was lucky not to get hit by debris or bodies when I walked out. Now look at me, about 14 years later and these bastards finally got me." Tears of anger stream down her face.

"For what it's worth, you're not making it easy."

Naomi laughs, "You're such an asshole. You do know that right?"

I smile, "So, I've been told."

Naomi reaches over the far side of the bed and picks up the book. "I hope you were not expecting me to finish this in one day. I'm sure my mother and brother are going to be here soon and once they get here, I will have no time to read."

"Of course not, I'm surprised you've gotten as far as you have."

"Well, I think I can finish this by tomorrow. I will make sure you get this back."

"There really is no rush. The book will still be here when you get out of surgery."

At that moment her mom walks in all bundled up with a big purse in one arm and a shopping bag in the other. Mrs. Brooks looks like a shorter version of Naomi. I walk over to her to help her with her stuff.

"Hi Mom," Naomi says weakly.

"Hey baby, I'm sorry I'm a little late but you know the trains don't run well on weekends." Mrs. Brooks takes off her hat.

"Hi Mrs. Brooks." I say as I give her a hug and a kiss on the cheek."

"How are ya, Louis?" She asks as she begins the process of taking off her rain coat.

"I'm doing well, you know, keeping our fighter company today."

"How's she doing?" Mrs. Brooks finally gets her coat off. She has on a festive green sweater and a pair of jeans.

"She's doing as well as she can be. She's a fighter, but she's tired." I can't imagine what Naomi's mom is going through. I remember when one of my cousins died about 15 years ago. He was at the wrong place and the wrong time. There was a robbery at a local bodega and he startled the crooks which lead to him getting blasted by a sawed off shotgun. The one thing my mother told me is the worse thing a parent can ever go through is the death of their child. I remember how devastated my aunt was. So, looking at Mrs. Brooks now, all I see is a strength that I'm not sure I have.

"I'm doing well enough to hear you. I'm not dead yet." Naomi responds with a weak laughter.

Her mom walks over, "I know you can hear us. Stop staying stuff like that." She kisses Naomi's forehead and they begin to talk. I stay in the back of the room causally packing my laptop into my bag. I don't want to make it seem like I'm in a rush so I take my time.

"Louis, is this the book you wrote?" Mrs. Brooks asks as she holds it up. I can tell that Naomi had put a paper to hold the page she's on.

"Yes, it is. That is just the proof. I'm still working on it. I just wanted Nayo to get the first read."

"This is great! I'm so proud of you."

"Thank you." I answer as I put on my coat.

"Leaving already?" Mrs. Brooks asks.

"Yeah, I have to get going. I promised the woman that we would go out to dinner tonight with her parents." I walk up to the bed and look at Naomi. "You gonna be OK without me?"

Naomi looks at me, "I think I can manage. I just need to rest a little before I finish your book."

I lean in and kiss her forehead. "It is ok Nayo, don't feel like you have to finish it. Just get some rest." When I pull up, Naomi's eyes are closed. She is sleeping. I look at her mother and she just nods her head indicating that it is ok for me to leave. She gets up and we hug again.

"Thank you so much for visiting and staying with her, Louis. You've always been such a good friend to her," she whispers.

"Keep me updated. I will be praying for her." I respond as we pull away.

She nods her head, "I will."

I grab my laptop bag and my gloves and walk out the room. I wipe my eyes because I don't want to lose a friend and today may have been the last time we ever speak.

A NIGHT TO REMEMBER

As a Syracuse alum that resides in New York, it's never hard to forget that's where you went to school. There's always something going on that revolves around alumni. There are several alumni associations that have meetings and happy hours for people to meet and mingle. I remember being told that there's nothing more powerful than the ability to network with fellow alumni because you never know what it might lead to.

Tonight was that night. There's a big party happening at the Latin Quarter for all alumni of color. Recently, there has been a push by the university to try to accommodate more Latino alumni within their programming. So announcing this happy hour at the Latin Quarter sparked a lot of excitement. I got here early because I didn't want to miss anything. While, I would love to see people I've graduated with, I'm here for a different reason.

The person who told me about this event was, of course, Lucy. I was a bit surprised that she still messaged me after my emotional display a few weeks ago. The one thing that Lucy told me was the Isabel was not planning on being there, but that's not why I anticipated going to this party. Rumor has it that Ellis may be here tonight and I've been dying to be in the same space as him. This whole thing has become about more than just him and I. About a week after I started my practicum, Frank called me to tell me that he spoke to Ellis. It turns out that I was not the only victim of Ellis' theft.

It's well known that Frank and I have a few things in common. We love video games, sports, sci-fi movies, and basketball cards. On rare occasions we would go to a toy fair or a comic book convention in Rochester to see what kind of stuff they have. I remember this one time going to a Star Trek convention and I saw Michael Dorn while Frank managed to find some rare basketball cards he was looking for. He would kill me in NBA Live playing with Charles Barkley and Danny Ainge (who never seemed to miss a shot in that game). I always found it weird that he loved the Phoenix Suns even though he was from Buffalo, but I digress.

His collection also included football cards, many of which were players from the Buffalo Bills. His two favorite players are Bruce Smith and Jim Kelly in that order. Frank comes from a long line of tortured Bills fans that have watched them lose the Super Bowl for three straight years. Despite that pain, he still rocks hard for his team and as a Mets fan I respect it. There is a deep love there that is quite understandable, especially for the players on that team.

Frank kept all of his cards in several three-ring binders just like the ones I have. The binders are filled with see-through plastic sheets that hold 9 cards per page so you can see the front and the back of the cards. He kept all of his binders in meticulous order by sport. From what I remember, he had six binders in total, four of which are for basketball and the rest are dedicated to football.

None of this is new information if you know Frank, so I can totally understand his anger when he told me that Ellis stole some of his basketball and football cards. This includes his Kobe Bryant rookie card and his signed Jim Kelly rookie card. I wish I wasn't so shocked when I heard this.

Apparently Ellis must have gone through his binders and picked out the ones that he either liked, or the ones that were the most valuable if he chose to sell them. The Jim Kelly card is by far the most expensive card in his collection and probably the one with the most sentimental value. This wasn't just a card that he bought at a convention, this was a card he actually had Jim Kelly sign in person.

Frank was pissed. I've rarely seen or heard him so angry. When he calmed down I asked him to check my binders to see if anything was taken. After a quick scan, it turns out that Ellis didn't go through my basketball cards, only his. I really felt bad for Frank. I know that I was angry when this whole thing with Ellis initially went down, but to find out weeks later that some of things you hold dear are gone, is rough.

So he did the only thing that he could do, which was call the police. I didn't think about doing that weeks ago, but it makes sense now. Of course there's nothing they could really do but file a police report. Ellis doesn't live in Syracuse anymore so he's out of their jurisdiction. I guess if he ever does come back they could nab him, but then what? Can we even prove how much those cards are worth?

That only thing left for Frank do is the same thing that I did, call Ellis and hope he picks up. I stopped this plan of action long ago because it proved to be hopeless and after awhile I just got too frustrated. There's also a part of me that thinks his mom simply stopped giving him my messages. However, Frank was able to reach him by phone.

El_Jander1: He picked up the phone?

Madawg_78: Yeah, I wasn't expecting him to. I thought I would get this mom so I was shocked when he answered.

El_Jander1: So what happen, what did he say?

Madawg_78: He acted like nothing happened. When he heard my voice it was like this big surprise to him. He thought I was calling just to shoot the shit.

El_Jander1: That's crazy.

Madawg_78: So I asked him what the hell his problem was. Why did he steal my shit? Guess what he said.

El_Jander1: He denied it.

Madawg_78: Nope. He said he just wanted something to remember me by.

El_Jander1: What? Are you shitting me?

Madawg_78: I wish I was. I asked him if he still had it and this fucking guy said "let me check."

El_Jander1: What? No fucking way.

Madawg_78: I could feel the steam coming from my ears when he put down the phone to go look.

El_Jander1: You mean the weed smoke.

Madawg_78: Whatever, fuck you.

El_Jander1: Temper, temper. I didn't steal your shit. Does

he still have your cards?

Madawg_78: He said he still has them and because we're boys, he would never sell my stuff. That's when I got really angry and told him that if we were really boys he wouldn't have taken my cards nor would he have stalked your ex-girlfriend.

El_Jander1: What did he say?

Madawg_78: Then he kinda flipped out talking about why motherfuckers always think the worst of him. When he was in jail nobody came to visit him.

El_Jander1: Damn. That may be true but what does that have to with stealing and stalking?

Madawg_78: I have no idea but he did say that you had all this shit coming to you.

El_Jander1: He said that? Why?

Madawg_78: Ellis was yammering about how this was payment for punching him in the face. Instead of fucking you up he was just gonna fuck your ex-girl.

El_Jander1: That's bullshit! That makes no sense.

Madawg_78: I know. Then he said that he would prove his point. Apparently he's going to that party in NYC with Ingrid.

El_Jander1: Get the fuck out of here.

Madawg_78: I'm just repeating what was told to me. But, I did tell him that if he doesn't give me back those cards I'm going to break my foot up in his ass.

That was how the conversation went while I was sitting at my desk today. I was fuming. So I did the only thing that I could do at that point which was open up a chat window with Ruben. Things seemed to have cooled off since the *Phantom Menace*. We still hang out less than we want to, but somehow we've both managed to keep our issues away from our parents. I didn't want to imagine how my stepmother would react if she got wind that we weren't really getting along all that well. She might blame Ingrid for it. Nevertheless, I needed to at least let him know that Ellis was planning on showing up to this event tonight.

El_Jander1: Hey man.

Destro99: What's up?

I half expected him not to answer since his away message was on. All it said was "busy" which could've meant anything really. Ruben could've been legitimately busy or he may not have been at his computer. He recently quit his job at a mental health insurance company on Wall Street since he got this modeling gig a few weeks ago. I didn't consider it a real thing until I saw his face on the 6 train. It was one of those typical subway cars advertisements we all stare at during our commutes to and from work. The product was something I'd never heard of before called TiVo. I guess it wasn't as fake as I thought it was.

El_Jander1: I just found out something interesting that you might want to know.

Destro99: Ok.

El_Jander1: I was just told that Ellis is going to be at LQ tonight. I think we should roll there. You down?

Destro99: I'm not sure. I have another audition tomorrow morning.

El_Jander1: Ok, well before you say no, I think you should reconsider. Frank spoke to Ellis and he told him that he was going to show up with Ingrid.

Destro99: Really? Why would he say that?

El_Jander1: I don't know. But, I need to settle all of this once and for all. I plan on going to this thing tonight so just let me know.

Destro99: Alright. I do have a few words for him but I doubt that Ingrid is going to be there. I think he's lying but I'll see you there.

Just as I knew he would, he agreed to come down. If it turns out that Ellis is lying then there's no real harm, but if he's telling the truth then there are going to be fireworks. I'm not sure whether to believe any of this or not, but Ellis has been that thorn in my side ever since he told me that bullshit story about Isabel.

I've already had two Coronas before I see Ruben walk in. I cut my conversation short with a few alumni to greet him. I can tell he's scanning the room looking for me when I come up on his left side.

"What up man," I say. We do the standard bro hug. "I'm surprised you're here so early. I know how you like to take your time to get ready." I smile.

"Yeah, well, for some reason I couldn't get in touch with Ingrid, so I'm even more curious about this."

It's still early with no sign of Ellis as of yet. The music level is comfortably loud and the DJ is playing current hip-hop. As time passes, the place gets fuller which will make it difficult to spot anyone we might be looking for. The only thing left to do is mingle and anticipate.

Several people recognize Ruben from his ads on the 6 train, which delights him. The man is in his glory with all the attention he's getting from people who largely ignored him in school. Lucy shows up as well. I give her a big hug as a way of apologizing for my behavior a few weeks ago. We begin to have a good time and for about a half an hour we almost forget why we're really here. The drinks flow and the music plays. The night moves forward and happy hour ends almost as quickly as it began.

Ruben and I settle up our tabs and we just look at each other laughing. The running joke all night is the fact that we are two guys out of college, (where we seemed to have largely been ignored) that are getting more attention then we thought we would. For the most part Ruben was good. He flirted without getting any numbers because he respects Ingrid as his girlfriend. I played it cool too. I really wasn't interested in anything because I knew that I'm just angry at everything these days. It wouldn't be fair to string someone along with the bullshit that's going on with me.

We head outside wondering where the night will take us. Most of the alums have left to go elsewhere, perhaps another bar or maybe to get something to eat. Ruben and I were on the same page and were both thinking about taking a trek to a strip club. The problem was that all the Manhattan clubs were mostly white and mostly expensive. For all the gigs he may have been getting, it didn't translate to good money as of yet.

As a result, we started plotting how we would get to our

favorite club in Mount Vernon called, Sue's Rendezvous. Both of us started heading to toward the train station debating whether to take the Metro-North up there or somehow borrow a car. We really didn't want to take a cab because that would be costly. The debate begins but it's interrupted when we hear a very familiar voice saying, "But he didn't do anything!" We turn around and we see a police officer patting down Ellis against a police car. Our jaws drop when we see who's standing next to him…Ingrid.

Ruben blurts out, "What the fuck is she doing here with him?" He moves quickly to see what's going on. I try to warn him to be careful when we see Ellis mouthing off to the cop.

"I ain't fucking do anything. Why you all on my shit?"

"I think you better watch your mouth wiseass before you find yourself in cuffs." The officer responds back. You can tell that people are starting to form a small crowd around this scene. New Yorkers, as a rule, are good at minding their own business and this is a commandment that Ruben is not about to break if I can stop him.

He walks up to Ingrid and grabs her by the arm a little too hard, and yells "What the fuck is going on here? Why are you with him?" Ingrid looks shocked to see him and begins to conjure up a hurried explanation.

"He asked me to come down here saying that he would give me the rest of the pictures and I believed him and then the cops just started harassing him…"

The officer pays no attention to Ruben. He's squarely focused on Ellis. Then I see the second officer emerge from the police car. "This one's got some outstanding warrants against him so we are gonna have to bring him in."

Ellis begins to spew all kinds of profanities as the officer that was patting him down starts to cuff him. This is not looking good. I head toward Ruben in case I need to grab him. "What are you arresting him for?" I ask. Both cops ignore me. The second office begins talking on his radio, "We have a 10-50, possibly intoxicated with outstanding warrants."

I look over and see Ellis giving the other officer a hard time. 'Fuck you man, you a fucking pig that kills niggas." Then somehow he gets free. I don't know how he did it but I push Ruben back because I'm not sure what's going to happen. In one swift move the officer pulls out his baton and cracks Ellis across the face.

There was a brief and profound silence. A huge glob of blood and teeth fly through the air and hit the pavement with a horrifying splat. Ellis lands on the floor, mouth bloody. The officer finally handcuffs him.

I look over at Ingrid and a look of horror flashes across her face. Tears of fear are streaming from her eyes and she says, "But he wasn't doing anything…"

I can tell that Ruben has no idea what to do. He begins to shush her.

"Step back everyone," The officer commands us as Ellis is pulled up to his feet. He opens his eyes and looks at me. A look of recognition comes across his face. He flashes a bloody jack-o-lantern like grin and begins to laugh. "This bitch thought I was going to give her some pictures but I had something else for her."

That is when we looked down and realized that his pants were unbuttoned. I look over to Ruben and I can tell that he saw the same thing. All he sees is red.

"You motherfucker," He screams as he lunges for him. I block him the best way I can to hold him back from doing something stupid.

The officer puts Ellis in the car. Ruben begins yelling even more aggressively. I ask the officer. "Sir, please let us know what's going on. We know that maniac. We just want to know why he's being arrested so we can at least tell his mother."

The officer looks at me and walks away. Before he gets into the car he says, "Why don't you ask his girlfriend? She seems to know him very well."

ENDINGS

It's been several days since the Latin Quarter party and I hadn't been able to get a hold of Ruben until today. He's been too upset to really talk about what happened with Ellis and Ingrid. I just hope that he's still going to his acting auditions, the modeling agency open calls, and go-sees.

Once I got through to him, we decided to meet at a place on Westchester Avenue called The Riddlers. It's a little after 7 p.m. when I walk in. Ruben is already at the bar nursing a half of a bottle of Corona. I'm not sure what I'm walking into. I know Ruben and Ingrid have broken up so I guess I don't know what stage of grieving he's in. This is one of the few times where I can say that I've been in his shoes. I know what it's like to have to go through a breakup. While Ingrid wasn't the love of his life, it certainly doesn't mean that none of this hurts.

I sit down next to him and order a beer from our smoking hot bartender, Jackie. She's showing tons of cleavage today, like she normally does, which makes her very popular around here. Ruben is sitting on the stool just staring at the beer in his hand like he's reading the label. I don't say anything nor do I feel the need to. I know why I'm here. He's still processing everything so it's my job to sit here and listen to him.

The only part of all this that I know is that after the police drove Ellis away, Ruben and Ingrid got into a huge argument. Words were said and they parted ways in anger. I almost feel bad having witnessed that terrible sight.

Jackie places a small napkin in front of me and then puts the bottle on top of it before she walks away to attend to another costumer. As I begin to take a swig, Ruben begins to speak as if we were already in the middle of a conversation. "The thing is, I should've known from day one the type of person she was. Ingrid has a consistent history of making bad decisions. I just thought that somehow all of this would be different. I think there was a part of me that really wanted to believe that you were wrong about her. I had no real business dating her and in the end, when I was sitting on the six train wondering what the hell I was doing, I realized I settled for someone I thought I wanted."

Ruben finished off his beer and signals to Jackie for another one. "So are you going to get into what happened?" I ask.

"Alright fine," he says as he slams his hands on the bar and sits up straight. He looks at me and says, "So check this shit out. Like a fucking pendejo, I go over to her place thinking that there has to be a reason she felt the need to meet up with this fuck. I'm thinking that this asshole must've tried to forced himself on her. There is no way, after all the phone calls, the tears, and her bullshit about how no guy has ever talked to her in that way that she would allow herself to even be in that fucking situation."

Jackie comes back with another beer for Ruben. We smile at each other and then I ask him, "So, you were able to talk to her then?"

"Yes. I did. I had to get the full story from her. I had to know why the hell she was there with him. We had a huge argument that I won't even get into with you. It was one of those arguments where everything that has been bothering the both of us came to light. But to keep it real short, she's attracted to his crazy ass."

"You're kidding." I had to put the bottle back down on the bar. I had trouble comprehending what Ruben just said.

"Nope. Apparently there was something deep down inside of her that really likes his craziness. He spoke to her in a way that she enjoyed and she was all kinds of curious about him. So when he 'offered' to give back the pictures she jumped at the chance." Ruben clutched the new bottle of beer as if another drink may help. He slowly presses his lips to the bottle as I begin to speak.

"I don't get it, this doesn't make any sense to me. Let's back this up a bit because I want to make sure I'm hearing all of this right. You're telling me that Ingrid, our ex-girlfriend, thinks that Ellis, my former friend, is so attractive with this psychotic behavior that she was willing to meet him on the street to see what may happen?"

"Yup. Crazy right?" Ruben takes another swing.

"She admitted this to you?"

"She didn't deny it."

"What does that even mean? You asked her this?"

"I sure did and it was almost like I caught her red-handed.

Look, she didn't cheat on me. They didn't fuck or anything like that, but I guess I just wouldn't put it past her. Who knows what would've happened that night had he not been stopped by the cops."

There's a brief pause in the conversation as if we had to mutually think about what may have happened. This gave us the chance to catch a few more gulps of our beers. I interrupt our brief mutual silence, "So why the hell did the cops stop him in the first place?"

"From what I pieced together they were in the Chase bank talking while getting money from the ATM and that is when they started arguing. I think some lady called the police."

I look at him with bewilderment. "So you Batman now? How did you piece this together?"

"I got some of it from Ingrid and the other parts by asking around before I went home."

"That's crazy, so you are Batman," I say and he nods. We both take swigs from our beers and I look around. The silence between us is much needed considering everything he just told me. I'm worried about his state of mind. I would be too angry to even be here, but he seems to be handling things well, all things considering. So I feel the need to ask, "So are you ok? You're a little too calm for my liking. I just want to make sure you don't murder anyone, unless you already have."

Ruben chuckles, "There's nothing about any of this that is OK. I'm fucking angry dude. It took me several days to get where I am right now. It's not just Ingrid and Ellis that I'm angry about because shit happens. I mean, it's not like I was going to marry this bitch anyway. I'm mad because I let this relationship get the better of me. I wasn't thinking about how all this would affect you and effect our relationship. More importantly, I'm mad at myself because I almost let Ingrid destroy us. We are family and it would've been my fault."

I can tell this is something that was weighing on him. "For what it's worth, this whole situation didn't destroy us, so try not to focus on what could've been. That's something I've done too much of this year."

"Agreed. How about we do this," Ruben lifts up his beer bottle. "Let's make a pact to never let a woman get in between us."

I lift my bottle and say, "I can drink to that. May we always find time to hang out." We tap bottles and drink. I put my bottle down and continue. "So, are we just going to pretend that we didn't witness some gruesome shit done to Ellis by the NYPD?"

"Fuck Ellis..." Ruben say emphatically.

"I guess that's a yes," I say under my breath

"...I hope they worked his ass over when they booked him. He deserves everything coming to him and don't give me a story about how his brain is fried from whatever drugs he took in college. That motherfucker is of sound mind. He steals your shit and then talks about payback for you punching him in the face?!? I wouldn't be surprised if this was all some sick plot by him to fuck Ingrid since he couldn't get with Isabel or Naomi."

Shit, I never thought about it like that. I knew he was holding a grudge because I clocked him a few months ago, but to take things this far? Just when I thought I knew how Ellis thinks, something else comes up that suggests to me that I really have no clue about anything he does.

"I guess the sight of him being all bloody makes me question how I may have wished bad things on him. People like to talk about karma and what goes around comes around. Rarely do we get to see the comeuppance."

****

I sit in this chair waiting for him to come out. I really didn't want to come here but I need to get answers. The last time Ellis was in jail, he complained that none of his friends came to visit him and to be honest we all had very good reasons not to. We didn't want to entertain his nonsense anymore.

I was willing to forget about him. While I was completely disturbed by what the police did to him on that night, I can't help but feel that all this shit he has done finally caught up to him. Thinking this way makes me feel guilty because according to many people, he truly wasn't doing anything. Perhaps he matched the description of a person they were looking for or perhaps they thought that his "blackness" made him a suspect. In either case, I recognize that Ellis is a victim of a type of a police brutality that we all hear about.

I suppose in the end he's lucky because he could've ended up like Amadou Diallo with 19 bullets out of 41 shots ending up in his body. Instead of visiting him in here I could be pissing on his grave somewhere. But, I'm here because he sent me a letter asking for a chance to redeem and explain himself. Ellis sent the same letter to Nayo and Frank and they both laughed and threw away their letters. I said yes to his request because I believe everyone deserves the chance to be heard.

Ellis walks in and sits down. The visitor's room looks like something straight out of *Law & Order* down to the bullet-proof glass and the phone we pick up to communicate with each other. Ellis looks thinner in his prison jumpsuit, which is about the only negative thing I can say about his appearance because he looks healthier. Maybe prison life agrees with him.

I pick up the phone a few seconds after he does. He looks at me and smiles. It may have been a sincere smile if his missing teeth didn't make it so tragic. But in that moment I recognize the devil in him. "Hey 'friend'. I didn't think you were going to actually show up."

"Yeah, well, I'm here so make it count."

"I see. No how are yous? No how you beens?"

"Contrary to what you may be used to, I'm not here to jerk you off."

"Fair enough. I wanted you to come here to clear the air about things. My wacko fucking therapist says I need to make amends if I ever want to get out of this shit hole. So I wanted to say sorry for all the things I've said or done to you and your family."

There is silence. He stops talking and it leads me to believe he asked me to come all the way out here just to say this half-assed bullshit apology.

"That's it?" I ask.

"Well I don't know what else to say."

"You make me come all the way here just so you can say that mess?" I look at him with disgust.

"You really didn't have to come," he responds smugly.

I hang up the phone then turn around to walk away. I hear him knocking on the glass. I look back. His head is down between his elbows with the phone in one hand as he continues to bang away with the other. I can't help but pity him now so I walk back and sit down. Then I a grab the phone. "What?" I say.

"I'm sorry man. You don't how tough it is in here. I've gotta be on my guard constantly and I don't know how to turn it off sometimes," he says in a low voice. It's almost like his voice was cracking but I can't be sure. This might be the first time I've seen the real Ellis.

"You sound like the same asshole to me," I respond. I refuse to give an inch. I still don't trust him no matter how human he may sound.

Ellis looks up at me and says, "I know I deserve that but I was really sincere in my letter. I don't expect you to forgive me but I really need to get much of this of my chest."

I look at him stoically. "Go on," I say.

Ellis pulls out some loose-leaf paper. I don't even want to know where that has been. He unfolds it a few times until it's fully open and he begins to read:

The person that I need to apologize to first is Nayo. She has been nothing but a good friend to me and everyone of us. I really do love her, but I had so much trouble trying to say it. The more drugs I took the more paranoid I got and I just could never tell her. I don't know what made me go to her room that night but I could not help myself. I'm sorry it came to that.

I'm sorry that I stole from Frank. I was so high at the point that it was just too easy to do. I lied to his girl in order to gain access to the cards. I'm sorry to say that I sold his Jim Kelly card to this dude for $75. I needed the cash to get back home.

I'm sorry that I took those pictures of Ingrid. I was looking through all of Louis' stuff and found nothing I could sell. I came across them and I remembered who she was. I was hoping to meet her and have sex with her. That whole thing just got away from me. Everything I did or said just came out wrong. I'm sorry to everyone I affected with my behavior.

Ellis turns the page over.

I apologize to Isabel for the things I said. She slapped me defending you, Louis. I lied because I thought it would be funny if she was actually flirting with another man. I know that sounds weird but when I'm high many things are funny.

I just look at him. His words do nothing for me because I'm still dealing with the havoc that he's caused. There's silence between us but our eyes are locked. I'm not sure if I believe any of this. How do I know he's not making all this shit up to appease his psychologist?

"You know what Ellis? I can't do this."

I hang up the phone and leave.

****

The one thing that I love about the fall in Syracuse is the foliage. The different colored leaves make everything look peaceful. Of course, fall in Central New York is always short lived due to the quick arrival of snow.

I stare out my window thinking about Carolina. She just left a few minutes ago after spending the night. I'm not sure how long this will last, but I'm still having a great time. I walk over to the new desk in my room and on there sits a computer that my dad ended up buying for me. He surprised me with it calling it an early graduation gift. Of course, this means no more late nights in the computer cluster unless this AOL connection goes bad.

I begin to pack my book bag that was sitting on the chair. I make sure to grab the envelope I placed on top of the keyboard so I wouldn't forget it. I pick it up and look at it to make sure I have the correct address. This is my final check to Isabel. I wanted to make sure that I paid her back every penny I owe her. It took me longer than I wanted, but this is the final $100. This means my debt to her is paid in full. Once I send this out, we are done, forever. I put the envelope in my bag. I will mail this out when I get to campus.

I remember that I need to check my email before I go to class. This is my routine now. I have a Yahoo! email account where I check random emails from groups and listserves I've joined. I'm actually in the process of creating my own website. Lucy had told me that after this whole Y2K nonsense was resolved everyone will be concentrating on having their own custom websites and I figured I should be a part of that in some way. Maybe I will create a blog.

I turn my screen on and maximize my Internet Explorer. I forgot that I was on the Yahoo! Personals page. I was trying to convince Naomi to consider this new internet dating thing that people are talking about. They even made a movie about it with Tom Hanks and Meg Ryan but she wasn't convinced because Eyewitness News did this segment about predators on the internet and she's been skeptical ever since. So, being the leap first and ask questions later type of person, I created a

Yahoo! profile for myself to see if I would get any hits.

Needless to say that I didn't get much. There were a couple of women that looked interesting but nothing that really caught my eye. Overall, there were three profiles that I liked and I responded to them by sending a friendly message. I wasn't looking in the Syracuse area because I know there is no way I'm staying here and there is absolutely no way I'm coming back. I think I've had too much of this place.

Before I log out, I notice that I have a reply from one of my messages:

Hey there,

I see you're into wrestling too. I'm a total fan of The Rock! I love him so much and I try to go to as many shows as I can. It's too bad you go to school in Syracuse otherwise I would love to hang out some time. How long is your program?

I also looked at your profile and I honestly see nothing wrong with comic books. I may not read them but I do try to read pretty much anything I can get my hands on. I should warn you that as a Bronx girl, I am prone to the Yankees. Maybe the Mets might make it to playoffs this year. ☺

I hope to hear from you soon. Have a great day! Xoxo

Raina.

She seems interesting. I think I'll write her when I get back from class. I put on my jacket, fling the bag over my shoulder and walk out of the room. Frank is at the door putting on his jacket.

"Good morning" I say in a chipper voice. I know that

neither he nor Madison are used to my positive morning vibes, but fuck it.

"Hey man, good morning," Frank replies. He doesn't seem to be in a great mood, which is not all that uncommon lately. Frank may still be upset with Ellis for selling that card, or the fact that he and Madison are not having sex as much (it's quite noticeable), or maybe he's just tired.

"Taking the bus?" I ask as I walk toward the door.

"Nah, I'm driving Madison's car today. Wanna ride to campus?"

"Sure," I answer. I totally forgot that Madison lost her job over the summer. It turns out The Direct Club was not doing as well as we once thought. From what Madison told me the ownership "took the money and ran" leaving all the employees high and dry. Since this was a franchised operation, the corporate offices took over leaving the showroom portion still running for members who already paid while shutting down the sales area. People like Madison and Serene found themselves without a job. However, she did get a pretty decent severance package. The problem is that all she seems to do is sit around and smoke all day. I sensed trouble in paradise when I came back for school.

We walk out of the apartment and into the parking area. It is a crisp day and I'm enjoying every moment of it. The sun seems brighter and air smells of grass. I wait for Frank to get into the car and unlock the door. I get into the front passenger seat and I can't help but smile a little thinking about my last memory of this car. "Thanks for the ride. How are things going?"

Frank starts the car and puts it into drive then he says,

"Things are OK, I guess. It was a long summer and I had a lot to think about since Madison lost her job."

"Come up with anything interesting?"

"I mean...why do we do anything in life?"

Oh Lord. I roll my eyes as I look out the window. I already know where this is going. The fucking blunted Confucius is about to speak his mind. "Nigga, don't tell me you started smoking early in the morning now..."

"No, listen, that's not the point. What I'm saying is why do we do this? Why do we feel the need to be with anyone? Check it, so Madison could have easily decided to be with you right?"

"I'm not sure why we are..."

"Right! I'm saying... all of a sudden she decided to go with me, why?"

"Um... I don't really..."

"I don't know either! That's what's been fucking with me since you left. There was no one in the house and I figured that we would do something like go to Darien Lake or maybe go to Niagara Falls, you know, something." Then Frank just stops. There's a pronounced silence in the car, almost as if he was just about to say something profound then forgot. We're at a stop light on Comstock and Colvin right in front of Manley Fieldhouse. The light turns green and he doesn't move.

I'm wondering what he's waiting for. I look both ways to see if maybe there's something I'm missing. The car behind us blows its horn. Then Frank peels out. "See, the thing is... I may just need to break up with her."

Once I catch my breath I say, "I don't think driving while high is legal."

Frank looks at me seriously, "Is there a problem Louis?"

"No. Not all. You got it."

"That's not what I'm asking. I'm saying is there a problem I'm not seeing? Because I think that I made a mistake and right now I think you're the only person who can see this clearly."

This is not what I expected to hear this morning for many reasons. I always thought that Madison and Frank happened a little too fast and I was never sure of the shelf-life of their relationship. What I do know is that she has gotten him into a habit he can barely handle.

"Are you asking me to tell you what to do?" I smile.

Frank laughs after grasping the irony of my question. He answers back, "Maybe I need to see if our answers match up."

Frank parks the car in the lot in front of the library and I continue the conversation, "Look, you've been a godsend to me when it came to Isabel and maybe I haven't mentioned it, but I'm not sure where I'd be right now without you and Nayo. It still hurts to think about her, but from the bottom of my heart I know that it's better this way. Maybe I will find a better person to be with, maybe it's with Carolina or maybe is with this woman Raina that just hit me up on Yahoo. The point is, if it doesn't feel right, you gotta move on."

We get out of the car and Frank responds, "Wow, you're getting pretty good at this. You're right though. I think it's time I grow up and make some adult decisions."

I bow to him and say with a smile, "When I left you, I was but the learner, now I'm the master."

Frank shakes his head, "You've been hanging out with Brian too long. Damn *Star Wars* nerds."

I head over the first mailbox I see and I pull the envelope out of my bag. "Please, like you haven't seen *The Phantom Menace* yet."

"I haven't."

I stop all motion and look at him in disbelief. "You poor little man. Why not?"

"Madison isn't into *Star Wars*." Frank says as he looks down almost embarrassed.

I stretch out my arms and then let them hit my sides. I give him a glare "If that isn't sign then I don't know what is." I give him a half-hearted smile and then I look down at the envelope.

Frank asks, "What are you about to do?"

I answer as I slip the envelope addressed to Isabel in the mail chute, "I'm about to make my first adult decision." I closed the lid the chute and I begin to snicker as I reminisce about something that was once said to me.

I walk away and Frank looks at me awkwardly, "What are you laughing at?"

"Vivienne was right."

Lucha Libros
April 5, 2016
6:53 p.m.

Before I go out there, I decide to sit alone in my thoughts. This has been a long road and somehow I find myself in an incredibly positive situation. My book came out today. The first thing I've ever truly created by myself is sitting on the shelves and it's a bit overwhelming. All my blog entries and Twitter posts cannot compare to actually holding my novel in my hands.

I'm in the bathroom of an independent Latino bookstore in Spanish Harlem. I was able to secure this location for my book opening through a friend of a friend. Tonight's agenda consists of a simple reading, some questions and answers, and then a book signing. While this might be standard procedure for all authors during a book release party, this is a brand new experience for me.

I take this moment to look into the mirror because I know the minute I go out there and mingle with all those people and take that microphone, is the minute that my arrival into the literary world becomes official. I'm not sure I'm ready for this. All my family and friends are outside waiting for me to debut this work and I really don't want to disappoint.

All my thoughts on how I got here flood my mind. The last few years have been a whirlwind of events that have come to define who I am. A divorce, a car accident, moving back to New York, and now writing this book.

There is a knock at the door. I open it and it's Zenia. She flashes a beautiful smile. "Hey Handsome, you planning on being in here all night?" She walks into the bathroom and closes the door behind her. She's such a welcome sight. Her obsidian hair falls past her shoulders down to the center of her back. Zenia decided on going with the short grey V-neck sweater that she debated about with her sister. I remember this because the jeans she bought the other day were a perfect combination with variety of tops that include this sweater and a turtleneck.

I smile back at her, "No, I'm just clearing my head."

Zenia starts straightening my tie. "Well, I've been sent back here to check on you. The event starts in a few minutes and your adoring fans await you."

Fans? I know she's joking but I never thought to look at anyone as a fan. But on a serious note, I suppose that's what family and friends are supposed to be, people who are rooting for you in times of great success. "I'm just a little nervous," I say as I stare at her. She's wearing her glasses.

Zenia smiles, "Honey, there's no reason to be nervous. You'll be fine. It's not like you haven't done public speaking before."

"I know but this time it's different. I'm putting myself out there. You know?"

"Yes, I know. But it's time to go." She gives me a quick

kiss on the lips and leaves the bathroom. I turn around to look into the mirror one last time. I take a deep breath. I can do this. I grab my tablet that was sitting on the top of the toilet and walk out the door.

The bathroom is located in the back of this tiny bookstore. All the bookshelves are up against the walls. Each shelf is set up with each particular genre. There are shelves for books primarily in Spanish, another one for famous authors, one for children's books, and one for local authors. There are a few people browsing the sections. The area for the book reading is actually one level below called "El Escenario de Barrio." Granted this is a small set up and the lower level itself probably fits no more than 50 people, but some of the most famous Latinos authors and poets have graced that stage. I find it difficult to accept being considered as one of them. I will just call it a stroke of luck.

When I get to the bottom of the stairs I see the room is packed. Family, friends, and a few people I don't know. I begin to fumble with my tablet. I already know which chapter I'm going to read. I just need to make sure that I have it ready. Zenia gives a nod to the bookstore owner who walks on stage and begins her introduction.

"¡Buenos Días! My name is Jasmin Bayamon and I'm the owner of Lucha Libros. For over four years we have provided this community with a place where reading and buying books from Latino authors is made simple. We call this area where you are right now, El Escenario de Barrio. We've had world famous poets and authors on this very stage like Piri Thomas, Sandra Cisneros, Junot Diaz, and Isabel Allende. That is just to name a few, but tonight we have a new author coming to the stage to read an excerpt of his new book, *The Book of Isabel.* Welcome, Louis Ortiz!"

316

People begin to clap as I walk up the center aisle. The conglomeration of faces look at me while clapping and I'm overcome with a sense of satisfaction and achievement. Maybe I've finally arrived at a place where I truly belong. Jasmin shakes my hand as I step on to the stage. The platform is more like a 4x8 skirted riser. Behind the riser stage is a projection screen that has the name of the bookstore in huge letters with my picture and the title of the book below it. In front of the screen is a stool with a bottle of water on it. She steps down off the stage, I turn to the microphone and survey the room.

Before I say my first words I see the crowd looking up at me. This is not a theater. There are no par cans to blind me from the fact that I'm the center of attention right now. I knew this would be a reunion of sorts, a collision of all my separate worlds. The front rows are filled with family members. To my left, Ruben and his girlfriend are sitting up front next to my mother and my brother. A few of my cousins fill in the rest of the seats in the front row. On my right, Zenia sits down next to her sister, Janice who is there with her daughter and their parents.

Scattered throughout the room are various friends and former students. I see Dopeness in the back sitting next to Brian who came down from Syracuse with his wife. Judy, my former assistant, who came down with him is sitting next to Jason and his wife Sasha. So many faces here, but the one that really takes me back is Naomi. She's sitting in the back toward the right. I know her well enough to know that she really didn't want to bring much attention to herself. She is thinner, but she did survive that surgery back in December. The doctors were able to remove the tumor and a wave of happiness hits me when I think about it. She's spent the last few months recovering and this is one of the few times she's left her house. This is almost perfect, most of my friends and family are here.

The only thing that would have made it better is if my dad was here. Once he moved to Florida, there was very little doubt in my mind he would be back for anything outside of holidays. We talked about this and I was ok with it. The one good thing about being an adult is the ability to fully understand your parents' decisions.

I smile and say, "Welcome." The sounds system isn't perfect. I'm then reminded that Frank is not here either. I invited him, but I wouldn't expect someone to drive five hours just for a book reading. I made sure there was a reception happening afterwards for people to mingle because I doubt I will be doing much talking during the book signing.

I continue, "Thank you all for coming. I love the support of all my peoples and my loved ones. Before I begin here I just want to say that this book is just the beginning. I feel like I've been writing all my life and this moment is when my hobby transforms into something more. I feel very blessed having everyone in this room right now. The love you have shown me means so much." I look down at my tablet and swipe the screen. Chapter one comes up. I look back up and before I can speak I see Frank walk in with Lidia, his ex-wife.

I'm taken aback for a second. I'm surprised that Frank even made it down here. He never said a word to me about coming. But to see Lidia, his ex here with him? The shock of it is unsettling. I need to pull myself together. I reach back for the bottle of water and open it. I take a big sip and look back down at the tablet to regain my composure. As Frank and Lidia find seats, I notice Zenia look back and then look at me. Her eyes say it all... *What the fuck?!?*

I take deep a breath and begin, "I waited for her. The airport was empty and the fluorescent lighting gave off a sense of a pale emptiness. At least I wasn't alone..." I read slowly.

The one thing I don't want to do is trip over my own words. I have a habit of reading faster than I speak, so every time I think I'm going too fast, I slow down. If I look up and see Lidia, I know I will lose my concentration. To avoid this, I focus my gaze upon my mother and Zenia.

Once the reading is over. I take some questions. The room is small enough that a microphone is not really needed for the people in the audience. Finally, I can be myself and relax. Since I'm used to talking in public I breathe easier. I sit on the stool because for some reason, I was not comfortable sitting and doing the reading. I take the standard questions of *how long did it take you to write this book* and *how much of you is in it?* Both questions are easy to answer but in the back of my mind I'm thinking about why Lidia is here with Frank.

It wasn't all that long ago that they were battling each other in a brutal divorce. It wasn't even that long ago that she kicked him out and started coming on to me. It was not that long ago that he was seeing Annette. Geez, poor Annette. It was because of Frank's feelings for her that lead Lidia to leave him despite everything that happened. But now this? What really happened with Paula? How did he even get here again? These are all questions that are in the back of my mind and yet, I haven't spoken to him in months.

Then Lidia raises her hand. It's the only hand raised. I don't want to call on her, but I have to. I point to her and she stands up. She looks very different from the last time I saw her. Her hair is now shoulder-length and I think she may be inappropriately dressed, which is not surprising to me. Lidia has on a tight turtleneck sweater dress that shows a lot of leg and boobs. "Yes, my question is how authentic is your writing in this book? It sounds like a very interesting story, but how much of that realism gets portrayed in your writing?"

The room is silent. I automatically get the sense that she's being very rancorous with her line of questioning. I chuckle, "I would like to think that I'm very authentic. The reader should be able to see the conflict within the protagonist. Of course, I can say that my writing is very genuine, but I would rather the reader decide for themselves." Someone else raises their hand and I take that question. I didn't want to give her time to follow-up with any other foolishness. I have no idea what she may be up to, but I do have a feeling that I will find out soon enough.

The next question after Lidia's turned out the be the last. Jasmin signals to me that my time on stage is up and I will need to move to the book-signing portion upstairs. People begin to clap and I thank them again for coming. When I get off stage my family greets me. There are smiles and laughs. Zenia motions that she'll meet me upstairs with her sister Janice. As they walk away I see Frank and Lidia head up the staircase.

Ruben comes up to me and says, "What was all that about?"

"Zenia or Lidia?" I respond.

"Well, we all know why Zenia and Janice are not fans of mine, but I was talking about Lidia."

He's right about one thing, none of us will forget that him and Janice dated years ago. "I have no idea what's going on here. I didn't think he was coming to this. In fact, I didn't even know they were together."

"That's right! Didn't they get a divorce?" Ruben asks as he looks at his girlfriend, Diana. It's a look that suggests that this is another juicy story he will have to inform her of.

"I thought they did. But who knows now."

I begin to head toward the staircase. As someone who has been on the event side of book signings, I'm not trying to be that person that takes forever to get to the book signing table. I've seen how hectic these things can be regardless of the size of the crowd. Lucha Libros has an allotment of 20 books to sell on consignment and I think they're about to sell out.

I get to the table and it's draped with a red tablecloth. A line has already formed. The people that stayed to get a their book signed are mostly those who I know personally. Judy is the first person on line and I can't say that I'm surprised. I sit down and pull out my orange sharpie. "You know I just had to be the first one on line," Judy says smiling.

I smile back, "Yes, I know. I would've been disappointed with you if hadn't been." Judy and I have kept in touch ever since I left Syracuse a few years ago. I thought she would have brought her fiancé but he had to work.

As I sign the book she asks, "Lidia huh?" I nod my head. "She gonna be in your next book?" She chuckles. I finish signing her book and give it back to her.

"She just might be, I'll let you know." She takes the book and steps aside.

Brian is right behind her with the book in his hand. "I always needed a reason to come to New York and you seem to be the only one," he says as he hands me the book. I laugh as take the book and sign it. His wife is right behind him. I always give him credit because he always seems to be the "white savior" in my life. The last time he was in New York was more than 10 years ago. He came and helped me drive all my shit up from the Bronx to Syracuse when I got the job in Diversity

Initiatives.

The three of them leave together with promises to meet me at the reception. The next few people are pleasant, I've never met them before, but they heard about the book reading from Twitter. Naomi is next and behind her is my boy, Dopeness. I get up from the table to give her a hug. "How are you feeling?" I ask.

"I'm good. The last few weeks have been better. I've been tired but the doctors have given me good news and right now I'm living one day at a time." She smiles, but I can tell she's still tired. I sign her book and ask her how's she's getting home. Clearly I'm worried about her still.

Naomi rolls her and eyes and Dopeness interjects, "Man, just sign my book. You know I will make sure Nayo will get home safe." I tend to forget that he also lives in Brooklyn. As I sign his book he also says, "I see you are finally paying me back for those *Phantom Menace* tickets." He smiles. That's right, I almost forgot about that.

"Yes, I am. I think I made it right under the deadline too."

Dopeness looks at his watch, "Yup, almost 15 years. You just made it." We both laugh as I give him back his book. They both head out. I know I will see them both later at the reception.

Janice is next with her daughter and she hands me the book and says, "I'm so proud of you."

"Thank you, I hope you enjoy the book," I say as I sign it. I give the book back to her and ask, "Are you OK with...you know?" I nod my head towards Ruben's direction.

Janice turns her head. "Please, I'm so over him," she laughs. "I won't see you at the reception because I'm dropping of this little girl at her grandmother's house. I got a hot date tonight."

"That's awesome." I wave goodbye as the next person gives me their book. A few of my cousins come up next. We laugh and joke about me writing a book. As they begin to leave the table, Lidia appears with Frank behind her. I stand up to give him the customary bro hug. I reach over to Lidia and we give each other the coldest kisses on the cheek this side of Onondaga Lake.

"I didn't think you were gonna to be able to make it." I say to Frank as I begin to sign his book.

"Well, it was a last minute decision. I didn't think we were going to make it either." Frank responds. I almost expected a joke from him but he seems to playing it straight right now. He's not even wearing his Buffalo coat.

I give him back the book and take hers. "Wow, so… this is…uh," I struggle for the right word.

"Unexpected? It's okay, you can say it," Lidia says.

"Well, yeah, its definitely unexpected. I mean, I haven't heard anything from you in a while there buddy, I was getting a little worried," I say looking at Frank.

"I know. I've been busy with work and all." Another short response. I know Frank pretty well and I feel like maybe he's hiding something. In any case, his answer doesn't explain the lateness of his payments towards the house. I may have to use another angle if I can.

I look at them. "So, you are voiding the divorce decree? Can you even do that?" I chuckle a little bit trying to be funny but neither of them are laughing. "Ok then, tough crowd." I begin to sign her book.

"We decided not to go through with the divorce. It was going to be a lot of money. At the end of it all, we decided to do the one thing we just weren't doing as a married couple and that was talk to each other." Frank says as he looks at her. I find myself gasping at this sight. Is he serious right now?

"I decided to listen. We hashed everything out. We told each other everything. There are no more lies between us," Lidia adds. I feel like I'm watching an eHarmony commercial.

"Wow, that's awesome. I'm happy for you both." I stack both books on top of each other and hand it to Frank and continue, "So wait, how's the house?"

"It's great. I moved in last year." Lidia says.

"Really. Well that's good." Maybe this is the real reason why Paula and him broke up. But why has he been so elusive with me? It does explain the roommates. There's no way she was going to allow anyone to live with them. However, it doesn't explain the lateness, or rather, the complete lack of payments. If they are living together then there should at least be double the household income. This is not making much sense at all but I'm not sure this is the right time to get into it.

"I would say so. But listen, Frank has a question for you before we go." Lidia says with a condescending look.

I look over to him and say, "Yeah..." Frank hands the books over to Lidia then flips over the table with such force that it takes everyone by surprise. I hear a loud gasps. I almost fall back on my seat. I've never seen him so menacing. I stand up as if I have some place to run to, but I have my back against the bookshelf.

He grabs me by my shirt and lifts me up like a rag doll. I can hear people screaming. I see the fear in Zenia's face from here. "Tell me something 'friend.' Were you ever going to tell me about you trying to fuck my wife?"

Frank punches me in the stomach and let's go. I fall to the ground wincing in pain. I clutch my abdomen as I try to catch my breath. I look up and I see Frank glaring at me. He takes Lidia hand and they both walk away towards the exit.

Zenia runs over to me as I begin coughing and struggling to stand. I feel embarrassed and hurt. "Are you okay?" She asks.

"No. I'm not."

ACKNOWLEDGMENTS

There are so many people that I wish to thank that I could write a whole other chapter just for them. I feel so fortunate to have so many people in my corner for this second book. *Hanging Upside Down* was such a new experience for me that I almost dread to read it now due to all the mistakes that were made in creating it. This time, the process was different. I took my time and really worked with people to come up with the best version of this story that I could tell.

I have so much love for Monique Thompson. She worked just as hard as I did on the editing side to make sure this was done in the way I wanted. I enjoy working with her and to be honest, she's a Godsend. We discuss ideas and she convinces me that I'm not as crazy as I think I am.

There are also not enough words for Andre Cole. I've learned so much from him. Even if he's yelling at me (over text message) to get back to writing, his constant encouragement has made these books easier to write.

Let's talk about this amazing cover. Sam Wilson hit me up some time after I was done with the first book and asked me if I needed a graphic artist. Sam, like my other two friends, graduated with me from Syracuse University so it was never a hard decision to work with talented people that I knew. Bottom line was that I had a vision of what I wanted the cover to be and he took that vision and ran with it. I thank him so much for that.

To the love of my life, Zulay, your drive to make yourself a better person has led me to do the same. I hope to be the great writer you think I am.

My test readers were amazing this year. I cannot thank them enough for taking the time to read this book. Some of you gave me the praise I needed while also giving me crucial critiques that made the story better. To my proofreader, thank you for being amazing.

Family comes first and I have to say thank you. To my father, my step mother, my brother, and my mother. To my nephew, Justin, and my goddaughter, Maya, I love you both more than you will know. To Ricardo, Karen, Liz, Ivonne, Olga, Pat, Sylvia, Theresa, Myrta, Debra, Fredrick, Jennifer, and Scott. To Josie, Darius, James, Debra, and Yvette. Thank you for always asking me how the writing is going. I cannot forget my Atlanta family either: Amelia, Cynthia, Tracy, Elizabeth, Jarrett, Tiffany, Ty, Cydney, and little Carmen. My other family, Carmen, Cathy, Justin, Faustino (Rafael), Ralph, Marisa and Jacob.

To the rest of my friends and colleagues…if you're not named it's not that I don't love you but I'm running out of space. Rahman, Maximo, Ynanna, Angela Morales -Patterson, Meghan, Jenn, Scott, Eddie, Peter, Cristobal, Yvette, Melanie, Julio, Gil, Hilda, Nancy Gutierrez, Chasity, David Pressley, Emma, Bridget, Henoc, Tiffany Dugan, Nakia, Jessica Urraca, Gladys, Radames, Angie Toribio, Rameer, Annamaria, Hayden, Raymond, Amani, Mike Frazier, Victoria, Wanda, Cassy, Lenise, Raquel, Alena, Misael, Michele Soto, Aaron Hudson, Tiffany Viruet, and Barry Wells.

Whew. I hope I get half the love and support you've given when the next book comes out.

ABOUT THE AUTHOR

Anthony Otero is an author/blogger with a BA in English from Syracuse University. In addition to his blog, *Volume 2*, he has written for the Huffington Post. You can follow him on twitter as @latinegro.